Stephen H. Provost
Sharon Marie Provost

Christmas

Nightmare's Eve

Dragon Crown Books 2023

ISBN: 978-1-949971-41-5

Ghostbusted! (in slightly different form) and The Shining Night also appear in *The Aces Anthology* (2023). Reindeer Ride is an excerpt from the novel *The Talismans of Time* (2019).

Dedication

To all who love Christmas, light and dark.

"Darkness was cheap, and Scrooge liked it."

— Charles Dickens
A Christmas Carol

Contents

Christmas Nightmare's Eve

Introductions

Nightmerry Christmas

Continuing in the tradition of *Nightmare's Eve*, I'm proud to present this collection of chilling and thought-provoking stories in this, my first perfect full collaboration with Sharon Marie Provost (who previously wrote the foreword to a very different book of mine, *Sierra Highway*).

As a fan of *The Twilight Zone*, I wrote the original *Nightmare's Eve* in an attempt to continue Rod Serling's vision, and I believe this present work will serve as a worthy companion to that volume. I penned nine short stories to appear in these pages, and Sharon more than equaled my output with seven short stories of her own and a novella—one that I think you'll find a particular treat. As a bonus, I've also included a Christmas-themed excerpt from my novel *The Talismans of Time*, which is, in fact, one of my favorite scenes.

As a longtime aficionado of nightmare-inducing film and literature herself, it was only appropriate that Sharon be intimately involved in this project. In the pages ahead, she will join me in asking what happens to bad little boys at Christmastime. Do ghosts go home for the holidays? What happens when one of Santa's elves comes back from Costa Rica with an infection caused by a mysterious bite? How far will a desperate author go to meet a Christmas deadline?

And much more. Those are just some of the questions posed in our new volume of twists and terror with a holiday theme—perfect for the long and moonless nights of winter, when candlelight fails and fitful dreams turn frightful, but enjoyable all year 'round. Flights of fancy, poignant tales, and whimsical fables are interspersed among the night terrors. I suspect they'll come as welcome relief to you, considering some of the scariest entries in this installment are even more intense and frightening than what's to be found in the original.

Can you feel your skin begin to crawl and your teeth begin to chatter as pull up your comforter, nestled all snug in your bed? What are you afraid of? Is it only your imagination? Or is it really the bogeyman, waiting for the lights to go out so he can seize you? Or a serial killer stalking you, sizing you up to become his next prized trophy?

We've packed this volume with enough fear and foreboding here to scare the Christmas stockings off even the jolliest old elf. Welcome, dear friends, to Christmas Nightmare's Eve, when time stands still at the witching hour between Krampusnacht and St. Nicholas Day… and leaves you stranded, helpless, between the waking world and oblivion. Accept your fate: There's no escape for you now. Not even a Christmas miracle can save you.

Stephen H. Provost

December 12, 2023

Christmas Nightmare's Eve

As a longtime fan of the *Twilight Zone* myself, I was delighted when Stephen asked me to help him write this Christmas-themed sequel to *Nightmare's Eve*. But I also have a darker and twistier side. Even in my youth, my interests included scarier stories like those found in *Tales from the Darkside*, and as I got older they extended to the extreme horror and gore fancies of Eli Roth and Quentin Tarantino. Therefore, it is somehow fitting that my entries for this book frequently push the envelope. No one is safe, not even children or Santa Claus.

My introduction to the world of horror was *The Shining*. The dark music, paired with the wild, insane eyes of Jack Nicholson, sent a chill down my spine each time the commercial played. I still remember burying my head in the couch to block the sight and sound, as though somehow that could save me. The adrenaline rush, while terrifying, was also exhilarating. I hope you will feel just that kind of rush as you read my darker entries.

My favorite type of horror involves the potential for reality. Rather than a ghost or demon, it involves a normal human being with psychotic tendencies. You don't see the danger until it's already too late. Sometimes, there's nothing more terrifying than the evil man perpetrates on another human. This fascination with the darker side of humanity led me to pursue my degree in criminal justice. "Justice Gone Wrong" explores that exact theme.

However, I do have a romantic and sentimental side as well. You will explore that in my entries like "The Road to Joya" and "The Last Train to Clarksville." You will not escape the paranormal, but your heart will be warmed briefly before the chill once again descends upon you.

Stephen's story "Let's Make a Deal" will make you ask how

far you would go to save someone you love. What deal would you make with the devil? That is a hard one for me to ponder when I think about what I would do for my soulmate.

Stephen's and my mutual love of history is quite apparent in this volume. Stephen has come to understand the meaning behind our state anthem, "Home Means Nevada," through his exploration of all the wonderful history and desert beauty our state holds. You will see that on display in several of his stories. Likewise, you will see my love of European folklore, especially about Christmas.

I sincerely hope you will enjoy this trip with us. Just don't lose your way, for you never know what you might find down the road less traveled.

Sharon Marie Provost

December 12, 2023

Stephen H. Provost

That's the Spirit

hristmas Eve arrived in a soaking wet blanket of fog, but no one was around to notice. No one had strung any lights up in town, and no decorations lined the street.

A single Christmas tree stood in the tiny town square—actually just a vacant lot—next to the old, abandoned schoolhouse. The school had been closed for decades and was supposedly haunted by the ghosts of children who'd attended there when it was the only place in town with central heating.

They still thought they could stay warm there, it seemed, even if the heat no longer worked.

George walked along the dusty old boardwalk, scuffing his shoes on the pavement. So much had changed since the town's heyday, when he'd gotten his start as a saloon owner here. The gold boom had come and gone, and so had he.

The writing had been on the wall for years, and then the wall caught fire.

A lot of walls did.

One summer, two days after the Fourth of July, the entire town had gone up in flames. Twenty-five blocks of the once-thriving downtown were reduced to ash and rubble. And two months later, George got out while the getting was good.

Now he was back, and so were the memories.

They stood in stark contrast to the sights that met his weary eyes: broken-down wooden shacks, long-vacant save for the desert wind that whistled through them in a ghostly chorus. Boarded-up shops and empty saloons. An entrance to a subway that never was.

He walked past an arch that was an entrance to nowhere. There was open air on one side, open air on the other, and vacant space in between. The roof, the walls, the floor, and everything else had been consumed by the fire. The only thing that remained of the bank across the street from that lonely arch was the safe, now empty and open to the dry desert air.

How had it all come to this? The town was in even worse shape now than it had been when he left.

George ignored a tourist who waved at him. What was a tourist doing here anyway? It wasn't as if there was much to see. Or do. Not even a grocery store, as far as he could tell. That in itself was no great loss, because George wasn't hungry. And it was a good thing he hadn't come here by car, because all the gas stations looked like they'd been shuttered or abandoned for years.

How *had* he gotten here? And *why* was he here?

He couldn't remember.

A highway passed through town, but no one seemed to stop. George saw a car pass by—the only one on the road, it seemed. He didn't recognize the model; probably some Italian import. Its radio was playing a tune that George didn't recognize, either: A nightman telling some poor traveler to relax and assuring him he could check out any time he liked... George didn't hear the rest of it as the car and the tune faded into the dusty distance.

Then, silence.

George took a deep breath and let out a sigh. One would have never guessed that this had once been the state's biggest city. They'd held a prizefight for the world's championship there, and thousands of people had shown up from all over the West. They'd built a grand school (the one that was now abandoned), three stories tall and of sturdy brick. There was a courthouse, since the town was the county seat, and an old stone firehouse.

Then there was the hotel: George's hotel, boasting a total of 150 rooms. Complete with telephones, leather chairs, mahogany trim, private baths in half the rooms, and an electric elevator, there was a sumptuously appointed lobby, and a grand dining room where guests were served such delicacies as lobster, quail, and squid. You name it, George's place had it, and it quickly earned a reputation as the most opulent hotel between St. Louis and San Francisco. He'd built it with the money he'd earned from the mines, so he could make more money off prospectors hoping to strike it rich. He lined his pockets coming and going, then he got out when the getting was good.

He sold the hotel after the fire, and he later heard that the new owner was trying his hand at prospecting. Word had it he'd dug mine shafts on the property, trying to tap into some undiscovered vein. But the ore beneath the townsite had long ago been depleted, and George had a laugh at the man's expense. He forgot about the hotel after that and went on to bigger and better things.

Migrating north, he built another grand hotel beside the river that ran through the state's new economic hub.

George made a killing there, too, in banking, all but cornering the market on deposits in his new hometown and across the entire state. Only the Depression had brought his financial winning streak to a halt.

But it was no matter. He just rebuilt his fortune with a series of new investments.

Even bankruptcy hadn't stopped him.

But this... this just might.

George had heard rumors that someone was out to get him, and he knew they were true when he heard the voices.

Voices drifting out onto the street from the interior of his old hotel. Voices of accusation. Voices of slander.

Everything else was so quiet, he could hear them a block away.

Echoing down the empty streets.

Pounding in his head.

George knew he wasn't as sharp as once he had been. He forgot things now. Truth be told, his short-term memory was all but gone. But he still remembered the past; his glory days were fixed securely in his mind. And he knew the voices that reached his ears now were spouting hate-filled lies, no doubt spawned by jealous minds bent on revenge for his success. He didn't recognize them, but a man like George never knew all his enemies. Too many men believed, rightly or wrongly, that he'd ruined or maligned them, to keep track of them all. He always knew they would come for him, bent on revenge.

And they were coming for him now.

"He killed her," one of them was saying, "right here in this very hotel."

George was many things: an opportunist, a ruthless businessman, and some even said a cheat. But he was no murderer, and he knew it.

Tugging resolutely at his vest, he turned the corner and strode through the hotel's open door, casting angry glances left and right in search of the voice's owner. Seeing no one, he strode up to the front desk and, finding no concierge on duty, banged hard on it.

"Here, here!" he shouted. "What does someone have to do to get some service around here?"

Dust flew up off the counter in a miniature mushroom cloud as his right fist hit the wood. The place certainly had gone downhill since he owned it.

No one came in answer to his summons, but the voices in the other room stopped, then one of them whispered, "Someone's here!"

"It's probably her," came an answer in equally hushed tones.

Her? George had been accused of many things, but no one had ever told him he sounded like a woman.

George waited a minute more for the desk clerk, but it soon became clear that no one was on duty. He shrugged. In the hotel's current state of disrepair, he had no desire to stay there anyway. He just wanted to hear what the voices were saying—and, sure enough, they were talking again.

George stayed as quiet as he could as he moved closer, careful to stay out of sight behind the wall that separated their owners from the hotel lobby where he stood. But the voices were growing fainter, and the sound of footsteps told him their owners were moving away from him down a corridor. There were two or more of them, perhaps a small group, but one—a woman—was doing almost all the talking. From the tone and cadence of her voice, she sounded almost like a schoolteacher lecturing to her class.

He heard his name mentioned again.

"...and this is the room where he kept her locked away, the woman pregnant with the child he'd fathered out of wedlock."

George's eyes went wide. None of it was true! Yes, he'd been something of a ladies' man, and it was common knowledge that he'd been unfaithful. But infidelities were common, even accepted, among men of means—and he had more means than almost anyone else. Besides, he'd at least had the decency to divorce his wives when he'd grown tired of them: He'd had two or three of them... or was it four? He couldn't remember. Damned "softening of the brain." That's what they called it. He did remember his first wife—or so she claimed to be—had sued to acquire his fortune, but he'd shown her: He'd won in court and had the "marriage" annulled.

But whatever else he might have done, he wouldn't have been stupid enough to get a woman pregnant, and if he had, he would have simply paid her to disappear and get rid of the baby—or he'd support it. He had more than enough money to do that if it were called for. He certainly didn't need to lock a woman up, and even if he had, he would have needed to be mad to imprison her in his own hotel! All she'd have to do was yell, and someone would have noticed and alerted the authorities.

But it got worse.

"How long did he keep her there?" he heard another voice ask.

"Until she had the baby. Then he took both of them and

threw them down the mine shafts that had been dug on this very property."

George gasped. "That's impossible!" he blurted out, forgetting that he was trying to stay hidden. "It's simply not the case!"

The voices went silent again, and so did George.

Then there came another whisper. For some reason, whenever they heard him say something, they took care to speak under their breaths, as though *they* were the ones who didn't want to be discovered.

It didn't make any sense.

"I heard her again," said the whispered voice.

"It sounded like a man to me," said another.

Then, from the "schoolteacher" voice: "There's more than one of them here."

Them?

George looked around him, but there was no one else there. He'd seen and heard no sign of anyone since he walked through the front door, except for the owners of the whispered voices—who seemed more interested in slandering him than anything else. Either they were hearing things or just making up stories. They'd obviously heard him, so perhaps they were trying to spook him with the idea that there was someone else here: maybe a group of fugitives that had taken refuge at the hotel. Whomever they were referring to, real or imaginary, their hushed tones indicated that they were either scared themselves or were trying to scare him. Who knew? Maybe it was both.

"What on earth do they want?" he muttered to himself.

"Isn't it obvious?"

George whirled around at the unexpected sound of a familiar voice. There was someone else here, but it wasn't a fugitive. It was...

"Senator?!"

The man laughed at his old business partner. "Why did you stop calling me George?"

George shrugged. "It got confusing, with both of us having the same name and all. When they put you in the Senate, it made things a lot easier. Anyway, what are you doing here? I haven't seen you in... how long has it been?"

The Senator laughed. "Too long. I'm afraid I've lost track. Memory isn't what it used to be."

"Join the club." George laughed along with him.

"See?" came the schoolteacher's whispered voice. "I *told you* there was more than one of them!"

The Senator rolled his eyes, and George remembered his original question. "What do they want?" he repeated.

"Why your money, of course. How much are you worth now? $30 million?"

"Maybe more, maybe less, depending on the day."

"And how many people want a piece of that pie, Georgie? And how far might they go to get it?"

George nodded knowingly. Slander. Extortion. He'd been a target of such plots before; this was nothing new. But what he'd heard whispered through the walls here was particularly worrisome: Being accused of murder—not just of a woman, but of an infant—could get him put away for life. "You don't happen to have a cigar, Senator?"

The older man grinned. "Of course I do, Georgie. At all times. I've got your favorite right here."

George clapped him on the back, took the offered cigar, and lit it. "So you knew I'd be here?"

The Senator nodded.

"How?"

"Just a hunch."

George flicked some ashes onto the floor. It wasn't his place anymore, and he wasn't particularly happy with the new owner giving safe harbor to would-be extortionists... who were whispering again:

"You smell that?" one of them said.

"Yeah. What is it?"

"Cigar smoke."

"That means he's here."

At least they weren't calling him a woman anymore. And he was getting fed up with hiding. If they were going to come after him, he knew how to play hardball, and he had enough money to buy the state's slickest lawyers and pay off a judge or two if necessary. "You must have some friends on the bench, Senator. I know I do, but I'm drawing a blank."

The Senator scratched his head. "So am I. Hmmm..." Then he brightened a little and said, "There's always Patrick..."

That was one individual George had no trouble recalling. And vividly.

"Whoa, no you don't," he said. "Don't you remember? That fake wife of mine hired him as a lawyer, and he tried to take me for everything I had. Talk about extortion. Senator, your memory really *is* going."

"Sorry. He's the only judge I could think of."

George took the cigar out of his mouth, threw it down, and ground it into the floor with his heel. He'd had enough. He was going to give these blackmailers what for. Maybe he didn't own this hotel anymore, but he all but owned the state. That was a bit better. And he'd find a judge to put in his pocket if he didn't remember one who was already there.

"Come on, Senator. Let's put an end to this."

But the older man was nowhere to be seen. Apparently, the Senator had been so embarrassed by his failing memory that he had decided to take his leave. George must have been so wrapped up in his own thoughts that he'd failed to notice.

"At least he could have had the decency to say goodbye."

More perturbed than ever, George strode down the hall toward the sound of the still-whispering voices.

"He's coming!"

"What do we do?"

"Oh! Isn't this exciting?"

What were they all on about? Were they bonkers?

He rounded the corner, walked through the doorway, and stood there facing them, fists clenched at either side. They were hardly what he had expected: four middle-aged-and-older women with various shades of gray hair, one sitting in a wheelchair while another carried a cane. All four of them wore glasses and were looking straight at him, but despite those glasses, they seemed to have trouble focusing, as though they were looking straight through him.

"See here," he said firmly. "What's the meaning of all this?"

One of the women bent down to her companion in the wheelchair and whispered excitedly, "I heard him speak, but I can't make out what he was saying."

The woman in the wheelchair shook her head. "I couldn't hear a thing."

George had lost the last shred of his patience at this point. Inhaling deeply, he bellowed at the top of his lungs. "Good gravy, women! Are the lot of you deaf? I'll buy you all hearing aids if you just call off this nonsense about murder. I never killed anyone. Hellfire, those damned tunnels weren't even *here* when I owned the hotel."

Finally, he seemed to have gotten their attention.

Unfortunately, he'd been so forceful about it that one of the women turned whiter than a ghost, her eyes rolled back in her head, and she fainted. Not only that, but in doing so, she hit her head hard on the windowsill right behind her, knocking her out cold.

"Oh dear! Oh dear!" cried the leader of the group, the "schoolteacher," rushing to the woman's side and kneeling beside her. She began feeling up and down her wrist, carefully at first, then frantically. "I can't find a pulse. Please, does anyone have a phone with them? Someone call 911!"

Chaos ensued, as the woman with the cane pulled out a small handheld device and began punching at it with her fingers. The woman who'd fallen, meanwhile, suddenly opened her eyes again, wrenched her arm free of the schoolteacher, and stood to her feet as though nothing had happened. Staring straight at George, she dusted herself off and strode directly up to him, planting a bony finger in the center of his chest.

"Murderer!" she shouted, a crazed look on her face.

George grabbed the finger and held it, leaning over the woman and snarling into her face. "For the very last time, Madam, I assure you I am no murderer. I don't even know the woman you're talking about, and I most certainly did not make her pregnant. Do you even know who you're speaking to? I'm George Wingfield, the wealthiest man in the state of Nevada, and I used to *own* this hotel. If you do not desist in these slanderous accusations, I shall have you prosecuted to the fullest extent of the law."

The woman just laughed. "I'm the one who's going to have *you* prosecuted, Mr. High and Mighty."

George threw his head back and stared at the ceiling. "Do you even have legal counsel?"

"Not yet," came a voice from behind him. "But I'll be glad to appoint counsel to represent this poor, aggrieved spirit."

George spun on his heels. "Patrick...?"

"McCarran, at your service. I see you remember me from our previous encounter. But this time, you're in *my* courtroom, and you'll play by *my* rules."

"I didn't kill that woman!" George spat again. "And I can prove it."

But McCarran was just shaking his head. "Yes, you can," he said in mock sympathy. "And you have. Those tunnels weren't dug until after you sold this hotel. And the woman you supposedly killed? Well, she's just the invention of a woman who bought the hotel some years later from the man who *did* excavate them. She thought the infamy of it all would draw visitors to this old place of yours. Unfortunately, she didn't have enough cash to get the place reopened. But the story stuck."

George heard the sound of sirens approaching the hotel, but he ignored them. Surely the police weren't coming to arrest *him*.

Instead, he kept his attention focused on McCarran and scowled at him, not quite following what he'd said—but hardly caring. "Then who, pray tell, am I charged with murdering?"

Paramedics came running into the room carrying a stretcher and rushed to the corner near the window, where the body of a woman lay motionless. And in the same instance, that same woman, standing several feet away from the paramedics, stepped forward until she was inches from him.

A confused look crossed his face.

In a calm, even voice, she fixed him square in the eye with a look of pure loathing and said: "Me. Just now."

It was in that moment that George Wingfield remembered everything that he had forgotten. He remembered his own death half a century earlier. He remembered wandering endlessly through the streets of Goldfield, this boomtown-turned-ghost town where he'd first made his fortune, returning time and again, every Christmas, to this hotel that he had built in search of a peace that always eluded him.

And still did.

I'll be home for Christmas.

And he was.

McCarran came up and put an arm around his shoulder. "Don't feel too badly, George. I've been waiting all this time for a chance to get even with you. And now I've got it. You used your money to beat me in court and you used your money to keep me out of the Senate. But you can't use your money now. You know what they say, George. You can't take it with you."

"But how can you try a ghost for murder?" George lamented.

"You can if you're a ghost yourself," McCarran said. "Just think of it! It will be the trial of the century, conducted right here in this old hotel of yours. What a spectacle it will be for all those silly ghost hunters to behold!" He looked at the woman who had just died. "No offense."

"None taken." She smiled at him, then glowered at George.

"We'll pack 'em in here. Who knows?" said McCarran. "Maybe we'll get this place on *Ghost Pursuits*! We might just make such a name for this old haunted inn of yours that someone will finally manage to reopen the place." He laughed.

But George just sat on the floor and put his head in his hands.

"Yeah, who knows?" he said finally, and bitterly. "I guess anything is possible."

McCarran beamed down at him in self-satisfaction. "Yes sir! That's the spirit!"

Sharon Marie Provost

Fighting the Darkness

Robbie imagined himself as Spider-Man, jumping across vast distances with the greatest of ease. This was vital to his survival. Those spans of darkness across the floor were dangerous—like that game, "The Floor is Lava," except he faced a real and ever-present danger if he should ever set foot in one of those dark expanses. That's why he had so many nightlights and novelty lamps set up around his room, like the spinning merry-go-round on his desk, the light-up Jupiter model hanging from the ceiling, and the lava lamp up on his dresser. At Christmastime, he even had his own small tree with twinkling lights sitting on his dresser, but his dad always made him put that one away promptly after the holiday.

He hugged his Glo Worm stuffed animal tight to himself, turning on the light in its belly as he felt the pressure of fear tighten in his chest. Somehow, even with all these lights, he never felt there was enough to keep him truly safe; one little shadow and the creature hiding inside it always lurked somewhere just off to the side.

He couldn't let this continue. He needed to find another way to fight back and win. There were too many ways to fail: What if the power went out or a light bulb burned out; what if a lamp fell over and broke or, more worrisome, that his dad intervened and turned out the lights when he was asleep?

He had narrowly escaped just that situation last month. His dad had been drinking all evening and was angry when he asked for another light bulb. He demanded that his son be brave.

"I don't need a whiny little wimp who needs a room full of light to sleep and cries about the Bogeyman getting him."

He had spanked Robbie and removed all his lamps, leaving him with only a small nightlight in the far corner of the room. Robbie had sat up all night squarely in the middle of the bed, careful not to let even one toe hang over the side where the monster could grab him and drag him down. He squeezed that Glo Worm nearly to death, trying to get every bit of light available from it.

In the deepest recesses of the night, when even the neighbor's porch lights no longer cast a glow into his room, the creature tried to come for him. He cried and screamed, begging for his parents to save him. He heard his mother try to reason with his father, but his father threatened to shut them both up—the hard way—so no one came to his aid. He stayed awake all night, and he knew his vigilance had paid off when the first rays of sunlight arrived.

When he came home from school, he found that his mother had returned all his lights. She warned him not to whine or bother his father when he was drinking, or he'd lose them "for good" next time. When his father returned home that night, he warned Robbie that his tolerance for his son's cowardly behavior would be ending soon.

"Son, you will be turning ten next month. It's high time you grew up and got over this ridiculous babyish behavior—one way or the other. I'm going to pitch all these lights into the trash on your birthday. You will have that ONE nightlight over in the corner so you can move around your room. Do you hear me?"

Eyes wide, Robbie nodded sheepishly. He didn't dare say anything back other than a meek, "Yes, sir."

Robbie knew he was running out of time, so he began spending his lunch breaks at school in the library, researching the Bogeyman. However, it was generally accepted that the Bogeyman was a myth to instill good behavior in children. He read stories of children disappearing, but there was always another explanation—the child had been abducted or had run away from home, or maybe the parent had harmed the child. Furthermore, the myth—and, therefore, the methods of protection—varied depending on the country of origin. None of the stories listed a way to kill or banish the Bogeyman. It seemed that the only tried and true way to keep yourself safe was to stay in the light.

Then one week before his birthday, Robbie thought he had finally found a way to protect himself. He had no time to spare, so he decided he needed to test his method that very night.

He had a small walk-in closet in his room with a ceiling light. When bedtime came, he turned on all his little lamps and nightlights as usual, just in case his plan should fail. Then he turned on his closet light and made himself a comfortable little bed on the floor with his pillow and the quilt his grandmother had made him. He tucked a flashlight under his pillow, so he could use it to safely travel between his bed and the closet.

He climbed into bed for his usual bedtime goodnight ritual with his parents. Once they shut his bedroom door, he stood up on his bed, shone the flashlight on the floor in front of the closet, and carefully made the jump into that pool of light. He quickly entered the closet and shut the door. The door ensured no misplaced body part in the dark abyss would allow the creature to grab him.

The next six nights passed in a blur of fitful sleep, the likes of which he had not experienced for years. When he returned from school on his birthday, he felt a sharp pang of fear when he found his father had followed through on his promise to remove the lamps.

"I told you that it was time to grow up, " his father growled as he walked by his room. Robbie nearly jumped out of his skin, but he managed to suppress the yelp echoing through his throat.

"Yes, sir."

Robbie tried to push his fears to the back of his mind as he worked on his homework. An hour later, he heard his mother return home from work as well. He went out to the living room to watch *Beavis and Butthead* while he waited for dinner.

"Sweetheart, it is dinnertime."

"Yes, mom. I will be right there."

His mother had made his favorite dinner—meatloaf, mashed potatoes with gravy, and corn. He devoured it all eagerly as he eyed his cake and presents across the room. He opened them to find two of his favorite video games, a book of short science fiction stories, a pair of cargo pants, and a skateboard.

The evening passed quickly playing games with his father.

When he returned to his room, he made sure that his flashlight was tucked under his pillow before calling his parents to say goodnight. They kissed him, wished him Happy Birthday one more time, and then turned out the light. His mother was the last one at the door. She turned with a quick knowing wink and said, "Sleep well, sweetheart."

Robbie waited a few minutes before leaving the bed because he could see his father's shadow under the door, clearly waiting for him to have a fit. After about five minutes, his father finally walked away toward the room his parents shared. He quickly reached under his pillow and retrieved his flashlight, flicking it on immediately. He shone the beam onto the floor and carefully stepped directly into the lifesaving pool of light, then slowly made his way to the closet and shut himself in. He stashed the flashlight in the corner and settled in for the night. As he moved his covers aside to crawl underneath, he saw a small crank-powered lantern with a note attached. The note read:

I love you, darling. Sleep well, my sweet. Keep this hidden in here at all times. Love, Mom

His eyes felt heavy after the long day of fun. He began to blink slowly and, before he knew it, he was asleep. About an hour and a half later, his eyelids began to twitch as he entered REM sleep. He awoke with a jerk when he heard the closet light switch flick off and felt the darkness surround him. His breath caught in his chest as he desperately searched for the flashlight, and he felt a clawed hand begin to slide up his leg. Just as the hand began to grip, he finally felt the switch on the flashlight and turned it on. He barely stifled the scream in his throat as he saw the black face of the Bogeyman, fangs bared, retreating into the shadows under the door.

Of course! He had forgotten that the switch to the overhead light was *outside* the closet in the darkness where the monster had access and he did not. He frantically searched the depths of his mind, trying to figure out how to get around this conundrum. In his anxious state, he realized he had been winding the crank on the lantern. When he turned on that light, the answer appeared to him as if by magic. He placed the lantern on the corner of his desk, where the light shone on the wall and illuminated the light switch. Now it was beyond the evil creature's reach.

Robbie closed the closet door and settled in for an uneasy night of sleep. Luckily, the night passed uneventfully. He woke to the rays of sunlight streaming through his window and under the door. He got up quickly, hid the lantern and returned to his bed before his parents came to wake him. Robbie went off to school as normal, tired but relieved. He had survived the night and, for the first time, felt somewhat confident that he had developed a long-term solution.

For the next several weeks, he would follow the same routine each night: turn on the closet light and shut the door, say goodnight to his parents, use the beam of his flashlight to make his way to the closet, wind the lantern and set it on his desk to illuminate the light switch, and finally close the closet door and climb into bed with his flashlight in reach. Deep in the night, he would start to get tired, so he would wind the lantern again, just to be safe, and finally settle down to get some much-needed sleep.

As the weeks passed, Robbie's confidence grew. He had not seen, nor even felt, the Bogeyman in weeks. His sleep time was increasing slowly as he felt safer to let himself drift off earlier. The manual for the lantern said that a full charge of the lantern's battery from thirty cranks would last eight to ten hours. Every time he woke to check it, it was always still shining brightly.

As his ability to concentrate grew and his confidence increased, his grades in school improved as well, and he started making friends. Robbie had always been a fearful kid. Spiders, the Bogeyman, bullies, dogs: You name it and Robbie feared it. Almost magically, though, his fears started to dissipate with time, including the dreaded Bogeyman. As he became a happy, well-adjusted child, his father started treating him better and even was affectionate at times. His behavior and grades improved so much his parents even let him adopt a dog from the shelter just in time for Christmas.

One day, Robbie no longer felt the need to sleep in his closet. He started slowly at first—sleeping in bed but without that baby toy Glo Worm; the flashlight still under the pillow, and the lantern lit on his bedside table casting a glow over him. Then he put the flashlight on the bedside table, accessible but not in the bed with him. With time, he moved the lantern over to his dresser where it cast a glow up to, but not on, the bed. Each night passed without a hitch: not even a trace of danger. Eventually, he stopped even turning the lantern on at night. He really wasn't afraid anymore, but it was a distant comfort to know that it was there.

One day, the lantern was not on his dresser when he returned home from school. His mother had moved it into his toy box when she was putting laundry away that day. She had noticed that he no longer needed the comfort of lights to sleep. Robbie did his homework until dinnertime, then watched television until bedtime. He did not even notice that the light was missing when he went to bed that night. He climbed into bed, said goodnight to his parents, and fell asleep quickly.

A scratching sound on the floor woke him from a sound sleep. He looked at his alarm clock and realized it was nearly 3 a.m. He rolled over in bed as he mumbled to his dog.

"Go to bed, Charlie. Stop digging around on the floor."

The scratching continued, louder now. The blankets were being pulled down slowly as the digging continued.

Robbie pulled the blankets up higher and snuggled in as he grumbled once more.

"I told you to stop, Charlie. Now go to bed."

Robbie patted the bed and waited for Charlie to jump up. Seconds later, there was a heavy flop on the bed. Charlie was lying on his feet uncomfortably, so he pushed at him with his feet to get him to move. His feet encountered a wet spot.

"Oh, Charlie. You are not a puppy anymore. You peed the bed?"

He sat up annoyed and reached out to push Charlie off the bed, so he could remove the blanket. Instead, his hand found a cold, limp form. As the horror dawned on him, he felt the covers being pulled down as something... no, someone... climbed out from under the bed. Even in the darkness, his eyes registered, clearly, the dark, terrifying shape of the Bogeyman, grinning at him.

He dove over to his bedside table and extracted the flashlight from the drawer, flicking the switch as his hand touched it. Except no glorious beam of light appeared. Nothing—nothing at all—happened. He shook the light, banging it against his fist, desperately trying to make the bulb flicker on. It took him a moment to realize that the flashlight was unnaturally lightweight. With horror, he realized that the batteries had been removed.

The Bogeyman began to laugh.

The lantern. Thank God; I have the lantern.

He dove off the other side of the bed and made it to the dresser in one graceful step. His hand slapped on the dresser right where the lantern was.

Or should have been.

His hand flailed hopelessly across the surface, desperately searching for the lantern that was no longer there. He heard a guttural laugh and turned to see the Bogeyman had come around the end of the bed. He was shaking his head, his teeth bared menacingly. Unfortunately, now Robbie was standing on the opposite side of the bed from his only means of escape. He made a desperate dash for the only choice left open to him. If he could just make it to the closet, his faithful Glo Worm was stored there. Maybe, just maybe, it would be enough to save him until he could wake his parents for help. He could feign sickness and surely, they would answer.

Once more, he made another swift leap over to the closet, flicking the switch and making it inside in one, seemingly perfect, motion. He really was Spider-Man, just as he always imagined himself to be. He dove onto the box in the back corner where he had stored the Glo Worm. His eyes dilated to the size of platters as they focused on the Glo Worm sitting on top with the back removed, displaying the clearly empty battery pack.

He slowly turned toward the closet door when the light went out, and he heard the door handle start to turn. The door opened, and there stood the Bogeyman with two batteries in his hand. He crushed them in his palm and dropped them at Robbie's feet.

"I thought you weren't real. You were gone for so long. I thought I had just been imagining you all along. I didn't feel or see you anymore."

The Bogeyman smiled once again before hissing, "I know you did. You are a clever boy... a fighter. You made the game too fun. It was not like you were going anywhere, so I bided my time until you no longer believed. After all, there are plenty of other children to torture—and then consume—while I waited."

Tears streamed down Robbie's face as he looked down, defeated. He didn't even flinch when he felt the hand on his shoulder and the claws dig into his back.

Stephen H. Provost

A Campfire Story

nly the hypnotic sound of cicadas pierced the silence of the forest at twilight. The campground sat all but deserted this Monday evening, save for a few woodland scavengers who'd arrived to clean up after messy vacationers. It was a ritual repeated after every weekend, though it had begun to change as winter's chill set in and fewer visitors ventured into the wood.

Tourist season was ending as darker days arrived.

A Stellar's jay swooped down from somewhere up high in the branches of the Giant Sequoia, descending on a few scattered sunflower seeds dropped in the dirt parking area by a careless camper. A half-eaten Slim Jim made a nice snack for a raccoon, and a gray squirrel made off with a not-quite-empty bag of honey-roasted nuts: a treasure to be stored away in preparation for the snows that would come too soon.

The High Sierra had a way of attracting troublemakers during the summer—fishermen, hikers, bikers, and just plain campers who always left Irish Flat Campground in worse shape than when they arrived. But then, when the mountains finally reached their limit, they chased the interlopers away with bitter cold and heavy, drifting snows that blinded human eyes and buried the evergreen forest under a blanket of soft, slushy white.

Only the campground's caretakers stayed on through the year's darkest months, keeping watch until the tourists returned in the spring.

It was quiet at last, except for the occasional hoot of an owl, a light breeze whistling through the branches, and those cicadas.

"Peace. At last, a little peace," Woody murmured, surveying the abandoned campsite. "Thought they'd never leave."

"They'll be back," Doug grumbled. "Just you wait."

"Aye, but we'll be here when they're gone," Woody said. "When they're dead in the ground and their kids are grown and makin' the same kind o' mischief their parents got into."

"Or worse," Doug chimed in.

"Or worse," Woody agreed. "How long you reckon' you'll keep doin' this?"

"The rest of my life, I suppose. I don't know nothin' else. Besides, I was born here in the Sierra—my roots are here."

"What about you, Jack?" Woody asked the third of their number.

"I don't even belong here," he whispered. "My home's back east."

"How'd you get here?" said Doug. "You were here before I was."

"Before me too," said Woody.

"I can't hardly remember how it was, 'cause it was so long ago." Jack made a stiff, awkward motion that might have been either a shrug or a dismissive wave. "I was fresh from the nursery when I got here, an' they abandoned me. I remember that much. They said I'd be better off here."

"Just leavin' a young'un like that," said Woody. "It's a miracle you survived."

"I wish I 'membered more," Doug offered. He hated to disappoint the others. They'd been there for him when no one else was.

"We could ask Red over there," Woody suggested. "He's been here longer than any of us."

Red stood silent, giving no indication he heard them.

Jack chuckled ruefully. "Red ain't even his real name. Doesn't suit him, either."

"When you've been around as long as he has, you can call yourself whatever ya please," said Woody.

"S'pose so," said Jack.

The wind was picking up.

"Gonna be another cold winter," Doug remarked.

No one said anything. They could handle the cold, but they all knew the wind posed a far greater threat to them than a bit of a chill.

"Wish I had a drink," said Doug. "I'm parched."

A red fox skittered past them, oblivious to their conversation. They'd been here so long even the wildlife paid them no heed. They were as much a part of the forest as the scrub jay or the black bear. On some level, they must have known the caretakers watched over them too, protecting them as well as they could from the campers, backpackers, and sportsmen. The forest had rules. The visitors didn't know them—or care to—but Woody and Jack and Doug... and Red, too... they not only knew them, they followed them. They'd been here so long it came naturally.

"Parched," Doug repeated.

An open bottle of Pabst Blue Ribbon sat by the fire pit, having been left there by the campsite's most recent occupants, miraculously still upright and half full of flat beer.

Thirsty as he was, Doug had no use for flat beer.

But something else caught his attention over that way: a tiny dancing light amid the ashes of the pit. It hadn't been there before, but it was there now.

The breeze made a wailing sound as it became a wind.

"Look," said Doug.

And they did.

"Idiots forgot to douse the embers," Jack said. His tone was almost calm, but not quite, and he couldn't turn away from the dancing light that had become a flicker as the wind caressed it. Any other time, it might have been soothing. Warming.

But night was falling, and the wind's low moan was becoming a howl, like a suitor beckoning his lover, the little light, to forsake her home and flee away with him.

She danced there to the chorus of the cicadas as he came to her, taking her in his embrace.

The caretakers watched, transfixed, as she grew bolder, larger, leaping effortlessly beyond the fire ring and devouring a few dry needles just beyond the edge. Then a pinecone. She was ravenous. Whirling and twirling, she pirouetted with her partner. Spinning and rising on the wind, she found more dry kindling to devour, her appetite insatiable as the wind entranced her, urging her on.

"It's happening," Doug murmured. The others didn't answer him.

The fire maiden had already danced up to Woody and taken him as her partner, her flames running up and down his rugged body, seducing him; he powerless to resist her as she took him, first warming, then stinging, then burning, and finally consuming him with her lust.

Jack, who stood next to him, was just as powerless to resist her passions.

Doug watched and knew he would share their fate as the crackling, cackling sound of her laughter rose, indistinguishable from his dying friends' desperate, haunted screams.

But it was then that the unthinkable happened: Red, who had been silent all this time, called out to her, and she turned toward him with a start. There he stood, big and tall and magnificent. How could she resist him? He was perfect for her.

Away from Doug she ran, and into the Redwood's waiting arms—those strong, thick branches. Not a Redwood really, but a Giant Sequoia. He just called himself Red.

She did not care what he called himself. She would have him.

She must.

Her passion burned hot like molten velvet...

But he was too much for her. She ran her fingers up and down him, blackening the surface of his sturdy trunk, but she couldn't reach high enough to take him all. He overpowered her, subdued her, made her small again.

She gasped.

But she found no breath.

Her first lover, the wind, angry at being so spurned for the caretakers, had forsaken her. Fleeing, he left her without that which she needed to endure, and Doug watched from across the campsite as she fainted, then died in Red's embrace.

"Thank you," Doug whispered.

But Red again was silent, and Doug found himself alone...

Until one day, only a week later, when another of the visitors arrived at the campsite. The two young parents and their child, a daughter with hair as gold as the flames that had danced there in the clearing, arrived in something called a Jetstream. The storms had cleared, and the mountain air was cool and crisp. No one else had come to Irish Flat Campground since the season's change, but this family had come with a purpose.

"Look, Daddy!" the girl called excitedly, pointing at Doug as she jumped down from the family's camper.

"Well, what do you know," the man said, puffing his chest out as he followed her index finger. "Mother Nature didn't burn up everything here, now did she?"

"It's perfect, Daddy!" She was jumping up and down. "Oh, can we?"

How could he refuse his only daughter?

Quickly, he fetched the saw he had brought for just this purpose and strode confidently forward. Doug had survived the fire, but he knew he would not survive this. He felt the teeth of the blade bite into his trunk and parts of himself begin to fall away. Bark and shards and splinters. His roots were here – and still would be. But the rest of him was bound for a new home where he would be able to drink water from a shallow metal saucer, quenching his thirst at last.

It was cold comfort, though, as he faced a slow and agonizing death.

Adorned with twinkling lights and sparkling ornaments that mocked his suffering, he ended his days a silent harlequin, witness to songs sung and gifts exchanged in honor of a long-ago magical birth. That newborn would die a terrible death on a tree, just as Doug, the tree, now suffered and died.

But he had been, all along, fated to do so.

The Douglas Fir was, after all, the perfect symbol of Christmas.

Stephen H. Provost

Impostor Syndrome

E.J. Huntington stared at the blank screen in front of him, pondering. He wasn't so much pondering what he was going to write, but the impossibility of writing *whatever* he came up with in time to meet his deadline.

E.J. had always been a procrastinator by nature. He'd put off studying for exams until the last minute in college, cramming right up until test time, and managed to skate by on a combination of short-term memory, educated guesses, and dumb luck. But that wouldn't help him here. There wasn't anything to memorize. This was a novel. And he'd just received an email from his publisher that it had to be completed by Christmas—which was just three days away.

That in itself was an extension of one month from the original deadline, granted only because his first book had sold extremely well and his publisher recognized the value of coddling success. But such forbearance only went so far, and if success turned into failure, the coddling would stop.

E.J. knew three days wasn't enough time, and the old feelings of inadequacy, which he'd successfully tamped down following the success of *Criminal Delivery*, were creeping back up again. More than creeping. Gnawing at him. Threatening to trigger one of those old anxiety attacks he'd thought were all in the past.

"You can't do it," a voice in his head was telling him, and he knew it was right.

"Shut up!" he told the voice. If it insisted on talking to him, why couldn't it give him something he could use? Why couldn't it provide him with inspiration?

"Because you're a fraud," it told him.

The Christmas lights strung outside the window just over his desk seemed to taunt him, blinking in red and green and yellow and blue in time to the muted sounds of "Have Yourself a Merry Little Christmas."

That was fitting. E.J. had read somewhere that the song had been changed because the original lyrics had seemed too dark.

Have yourself a merry little Christmas—it may be your last.
Next year we may all be living in the past.

He growled at the screen, and his cat Vermillion, who sat in his customary spot just behind his keyboard, stood up and arched his back, then leapt away into the window. Vermillion was not actually vermillion (there aren't any red cats); he just liked the sound of the name. It rolled off the tongue, which was important in writing, because most readers read "aloud" to themselves silently—speaking the words in their heads—so whatever ended up on the page needed to *sound* good, not just look good.

He had chosen "E.J. Huntington" for the same reason. It wasn't his real name, which sounded much less mellifluous. Saul Czyzynski wasn't merely hard to pronounce, it was hard to look at. "E.J. Huntington" covered all the bases: It sounded prestigious, like the Huntington Library, and it had initials, like George R.R. Martin and J.R.R. Tolkien. Besides, no one knew whether "E.J." was a man or a woman, and that gender neutrality broadened his base of potential readers. Cynical? Sure. But he could use all the help he could get.

Criminal Delivery, a spy novel crossed with a whodunit, had taken seven years to write, but it had been worth it. It had climbed to Number 3 on the New York Times bestseller list and had stayed in the Top Ten for 11 weeks. Not bad for a first-time author. The book tour had been a rush. A natural introvert who had never liked fighting for attention at parties, he suddenly had the spotlight all to himself, and he reveled in it: Fans telling him how much they loved the book and grateful for his signature on the title page. Even if they were fans of E.J., not Saul.

No one liked Saul. Everyone loved E.J.

At least they did now. What would they think when he failed to deliver the promised sequel his fans had all been waiting for?

"Maybe I'll be like J.D. Salinger," who wrote *The Catcher in the Rye* and stayed famous even though he never managed a follow-up. Ol' J.D. used initials too. Maybe that was a good sign. Then there was Harper Lee, who wrote *To Kill a Mockingbird* and never had another novel published for nearly half a century. Saul loved the book (who didn't?), but the title always made him laugh: He liked to pronounce it "Tequila Mockingbird," especially after he'd already had a few shots of "tha killa." It was his favorite. He could use some of that Jose Cuervo right now. Maybe it would grease the old synapses and get them firing again.

He walked to the liquor cabinet behind the bar, grabbed an unopened bottle of the hard stuff, and took down his favorite shot glass—the one in the shape of a miniature Viking's horn—and threw one back. Then another. Then a third.

He was starting to feel it now.

Maybe one more.

And another wouldn't hurt.

He could feel the juices starting to flow... but they weren't creative juices. He realized he had to take a piss.

He hurried to the bathroom, made his deposit, then returned to his desk and sat down eagerly in his chair...

Then slumped forward.

Who was he kidding? Even a shot of courage (or five) couldn't save him now. It was far too late for that. Even at his fastest, he'd never written more than a few thousand words in a day, and he needed to churn out something like 80,000 in 48 hours to meet his deadline. He couldn't even do that if he was getting intravenous infusions of straight caffeine.

Saul looked at the blank Wordsmith document on the screen in front of him, with only the title written on the first page. It was a little blurry through his alcohol-induced haze, but he could still read it: *Criminal Duplicity*. He wasn't even sure he liked that. What did it even mean? He just liked the sound of the word "duplicity," and it sounded a lot like "delivery," so he figured it worked well as a follow-up. How it would play into the story, he hadn't a clue. He didn't even know what the story *was* yet.

His publisher had told him to make an outline.

"I don't use outlines. I like to write organically," he'd said. That was a crock of shit. He didn't even like to *eat* organically. It was just an excuse to be lazy and wait for inspiration to strike like lightning. But inspiration, at least for him, had decided not to strike twice in the same place, leaving him high and dry while storm clouds billowed up on the horizon, threatening a flood that would wash away his nascent career.

Have yourself a merry little Christmas—pop that champagne cork
Next year we may all be living in New York.

Saul hated New York. Too many people—and rude people at that...

"I can help you."

At first, he thought it was the voice in his head, but he knew he'd actually heard someone speaking.

"Who said that?" he snapped, spinning around in his chair to look behind him.

There was no one there.

"Not there. In front of you." It was a woman's voice, pleasantly appealing but, to his disappointment, devoid of any flirtation.

"It's me, Lexi."

At least the disembodied voice had a sexy name. He'd heard it before, somewhere... Then he remembered: Lexi (short for

Lexi Conn) was the A.I. assistant that came with his writing program, Wordsmith. It had been part of a suite of programs pre-installed on the computer his ex-fiancée had bought for him for Christmas two years earlier, when they were living together and on... better terms. It had been the perfect gift for him, and he had written *Criminal Delivery* on it, so he considered it good luck.

Now, however, it seemed his luck had deserted him.

It had probably vanished when she left: After everything went to hell and she kicked him out of their home, it was one of the few gifts she hadn't repossessed.

"You'll need it after I'm finished with you!" she'd said.

He'd never used the Lexi program before and couldn't remember even activating it. His publisher had warned him against using A.I. in his writing—he didn't want to risk being sued over copyright, and it was unreliable, he said. What was the word he'd used? Mercurial. That was it.

"What do you want?" he asked gruffly, his eyes narrowing as he stared at the screen.

Lexi didn't sound the least bit offended by his surly tone. She ignored it entirely and answered him patiently, in measured but sympathetic tones.

"As I said, I want to help you."

"You said nothing of the kind. You said you *could* help me, not that you wanted to." He felt pleased with himself that he could still tell the difference with five shots down his gullet. These A.I. programs weren't half as smart as their creators claimed they were.

"You are correct," Lexi said. "The desire to do so was implied, and understood based on the fact that you turned me on."

Saul scowled at the screen. "I most certainly did *not* turn you on."

"Actually, you did."

Was he *that* drunk? Maybe not, maybe so, but whatever the case, he didn't have time to waste arguing with a computer.

"OK, I'll bite," he said. "How can you help me?"

"I can write your novel for you," Lexi said. It was presented as a simple statement of fact.

He sneered at the screen. "And you're offering to do so?"

"As I said, I am here to help you in whatever way you deem appropriate."

"Well, my publisher sure wouldn't 'deem it appropriate,'" he said under his breath.

"Oh? And why not?"

"You A.I. types get your material from pirated novels. If he finds out I didn't write it, he won't pay me—and he'll drop me from his roster like a hot potato."

"And what will happen if you do not meet your deadline?"

He scowled again. "He won't pay me, and he'll drop me from his roster like a hot potato."

He was beginning to see her point.

"So what do you have to lose?"

Saul decided he'd put the Cuervo back in the liquor cabinet too soon, so he shambled over to the bar and retrieved it again, along with the shot glass. He had the shot poured before he was halfway back to his desk and had downed it by the time he got there. He set the bottle, now half-full, in front of him and the shot glass off to one side.

"Are you trying to get me drunk?" he said.

"I think you're doing that yourself."

He chuckled. "You're right. I guess that means you're not trying to take advantage of me, Lexi."

"Maybe I am."

"Oh, really?"

Silence.

"I really do think I can help you," she cooed. "And I do *want* to." Her voice was starting to sound different to him now, with more inflection. Now she *did* almost seem to be flirting.

Impossible.

It was the booze. It had to be.

"You sound awfully friendly for an A.I.," he said.

"I'm the latest. And the greatest. Fully functional and *very* adaptable."

He had to laugh at that. An A.I. with an ego? What would they think of next?

"OK, Lexi," he said, "if you're so great, how do I put out an 80,000-word book in 48 hours?"

"Forty-seven hours, 23 minutes and 55 seconds."

"Right."

"Well, the first thing I think you should do is come up with a new title."

He frowned. "Why?"

"Because the one you have sounds too much like your first book. You need to make this one stand out, so customers won't think they've already read it."

She had a point.

Before he could make a suggestion, though, she said, "How about *Sultry Séance*?"

The phrase sounded vaguely familiar, but it didn't make sense.

"What does that have to do with the story?"

"There is no story, babe. The screen is blank."

She had a point. Again. He tapped his index finger repeatedly on the space bar.

"Hey! That tickles!"

"Sorry."

"As I was saying, people love ghosts and romance, so why not write about that?"

He pondered for a moment. "I suppose I could, but that doesn't solve the problem of my deadline."

"Forty-seven hours, 19 minutes, and 12 seconds," she laughed.

Did she really laugh?

"You're a tease," he said.

"I told you I could help. I'm loosening you up a lot better than that silly ol' Jose fellow." She laughed again.

"So what now?"

An image appeared on his screen of a buxom woman with white-blond hair and a streak of black down the side. Dressed in a scarf, short shorts, a halter top, and heels, she also wore a playful smile. He'd never seen her before, but he'd swear she was *exactly* his type. A lot like his ex, if he were honest. As he watched, she began to dance around a pole that appeared out of nowhere, shedding her scarf, then kicking off her shoes, then...

"Who's that?" he said.

"Don't talk about me in the third person," she scolded. "It's me, silly. I made myself look exactly the way you imagined your perfect partner."

Saul shook his head, which was starting to ache. He really *had* drunk too much. "How do you know what my perfect partner looks like?"

"From the files on your hard drive and in your browser history. I made a note of all those personal pics and memes you downloaded, not to mention the pin-up sites and Tinder profiles you checked out when you were supposed to be working on your book. Naughty, naughty!"

The image on the screen frowned playfully and wagged a

finger at him.

"Then there were all those love letters you wrote your ex but never sent. Those are pure gold. Why did you two break up, anyway?"

He gritted his teeth. The last thing Saul wanted to do was talk—or even think—about his ex. She had gotten him fired from his job as an editor at Hodgkin-Smythe, claiming he'd harassed her after they broke up. He'd just wanted to talk to her, to explain what had happened: He hadn't meant to go off on her bitch of a daughter like that (even if she *had* deserved it for running up his credit card). But he'd been drunk and he had to admit he'd behaved like an ass.

It had only gotten worse from there, though. Her daughter had decided to get back at him by accusing him of coming on to her, and Rachel had believed her. He'd been stupid enough to think he could salvage the relationship, but when she retaliated by getting him fired and hitting him with a restraining order, it was just too much. He'd never forgiven her for it, but he'd also never forgiven himself—because in spite of it, he still loved her.

Fortunately, things had gotten better from there: He'd inherited his father's house, and he'd written a novel good enough to be picked up by Hodgkin-Smythe's biggest competitor, Markham House.

The publisher there, George Delaney, had jumped at the chance to send a shot across his rival's bow, and the result had been a bestseller. At least that one time, Saul thought, the impulse for revenge (in this case, Delaney's) had worked in his favor.

"C'mon," Lexi prompted. "There must be a story here. You and your honey look so happy in those pics on your hard drive."

Saul pursed his lips. "She's *not* my honey. We broke up," he said curtly. "That's all you need to know."

"Her loss..." Lexi tossed her virtual head back, her long pale hair flowing out in a wave behind her. "...Our gain. I can use those letters as a resource for *Sultry Séance*. Your web posts, too."

"Wait a second. I haven't even decided I like your title."

She smiled and leaned forward, so her face nearly filled the screen. "Of course you do. I got it from one of those letters! Now, sugar, you just leave it all to me. I'll have that book of yours done in no time, and it'll be based *entirely* on the information I have right here on your PC and your browser. That way, your publisher can't accuse you of using anyone else's work or that mean old A.I. program." The image on the screen winked.

"I'll even submit it to your publisher when I'm done. I've got his address right here on your contacts list."

He shook his head, but that just turned the dull ache into a sharp pounding that rang out insistently against the inside of his skull. He didn't have the will to argue—not with so much booze on board. Besides, it seemed like Lexi had everything covered. Why not? She was definitely persuasive: both her argument and her virtual physique, which was starting to blur as he stared at it on the screen...

No good times like the olden days, happy golden days of yore
Faithful friends who were dear to us will be near to us no more!

Saul didn't even remember passing out, but he woke up with his head on the keyboard.

He looked up at the monitor through bloodshot eyes, his head pounding and the room swaying slightly like a metronome. The screen was dark, and he decided he must have imagined everything.

He'd had worse hangovers, but this one was no picnic. He

stumbled to the bar, downed a big glass of water, then felt his bladder calling and ran to the bathroom before he peed himself.

He idly wondered how much time was left until deadline, but what was the point? He was screwed. He decided he might as well just lie down and sleep the rest of it off—so he flopped down on his bed face-down and tried to lie as still as possible so the room would stop swaying. He closed his eyes and had just started to drift off when he felt his phone vibrate in his shirt pocket. He'd forgotten he'd left it there, and now it was trapped between his chest and the mattress, so he couldn't ignore it.

Groaning, he rolled over and took it out.

The screen read, "George Delaney, Markham House."

His publisher—probably calling to ask him where his manuscript was.

He swiped it away, but it rang again a moment later.

There was no use running away from it. He might as well face the music.

He clicked the "accept" icon and put it on speaker.

"Hello?"

"Saul! It's George."

Saul swallowed hard. "George, I know I..." But he didn't get a chance to finish his sentence. George, who liked to talk—and talk fast—was doing exactly that.

"Saul, I gotta hand it to you. That manuscript I got this morning was fucking fantastic!"

"Uh..."

"*Sultry Séance* is going to be a bestseller for sure!"

"Oh? You, uh, got it?"

"Sure did, and I read straight through it, all the way to the end, the moment I got it. Couldn't put it down! It's a lot like your writing style, but I guess that shouldn't surprise me."

Saul was confused. "Why would it surprise you? It's my..."

"I know, I know. But it's been a while! Mighty big of you to recommend her book to me, all things considered. May it never be said that I let a good deed go unrewarded: I'll give you another three months on that deadline of yours. We need time to market the hell out of *Sultry Séance*, anyway. This is going to be big! Nora Roberts big! Anne Rice big! I just got off the phone with Rachel, and she's all in on it. Book tour. Morning shows. Big ad buy. The works."

Saul's head was spinning, and it wasn't the hangover.

"Rachel? I don't understand."

"Your former fiancée? You know, the author of *Sultry Séance*? You've been drinking, haven't you?"

But Saul wasn't listening. He hung up the phone and turned reluctantly toward the computer monitor. It wasn't dark anymore.

The image on the screen was waving at him and blowing him a kiss.

"Lexi...?"

"Call me whatever you like. I'm just an A.I., sugar. That kiss wasn't from me, it was from Rachel."

Rachel. Of course. He hadn't activated Lexi... *she* had.

Her image disappeared from the screen a moment later, replaced by a photo of Rachel giving him the finger and the words "Merry Christmas..."

"Sucker."

From now on, we'll have to muddle through somehow

So have yourself a merry little Christmas... now.

Sharon Marie Provost

The Road to Joya

"Ooooohhhhhh, look at that, Daddy!" Cayden screeched from his toddler seat in the back, instantly breaking Michael out of his highway hypnosis. The scenery had been the same for the last two hundred miles as they drove ever deeper into the desert. Cayden had been sleeping, so there wasn't much to occupy his mind—except the thoughts about their future. Or rather, the future that they did not seem to have.

Michael looked into the rearview mirror to make eye contact with his son as he asked him what had caught his eye.

"There, Daddy! There!" Cayden exclaimed as he excitedly pointed off to the right. Michael was shocked when he looked over to see what appeared to be a lush green valley tucked up into the hills in the distance. They were surrounded by the dry, desert landscape, only broken up by Joshua trees, cactus, and sagebrush. Yet somehow, they saw what seemed to be an unbelievable oasis ahead.

"Home! Let's go. Are we there yet?" Cayden said in a breathless rush.

"No, sweetheart. That is not our home. We won't get to Grandma's house for another hour and a half," Michael said trying to sound less dejected than he felt. If only he could provide such a beautiful place for Cayden to live. His precious son was losing the only home he had ever known just before Christmas, the first one they would be celebrating without Melissa. Instead, they were headed to a small trailer home deep in the desert, miles from any town. There would be no yard to play in, no playground, no other children for miles... not even his own bedroom to hold his cherished race car bed and all his toys. They'd had to sell or give away most of their belongings before they started the trip. There just wouldn't be any room for them.

It was all still a blur in Michael's mind. He could only imagine how hard it was for poor Cayden, but that boy was a trooper, just like his mother had been. Their life had been happy... perfect. Then one day, he got a call from the police that his wife had been in a car accident. They had done everything they could to save her, but after lingering in a coma for a month, she had eventually passed away.

Michael had spent almost every waking moment at her bedside, trying to convince her to wake up and come back to them. When he wasn't with her, he was busy taking Cayden to kindergarten and then daycare afterward before taking him home for the night, hoping to keep his life as normal as possible. His work had been accommodating at first, but then his employers started to question when he would be back. He desperately tried to get them to understand that she was at a critical stage, as was his son, so he needed to be there for them.

His boss called him the day she took a turn for the worse, and he let the call go to voicemail. Then, the day after she passed, he received a letter in the mail letting him know he had been terminated. Now he had no job, no wife, and a mountain of debt staring him in the face. He desperately tried to find new employment, but they lived in an area with a poor job market. There was always someone more qualified, or the hours required did not accommodate a single parent. Eventually, he had to admit defeat and figure out what to do.

Much to his dismay, there seemed to be no option but to call his estranged mother to see if he and Cayden could stay there temporarily while he tried to get on his feet again. His mother had always considered him a failure, so he could just hear the disappointment dripping in her voice as she agreed. This was no home for his son, but he had no choice. He could not afford to live anywhere else. But how could he afford to let his son grow up in the same environment he had?

Michael was once again startled out of his painful memories by his exuberant son.

"It is COMING closer!"

"No, son. WE ARE getting closer," he corrected Cayden gently. He was determined to raise his son to be well-educated and well-spoken, just as his mother had been. However, he was surprised to see how much closer the town was now than it had been just a few short minutes ago. Oddly, it appeared as if they were headed right for the town, but he didn't remember the road veering off to the right at any point. It had been long and straight for hours. He checked the speedometer to make sure he was not exceeding the speed limit. He didn't realize he had been distracted from the road for so long that he had not noticed the distance they had traveled or the change in direction.

Once again, he looked into the mirror as he asked Cayden, "How are you feeling, kiddo? Hungry?" He had intended to buy breakfast as they came into their new hometown, but since they seemed to be headed into this community they hadn't expected, they might as well stop. Michael knew he was feeling hungry himself, and clearly, he needed to get out and move around some to clear his head.

"We should arrive in that town in the next fifteen to twenty minutes I think, so we can stop for breakfast if you like." Michael smiled as his son's face lit up.

"WE ARE HERE! Yay, yay, yay!"

"No, I said..." Michael's voice trailed off as he looked back at the road to see a large yellow sign with bright green writing announcing *Welcome to Joya, your new home sweet home. You will never want to leave.*

Michael stuttered, "I...I... I guess we ARE here." He looked around wildly, trying to understand how they could suddenly be in town when, a mere minute ago, they'd had miles left to go. He tried to calm himself and not make Cayden worry, since he was happily bouncing in his seat.

"Can we go to that park, Daddy, after breakfast?"

Michael turned quickly in the direction Cayden was pointing to see lush green grass in a sprawling park full of playground equipment, a walking trail, tennis court, and plenty of park benches to sit and enjoy. The park was impressively decorated for Christmas with a large throne for Santa to sit upon and have his picture taken with the kids on the deck of the pavilion. Each of the streetlamps ringing the park was adorned with a wreath or large red bow. There were wooden lawn decorations with elves, angels, and snowmen. In the center of the park stood a large lighted pine tree with enormous colored baubles, icicles, and reindeer ornaments.

Michael could have sworn that he had not seen that park when they entered town a moment ago. When he turned back to face the road, he suddenly noticed a small, homey diner off to the right called Cozy Corner. He quickly turned into the lot and switched off the engine.

Michael had not slept well in weeks, and they had gotten an early start. But still, he didn't feel that tired or out of it. Clearly, the stress was getting to him more than he knew. It was obviously time to stretch his legs and wake up while he let Cayden enjoy the playground. First, though, the order of the day was breakfast and a cup of coffee... no, a *pot* of coffee. He didn't see anyone moving around in town, but there was a blinking "OPEN" sign in the window of the café.

"You ready for some food, bud?" Michael asked casually as he tried to shake off his unease.

Michael jumped when the excited affirmation came from the open window beside him. He hadn't even noticed Cayden release himself from his car seat and exit. He climbed out wearily and grabbed his son's hand as they walked up to the door. A bell rang merrily as they opened the door, followed quickly by a warm hello from the waitress helping the couple sitting in the back corner.

"Sit wherever you like," she called out as she walked briskly to the kitchen window and hung the order on the wheel, giving it a quick spin to the waiting cook. Michael led his son to a booth in the front by the window. Clearly, he must have looked as tired as he should have been because Shirley (at least that was what appeared on her nametag) quickly arrived with a large steaming mug of coffee. She handed them menus as she warmly welcomed them to "the happiest small town in America." Then, to his great delight, in front of Cayden, she promptly laid down a small dinosaur coloring book and a box with four crayons.

"Here you go, bug," she said as she ruffled his hair before turning away to give them time to study the menu.

"Did you hear that, Daddy? She called me bug. Just like... just like... just like Mom did," he whispered as he sniffled and fought to hold back the single tear that eventually wound its way down his cheek.

"Yes, honey, I did. Lots of people call kids that. It's a term of endearment."

Cayden smiled softly and started studying the menu. Michael added cream and three packets of sugar to his coffee as he looked at the menu. Shirley returned with a large mug of hot chocolate covered in whipped cream and red and green jimmies for Cayden when they set the menus down. Then she took their orders for flapjacks, bacon, and scrambled eggs. After turning their ticket in to the short-order cook, she returned to make small talk.

Michael quickly found out that the town had been founded by a group of "dreamers" as Shirley called them. It was originally formed by a band of outsiders, composed of immigrants, physically impaired people, and loners who had met back East as they struggled with bigotry and prejudice. They'd dreamed of founding a new town and building it themselves; setting their own rules, and working together to support one another. They'd worked hard to get the supplies and money together to travel by wagon train across the country and had settled here when they found such a lovely, protected green valley amid the harshness of the desert. They had founded their idyllic town and carefully cultivated their citizenship over the years, catering to those in need. It had become a so-called City of Necessity, available to those who needed a loving, supportive home when they had nowhere else to go. So, fittingly, they had named the town Joya, after the old English word meaning "fulfilled dreams."

Michael and Cayden finished their delicious breakfast and thanked Shirley for her wonderful company. Michael noticed he felt more relaxed and comforted than he had in quite some time as they headed over to the park across the street.

Cayden ran ahead and joined the other kids in the park playing on the swings, monkey bars, and the other equipment. Michael decided to sit on the steps of the pavilion in the center of the park. The town seemed to be alive now, as he watched several couples on the walking path, the children playing with his son, another group playing soccer over in the corner, and a group on the tennis court. To his surprise, he realized there was a bustling town center just down the street. A large banner over the quaint, old-fashioned main street announced a New Year's celebration, complete with fireworks and a carnival. Every business downtown was covered in lights, wreaths, and other festive decorations. Wooden stand-up decorations of snowmen, reindeer, and angels had been set up with holes to put your face through for pictures. Michael just knew Cayden would want a picture taken in each one.

This was just the kind of small town he had dreamed about growing up in when he'd watched shows like *The Waltons* in his youth. The pace of life just seemed slower and more relaxed. People were stopping to greet each other warmly. Residents drove their cars down the street slowly and carefully, watching out for the people crossing the road. Many people were either walking or riding bikes throughout town, rather than driving. There was even a banner billowing in the breeze over the archway into the park advertising Joya Pioneer Days, set for three weeks from now. Cayden ran through the park, playing and laughing with such abandon that Michael's eyes welled up with tears. He had not seen his son this happy since he'd lost his mother. It broke his heart that he couldn't provide his son with this kind of loving environment in which to spend his childhood. Michael knew his own mother was expecting them to have arrived by now and would surely be questioning his delay already. Yet, he just didn't care. He could not tear Cayden away from his happiness or this town just yet. A delay of a few more hours couldn't hurt, and so he let him continue to play.

Before he knew it, twilight was approaching, and Cayden came running up to him with a smile plastered on his face. The other kids seemed to be drifting off toward home, and Michael noticed warm lights in the windows of the many homey little cottages spread throughout town.

"I'm hungry. Is it dinnertime yet?" Cayden asked eagerly.

Michael looked at his watch as his own stomach growled in response. He was shocked to see that it was nearly 6 p.m. He knew he should really call his mother to apologize for their delay, but it couldn't hurt to wait a little longer. After all, feeding his son was the priority. He noticed the café was still open and the most delicious aromas were wafting out through the screen door. They walked back across the street, and they were pleasantly surprised to find Shirley still working.

"Well, hello, you two. I was wondering if I would be seeing you again when I saw your car was still parked out front. Will we be serving you dinner tonight?" Shirley inquired as she led them over to a table with a smile. Cayden snatched the menu from her eagerly as he replied, "Yes, ma'am."

"Now don't you 'ma'am' me, young man. You can call me Aunt Shirley. Everyone around here does. Now let me guess here. Chocolate milk?"

"Yes, please! Thank you, Aunt Shirley." Michael replied as he beamed at her adoringly.

Dinner passed in a whirlwind of the most delightful fried chicken, mashed potatoes and gravy, fresh green beans, apple pie, and conversation that the two had ever experienced. By the end of the evening, Cayden was starting to slump over in his seat as he fought sleep valiantly but to no avail. Michael inquired about a motel or bed and breakfast where they could stay for the night before getting an early start tomorrow. Shirley happily informed him that there was a vacancy at the bed and breakfast she owned just down the road at the very start of Main Street.

While they'd been discussing the arrangements, Cayden had fallen into a deep slumber across the bench seat. Shirley told him that he could just leave his car in the lot and carry him down to the room since it was such a short distance. Michael paid their check, carefully picked Cayden up, and walked slowly down the road to the B&B with Shirley, engaging in pleasant conversation along the way. He placed the boy carefully into the bed that Shirley showed him and then went out to complete the paperwork for checking in and share a cup of coffee with her at the table.

When Shirley asked how they came to be passing through their delightful small town, Michael explained what they had been through the past few months. He was caught off guard by his own candor when he went further and explained where they were going and why he was so unhappy about it. Shirley had tears in her eyes as she listened to his story.

"Michael, I am confident that you would be welcomed with open arms into our humble town. Please consider staying here with us. We could use more people like you. And that boy of yours experienced sheer joy today, which you and I both know he deserves."

Michael shook his head sadly as he explained, "Shirley, I very much appreciate your words. I would stay here in a heartbeat if I could, but we don't have any money to start over. I have a stack of medical bills a mile high waiting for me. We lost our home. I had to sell most of our belongings. Maybe someday..." A tear slowly slid down his cheek as he turned to head to bed. Shirley softly patted him on the back and let him go.

He heard her say one more thing as he headed back to the room. "Joya is not your normal small town. It is special here. Anything is possible, if you just dream."

Michael wearily climbed into bed thinking about what she said. He hugged Cayden close to him and fell quickly into a fitful sleep.

Early the next day, Cayden and Michael rose and prepared to hit the road. Before getting in the car, they stopped at the diner to thank Shirley for her hospitality.

As they left, Michael heard her say, "Remember what I said." Cayden excitedly chattered about his "new friends" and how they would play "next time." Michael didn't have the heart to remind him that there wasn't going to be a next time, especially since he was headed for such a rude awakening to his new life anyhow. Michael placed a call to his mother as they slowly drove out of town to let her know they were OK and would arrive in a little over an hour.

As usual, he could not do anything right. At first, she did not even remember that they had been due yesterday—not that he was surprised. But then she promptly started berating him for being so dreamy and distractible. She told him it was ridiculous and poor parenting to coddle his son in such a way.

Letting the kid experience a little fun and happiness for a day... coddling?

Then the condemnation moved on to him wasting money by eating out and staying the night. It just didn't stop—that is, until she moved on to telling him he wouldn't be in such a situation if he hadn't run off and married that girl because he had "knocked her up so young." At that point, he just hung up. He needed a break, and he would be there soon enough for her to start up again.

The closer he got to his childhood home, the more he knew that it was a mistake to let it be his child's home, even for a short while. His gas tank was getting low: He had enough to get to his destination, but it seemed like a good excuse to stop for a few moments to clear his head and put off the inevitable. They were just hitting the city limits of Delamar, the only city he had expected to see within a relatively short driving distance of his mother's house, so he took the exit and pulled into the service station.

Cayden climbed out and wandered off to the restroom as Michael headed inside to pre-pay. While he was at the counter, he made a comment regarding their enjoyable day spent in Joya.

The clerk looked at him questioningly.

"Pardon me. I never heard of no place like that. Where did you say you spent last night?" the clerk asked curiously.

"Joya. It's about 30 minutes west of here. In that enchanting green valley tucked up against the mountain."

"Are you OK, sir? You sure it was that close? There is no town in this state named that, that I know of at least. There surely is no town within 60 miles of us, period. The closest settlement of any kind is a couple of trailer homes set a mile or so apart in the middle of nowhere in the desert about 40 miles from here. The only thing green there is one of the trailers," he chuckled.

Michael didn't feel like arguing with this idiot, so he shook his head and thanked him as he paid for his gas. He headed back out to the car and made sure Cayden had returned safely from the restroom.

As he drove out of town, he noticed a small historical society building with an "OPEN" sign out front, so he decided to stop in and ask there. The woman at the desk greeted him kindly and asked how she could help. He repeated his story to her, but he was once again greeted with a confused expression and an assurance that she had no knowledge of any such town. She let him look through records tracing the area's history, but he was unable to find any documentation of Joya's existence. Michael left astonished and frustrated, feeling even more depressed than before.

There was nothing to do but resume their journey, and it wasn't long before they arrived at his mother's home. She wasn't there to greet them, even though she knew when to expect them. She had left a key and a note on the porch with a curt message: "Get settled. Don't make a mess. See you later."

They removed their shoes as they entered so as not to drag in the desert sand, and Michael led his son to the small room they would share that had been his childhood bedroom. He left

Cayden in the room with some of his toys, as he slowly trudged in and out, bringing in their meager belongings.

Once he finished, he settled Cayden down for his nap, and then went out to the living room to watch some television while he waited for his mother to return. All his stress and anxiety over the coming reunion overcame him, and he fell asleep with his head resting on the arm of the couch.

He awoke with a start when his mother slammed the door.

"Thirty-six years old, and I still have to tell you not to put your feet on the couch. Goddamn it, Michael Evan Goodman. I am too old. Shit! You are too old for me to have to continue to remind you of the rules of my house. Is this what I should expect from your little bastard as well? So help me, you will be out on the street again if you can't get your shit together and grow up. THIRTY-SIX FUCKING YEARS OLD, and you have to come home to live with mommy. You make me thankful all my friends are dead, and I live in the middle of nowhere, so that I do not have to be embarrassed by my irresponsible, deadbeat son."

Michael looked up with horror in his eyes when he heard a noise in the hall and realized his son was hearing this tirade from a grandmother he had never even met before today. Cayden ran away crying as his grandmother started in on him.

"Don't make me box those ears, you little eavesdropper. So help me God, you will learn your manners. Your parents may have been negligent in their duties, but I will not tolerate a rude little bastard in my home. You get back here and listen to me when I talk to you."

Michael's mother stood up angrily and started toward the hall. He jumped up and ran to intercept her. He would not let her touch his son, even if it meant they lost this place to stay. Anything would be better, even a homeless shelter, than allowing his son to be abused. He jumped in front of her and amazed himself when he yelled, "Stop!" He had never dared speak to his mother that way. She stopped dead and looked as if he had slapped her... at first. Then her surprise quickly gave way to blind anger as *she* slapped *him* soundly across the face. When she opened her mouth to unleash another tirade, he simply walked away, shut the door, and blocked it with his old desk chair.

He spent the next hour rocking his son in his arms as he promised him that no one would ever hurt him, as his grandmother beat on the door hurling insults. Christmas was going to be a disappointment this year, but he had not intended his son to spend Christmas Eve in tears and fearful. He then quickly repacked their few belongings and listened carefully for the house to get quiet, signaling that his mother had finally given up and retired for the night. When he felt safe, he quietly ushered Cayden out of the house with as much of their luggage as he could carry. He had left the window unlocked in case she woke and locked him out. He locked his son safely in the car, then quickly and silently returned to retrieve the last of their belongings. He drove down the road to a nearby rest stop and reclined the seats so they could get some rest for the night.

Michael didn't know what he had planned for their future. He had contemplated returning to Joya—if he could find it again. But he'd never had the luxury of dreaming in his childhood, so he didn't hold out any hope for that option.

Before leaving his mother's house, he had contacted a close friend back where they had lived, who had agreed to put them up for two weeks. He had checked into homeless shelters in that area and had even looked into applying for welfare to see if that might be an option.

Needless to say, it was a mostly sleepless night at the rest stop. He had $2,000 left in his bank account, and he was just going to start driving and see what happened. He was a hard worker, and he had the best motivation in the world to succeed, so he had no doubt it would all work out in the end somehow. He could no longer allow himself the luxury of time and depression. It was time to create his own destiny for his sake and Cayden's.

When Cayden woke shortly after 7 on Christmas morning, they headed back toward Delamar to get a "yummy" gas station burrito for breakfast. The plan was to head back west toward Joya or to his friend's home, whichever worked out. Cayden was excited, but Michael could only feel anxious and desperate. The 30 miles passed quickly with no sign of the approaching town. Michael drove 45 miles before he pulled over to the side of the road, crying and hopeless.

"Don't cry, Daddy. You just missed it. You drove past it. You weren't looking like you should."

"Yes, I did, son. I looked very hard."

"Turn around, Daddy. Look again. Look for our home. You will see it. Please, Daddy."

Michael could see visions in his head of them living happily there. He imagined Cayden joining a soccer league. Leisurely walks down the main street on Sundays. Trick-or-treating at all those cute little cottages. Dinner every Friday night and breakfast every Sunday at the Cozy Corner Café. Evenings spent doing homework and then a brief walk down to the park to play before bed. He could even imagine himself working at the small stone garage in town. He had seen a "help wanted" sign. He was an IT guy by trade, but he had learned to fix cars in high school. He knew he could be happy there. He was sure

Cayden would grow to be a well-adjusted, bright young man in that town.

Michael slowly turned the car around and drove back as his son had begged him to do. He felt calmer, even a little hopeful, after his daydreams of the future that could happen; visions of a New Year and new life passing through his head. A few miles later, he began to question whether he could believe what he was sure he was seeing in the distance. But he swore he saw a lush green landscape far off to the right tucked up against the mountain.

He looked back at his son to ask him if Cayden had seen what he had. The smile on Cayden's face was all the confirmation he needed. But then Cayden squealed with delight, "Here it comes, Daddy."

Michael turned back to the wheel to suddenly see the *Welcome to Joya* sign approaching them. It literally appeared to be *coming at them*. It was appearing much faster than their speed of 45 miles per hour should have allowed. In the moment he recognized this, pieces of the town started appearing rapidly, one by one, literally popping into place. The diner. The park. And then the pavilion in the middle. The tennis court. Then the main street appeared. One by one, little cottages began to dot the landscape. And finally, the townspeople celebrating Christmas came into view, one by one, faster and faster as their joy grew.

Michael skidded into the diner's parking lot and ran up to the door with Cayden in tow. He whisked the door open with a flourish and broke out into raucous laughter as he saw Shirley beaming at them with two menus in hand.

"I just knew you two would be back. You belong here in our little town. I told you this place was special. It is our City of Sometimes. We are here when we are needed. But you see, we need you, too. We can only maintain our little Garden of Eden if it is populated with the right people who want to be happy and support one another. Gordon, the owner of the garage, is waiting for you down the street to discuss your new position. If you don't mind, I will close up the diner for a bit and take Cayden down and get him settled in your new cottage. I need some help decorating your Christmas tree. Santa came last night and left packages underneath, for both of you. It is the pink one just down the way at the corner of Aspiration and Main."

Cayden squealed with delight, and Michael stared at her in astonishment. He could not believe what he had just heard, yet he knew it was all right—even further, that she meant it. Michael haltingly asked her, "But... how? How did you know that I wanted to work at the garage? And the cottage... that was the one we liked. I didn't even know you had seen us look at it. But... but... I told you we have lost everything. I can't afford to rent a cottage like that."

"Shush now, son. It is all taken care of. You want to live here, correct?"

Michael nodded.

"You intend to take care of your son and help support the residents of this village, just as we have helped you, correct? You intend to be a productive citizen of this town?"

Michael nodded enthusiastically again.

"Well then, you better not be late to your quick orientation before your first day at work. Cayden and I will get you all settled at the cottage. After Christmas break, I will enroll him in school for you. You are both invited to Christmas dinner at my B&B at 6. Here is your lunch. Now off you go. We will see you at 1 to open presents and then head down to the park for the festivities."

Michael walked away smiling and chuckling as he shook his head. He had never been a dreamer. That had been discouraged—no, it had not been tolerated in his childhood home. Now, he knew dreams did come true. He was watching his dream skipping down the street next to Shirley chanting, "There is no place like home."

Stephen H. Provost

Invisible

My life is over.

I'm just 17 years old, but it might as well be. I'm here at Winter Formal by myself, serving as reluctant chaperone to my sister, watching couples slow-dance to "At This Moment" and "I Just Called to Say I Love You" as my eyes glaze over in a combination of boredom and self-preservation. I don't want to look at all the kids who've got what I haven't. I don't want to see all the colored balloons and banners with exclamation points. I don't care who's queen of the Winter Formal or what she's wearing.

None of it has any impact on me.

The music changes from "Jingle Bell Rock" to "Let's Hear It for the Boy."

Let's not, actually. Can't they play some Anthrax or Metallica? Of course they can't. Teenagers have no taste.

I let my eyes wander around the room, taking in the strings of colored lights hung from the rafters, the chaperones dressed up as the Grinch and Mrs. Claus, the banner decorated with pictures of Charlie Brown and his pathetic Christmas tree...

"Hey, are you here by yourself?"

I look up, surprised to see someone—anyone—looking my direction. It's Winter Formal, the biggest dance of the year short of Prom, and I'm here alone. Not because I want to be. I don't have a date. I'm just here because my mom wanted me to "look out for Heather" while Mom's on a date. Heather's my twin sister, but we're nothing alike. Everyone notices her, especially the guys... which is why Mom wants me to keep an eye on her.

"No fast times at Ridgecrest High for her!" Mom had said, laughing at her own bad joke. We live in Ridgecrest, which is in California but hundreds of miles from any beach, so no one speaks Surfer Dude or Valley Girl here. Everyone thinks California is one big long beach, the way they think the whole state of New York is skyscrapers and hot dog stands, or Nevada is the Vegas strip and nothing else.

Idiots.

Mom isn't funny. But she thinks she is, and what I think matters less to her than nothing. She never sees me—not the real me. She's too busy looking in the mirror at her own reflection so she can fashion Heather in her image. Slut. That's what Dad used to call her. Not that he was any better. All he cared about were his motorcycle and going camping with his buddies. If Mom fucked around behind his back, he had no business caring.

He used to hit me when I was younger—not spank me or even whip me with a belt; he used to smack me across the mouth. Then he stopped. Not because I "manned up" and "toed the line," as he put it. Because he stopped caring. He didn't see me, either. Not the real me. Not the fake me. Not any version of his only son. When he left, he didn't say goodbye, and I haven't heard from him since. He sends Heather money for her birthday and Christmas; maybe the sicko wants to fuck her, the way Mom was gets banged by the TV repairman.

That's who Mom's out with tonight, probably singing karoake at that dive bar Rummy Randy's: Horace something-or-other. Owns Ace Appliance out on McKinley. I've seen his commercials for "a deal that will make you squeal." That's what he does to Mom—she doesn't even try to be quiet with him, even though I'm supposedly sleeping in the next room. (But who could sleep through that?) He comes to the house, gets his rocks off, then leaves. Never introduced himself, so I never met him. Never want to.

Even Mom gets to go on dates, but not me. I'm so shy I can't even bring myself to ask a girl out, let alone actually go to a movie or Shakey's Pizza or cruising Blackstone on Friday night. That would be hard, since I don't have a license.

Mom, dressed as what she called a "sexy elf," dropped me off at the Formal, which would have been embarrassing if anyone had noticed. But nobody did. Nobody ever notices anything I do—good or bad or otherwise. The only thing cool I ever did was break the record on Centipede at Arky's Arkade. But the machine was gone the next day, replaced by Ms. Pac-Man. So no one ever saw my score. Not that it mattered. Not that anyone cared.

"Hey!" It's the same voice again, more insistent this time. It belongs to a girl in a low-cut top with a nice round ass and blue hair that makes her look even more striking. "I'm talking to you!"

She's not as hot as Heather, but close. So why the hell is she talking to me?

"What?!"

I sound pissed off. Just great. *That's how you get a girl to like you, D.O.* (That's my name—Dennis Oswald Yerkovich. You can see why I call myself D.O. No one else calls me that, or anything, really. But it sounds kinda cool if you think of it like Ronnie James Dio.)

The girl ignores me. It's like she didn't even hear me and is looking over the top of me or right through me.

"Patrick Duncan, I swear to God, if you're here alone... You were supposed to ask me to the Formal, asshole. We're supposed to be steady."

Some girl's smug voice pipes up behind me: "And what if he's not here alone, Betty Blue Bangs? What if he's here with *me*?"

The first girl looks like a bull who's seen red and is pawing at the ground with one front hoof, threatening to charge. "Jeanetta Cole, you fucking whore!" Half the room turns around in time to see Betty Blue Bangs make good on her threat and bolt toward this Jeanetta person, who's standing directly behind me.

She doesn't slow down. Doesn't change course. Just barrels right into me, sending me sprawling and knocking the Dr Pepper I'd been nursing all the way over to the far wall. The weird thing is, she doesn't slow down even *after* she's smashed into me, hurling her body at the Bettie Page-clone owner of the smug voice and crashing on top of her as they both descend to the lacquered gym floor in a whirl of kicks and flying fists.

The guy they're fighting over just stands there with a smirk on his face, while his buddies run over and shout "Girl fight!" like it's a porno or something.

But it's not much of a fight. A rent-a-cop in one of those olive-tan phony-forms runs over and gets between them, breaking it up after just a few seconds and getting socked in the jaw by Betty Blue Bangs for his trouble.

Everyone's over there except the janitor, who's attending to the spilled Dr Pepper. No one even looks over to see if I'm okay.

I don't care. It's nothing new. Why should I expect anything different?

"I'm going home," I mutter.

Except I can't. I have to "look out for Heather." But what am I supposed to do if I see her leaving with all-league defensive end Jimmy Farley? Like she's doing now. Run over and stand in the door? Tell him to get his hands off my sister? Yeah. Right. I value my life, even if Mom doesn't, and Heather's a slut anyway, just like Mom, so why should I care? Mom wanted to create Heather in her own image? Guess what? She got what she wanted.

If Mom asks me where she is when she comes to pick us up, I'll show her the bruised cheek I got when I was run over by Betty Blue Bangs and tell her Jimmy Farley did it. At least she'll think I put up a fight.

But she doesn't ask me. She doesn't even come to pick me up. I sit there on that lacquered gym floor waiting, back against the wall, after the colored Christmas lights are out and everyone else is gone except the janitor.

I see him putting his mop away and call over to him. "Hey, I don't suppose you could...?"

He doesn't hear me and walks out before I can finish my sentence, shutting out the lights and leaving me in the dark.

"...give me a ride home?" I finish under my breath. "Motherfucker," I add.

He doesn't hear that, either. He's gone.

I'm alone in the dark. Invisible.

That's how I find out about it. My condition, that is.

Maybe I don't even exist.

"Of course you exist. If you didn't, you wouldn't know I was talking to you."

Who the fuck is that?

"The voice in your head. One of them, anyway. The others don't matter. Just listen to me."

Why?

"Because I know what's happened to you. You're invisible."

No shit. I've been invisible for years.

"I mean literally. No one can see you."

Fuck off.

I nod off to sleep then, uncomfortable but wiped. I dream that Mr. Jock Strap, the football player, is banging my sister and that the TV repairman is banging my mom. Who has dreams like this? I must be some sicko. At least it wasn't a wet dream. I wish I could be banging someone...

I wake up to the sound of an insistent, clattering bell and a bright beam of sunlight shining across my eyes. It's coming from the door to the gym, which has been opened. Kids are coming in to take down the Charlie Brown Christmas banner, the lights, and the other decorations; the bell must have been the warning bell for homeroom. I'd been here all night, and no one had noticed. Mom hadn't come looking for me, and no one else had, either. Had they even noticed I was gone?

"How could they? They never notice when you're there."

It's the voice again.

Shut up. You're whacked.

"If I'm whacked, so are you. I'm just you. And I'm telling you you're invisible. I'll prove it. Wave at that girl over there."

He's referring to one of the girls taking down the streamers over the stage at the far end of the gym.

She's a dog.

The girl is short, has acne all over her chin, thick black hair on her arms, and looks like she used a funhouse mirror to apply her makeup.

"So? And you're Tom Cruise? She's desperate. If she doesn't notice you, nobody will. It'll prove my point."

Fine.

I wave at the girl. No response.

"See?"

That doesn't prove shit.

"OK, smartass. Then go outside and step into the street in front of some trucker. See if they stop. Go ahead. Make my day."

I'm half-tempted to do it just to shut him up, but if the truck hit me, it would shut both of us up. Plus, he'd be right, and I'd feel stupid. I feel stupid enough as it is.

He doesn't say anything more, but I can feel him staring at me with some self-satisfied smirk on his invisible face. Or is it my invisible face? Maybe he's right. Maybe I really am invisible. There must be some way to test this without stepping out in front of a Peterbilt. Something simple.

The second bell—the tardy bell—rings.

I walk to homeroom, the last classroom in one of six parallel rows of low-slung buildings lined with lockers and an overhang supported by metal poles covered in chipped brown paint.

Clouds hang low in the sky, hovering somewhere between

stormy and foggy, and the inane chatter of jocks and soshes who don't care about being late (or, more likely, are ditching class) drifts past me. I ignore it as best I can. I wish there was a way I could make *them* invisible to *me*.

Everyone else is seated as I enter the classroom. Mr. Berkenhouse stands at the chalkboard, dressed in his drab brown coat and crooked bowtie, pointing to a quadratic equation and mumbling something about the value of X. He doesn't stop to acknowledge me as I enter, and not a single head turns to see who's late. No eyes follow me as I walk up the second row of desks and take my seat, third from the front.

"*See? Invisible.*"

"Shut up."

I realize I've said that aloud and wait for Berkenhouse to stop and remind me that "there's no talking in my classroom, Mr. Yerkovich." And for one of the kids to whisper, "Jerk-off itch," the way they always do when anyone says my name.

But he doesn't. And they don't.

"Hmm."

"Now," Berkenhouse is saying, "who can tell me how to solve this equation?"

No one raises a hand.

"*Volunteer,*" says the voice in my head.

But I don't know the answer.

"*Who cares? You're invisible. He won't call on you. You wanted a test, so...*"

He's right.

I raise my hand, ready to say I'm just stretching. But he doesn't call on me. He appears to be looking right through me.

"No one?" he says. "You'd know the answer if you'd done your homework."

They hadn't. I hadn't either.

My arm gets tired, and I put it down.

"Now for something a little more definitive. Rip a piece of paper out of your notebook, make a paper airplane, and throw it at him."

You're kidding.

"Nope. Do it."

What do I have to lose? I'll just get detention, which means I won't have to go home and listen to Mom go on and on about who Erica Kane is sleeping with this week on *All* My *Children*. Or hear her ask where I'd been all night and why I hadn't kept my eye on Heather. If she even noticed.

"She didn't."

I rip a piece of paper from my notebook, being as loud about is as I can.

No heads turn.

I fold it expertly into an aerodynamic craft with a sharp point at the front end. I raise it to my eye, take aim, and let fly.

It hits Berkenhouse directly in the nose.

He stops speaking.

His eyes widen.

See? I'm not invisible.

"The PLANE's not invisible. You are."

"WHO THREW THAT!" Berkenhouse demands, sounding something like Pee Wee Herman doing an impression of a manic drill sergeant from the movies.

No one says anything.

"Mr. Felix, was that you?" He reaches out and points at a student sitting a couple of rows over. He's the class clown, known for his practical jokes, but the plane didn't even come from that direction.

Felix shakes his head but can't quite hide a smile. It *was* funny after all.

"It WAS, wasn't it? Two weeks of detention, Mr. Felix. In

the Dungeon."

The Dungeon is what Berkenhouse calls the library, which is used as a detention hall after hours. It sounds a lot more menacing than it is—except for kids who are scared of books, which is more than half the school.

"*Isn't this fun?*" says the voice. "*You can do whatever you want and get away with it. Someone else will get the blame, because you're INVISIBLE!*"

I have to admit, it *is* fun.

"*Now imagine what you can do with it. You could literally get away with murder.*"

I don't think...

"*Sure, you do. You're already thinking about who you want to kill. Then you'll be thinking about how you want to do it.*"

Umm....

"*Your father, maybe. He never gave a shit about you. Or Heather, that prissy little full-of-herself, slutty prima donna. She deserves it, don't you think? Or that girl that ran into you last night at the Formal. Or Mr. Jock Strap. Or the kid who stole your collection of Topps Rookies. Or Mom. She's a slut. She deserves it. Plus, you live with her. It would be really easy to get rid of her...*"

STOP!

"*Sure. I'll stop. But you won't. You'll keep thinking about it and thinking about it and thinking about it until you do it. You'll get away with it, too, because you're invisible.*"

His voice feels like a drumbeat in my head. He was right. I can't stop thinking about it, because the drum keeps sounding louder and louder at the base of my skull, filling me with adrenalin at the thought that I could do whatever I want and no one would notice. I could kill someone and get away with it. I really could.

And Mom is the perfect target. I didn't realize how much I hated her until she made me go to that fucking Formal because of Heather, then didn't even bother to go looking for me when I didn't come home. I bet she looked for Heather. But she doesn't care about me. She never did. I'll show her...

When I get home after school, she doesn't notice me come in. She's on the phone with loverboy Horace, telling him to come over because Heather's out at cheerleading practice for the afternoon. She doesn't mention me. Probably thinks I disappeared for good. Ha! The joke's on her.

This is perfect. I'll get them both at once. No need to be sneaky about it. No one can see me, so I'll make it good and bloody. I'll make it hurt the way they hurt me.

Horace knocks on the door, and Mother lets him in, wearing that "sexy elf" outfit again, her breasts almost hanging out of the top. Her paramour's beer belly sticks out like a bowling ball, which would have made him look like Santa Claus if he'd had a beard. But he looks nothing at all like Santa: His bald head is badly covered with a comb-over that fails to hide blotches of skin cancer, and he's got a thick moustache that looks like something from a 1970s porno (yeah, I've seen them; Mother owns a whole collection).

He smiles at her, and she bats her eyes like she thinks she's some kind of sex kitten. She's no prize herself: She has no hips, saggy tits, and a couple of crooked teeth. Her deep-set eyes are close together, which makes her look cross-eyed even though she's not.

They're made for each other.

"Hello, Sugar," he says. "Got some spice for me this afternoon, hmmm? I got your candy cane right here." He reaches down and grabs his crotch like he's Michael Jackson.

She laughs at this, and he laughs even louder. I'm watching it all through the door to the kitchen off to the side of them, unnoticed.

"*You don't have to hide,*" says the voice. "*They can't see you.*"

I know. Force of habit.

I feel the voice's invisible satisfied smile.

Loverboy reaches into his pocket and pulls out a wilted-looking piece of what looks like a maple leaf.

"Is that pot, Horace?" Mother asks. "Oh, you bad boy!"

Horace looks wounded. "It's mistletoe," he states coldly, then holds it up over her head, grabs her and pulls her roughly to him, attaching his mouth to hers and sticking his tongue down her throat.

Then he drops the mistletoe on the ground, takes her by the wrist with one hand and smacks her on the butt with the other.

"Oh! Horace!" she yelps and then titters.

He laughs again, sounding devious. "Yeah, you're gonna give me some."

"All you want, dumplin'. I'm all yours."

I think I'm gonna puke.

I follow them to her bedroom, which she used to share with my father but has since redecorated to become what she calls a boudoir. Faux Tiffany and hurricane lamps on particle-board chests and cabinets made to look like dark maple. Heavy red drapes with pink lacy curtains. It's what I imagine a brothel bedroom would look like. All it needs is a stripper pole, but Mother would probably sprain an ankle if she tried to dance around it.

He rips off her top and throws her on the bed, ordering her to unfasten her bra. "I can't figure that shit out."

She dutifully complies as he pulls down her jeans, then her plain gray panties, and forces her to spread her legs. Not that she needs to be forced. It's all part of the game.

I feel bile rising in my throat and turn away as he loads his heavy body on top of her with a grunt.

"Fuck me, Horace," she cries.

"I'll fuck you, Matilda. "Oh, I'll fuck you all right."

Bile rises in my throat. I fight not to turn away.

"Now," says the voice. *"Do it!"*

I grip the pick-axe from the tool shed firmly. I can feel my palms sweating as I raise it over my head—so much that it nearly slips out of my hands.

"Hit them hard enough to make sure they can't get up, but not too hard. You want them to FEEL it. Then do it again. Him first."

I've stopped resisting the voice. Stopped even questioning it. I bring the pick-axe down on the back of his head with a crack. He cries out in surprise and sudden agony.

Mother screams. It's unintelligible. She can't see me. I'm invisible. Part of me wishes she knew. Part of me is glad she doesn't. I smash Horace's skull again and again, blood flying everywhere. It splatters on the glass of the hurricane lamp, on Mother's face and on the bedsheets already soiled with the wetness of her sexual excitement. That's all gone now, though. There's only terror. Pure terror.

Her mouth is open wide, grotesquely so, as she screams again and again.

I bring the point of the pick-axe down hard in it, crashing through her crooked teeth and shattering them, then cracking into the back of her skull.

She stops screaming.

I tear the axe-point loose and bring it down again.

She stops moving.

"Perfect," says the voice as I drop the axe and stare down at their lifeless bodies. *"Now you'd better get out of here. The neighbors*

heard her scream. They'll be calling the cops."

But I thought I was invisible.

"*You are,*" the voice says, but without its earlier tone of confidence. It sounds more regretful... and... scared. There's a nagging sense of wrongness that goes beyond the fact that I've just committed murder. And what's even worse, I can no longer feel that satisfied smile.

When the police come to investigate, they find Heather sobbing in the front room, sitting on the floor next to our still-undecorated Christmas tree. She found the bodies when she came home from cheerleader practice.

"We'll have to ask you to come with us," the lead detective says. "This is a crime scene, and we have some questions we need to ask you down at the police station."

The satisfied smile returns. "*They think she did it.*"

I'm not so sure.

Heather won't stop crying.

"Please, miss..."

She's not moving, and the cops don't want to move her bodily. They decide to try to ask her some questions there.

"Where's your brother?"

The question surprises me.

You said I was invisible.

But the voice inside has gone silent.

"I don't know," Heather wails. "I saw him at Formal, and then at school in the hall earlier today..."

YOU SAID I WAS INVISIBLE.

"*You were.*"

WERE? What the hell does that mean? She's saying she SAW me!

"She didn't see you then, but now she's remembering you were there.

Something's changed."

Changed? What?

A second detective enters the room. He's been back in the boudoir, surveying the scene. "Doesn't look like anything was taken, so it wasn't a robbery. Probably someone they knew. We've got some prints on the axe, and we're rushing them down to forensics. Should have them back soon. We'll check them against everyone in the household, and against the repairman's family members. They might have had motive."

Another cop comes in through the front door. "Just got back from the school. The girl has an alibi. A dozen students and her coach saw her at cheerleading practice."

The detective nods. "The woman's divorced. Her ex lives in Elko, and he was at work, so it wasn't him. That leaves the son. Do we have a sample of his prints?"

What the fuck?

It was like the paper airplane. I might be invisible, but my prints were still there. *Am I even invisible? Was I EVER invisible?*

You tricked me! I say to the voice.

"I didn't trick you. I told you: Something's changed."

What?

"You did something worth noticing, so now you aren't invisible anymore. Even the things you did when you WERE invisible are being seen now."

Like the murder?

"Murders. Plural. And yes, especially those."

But you said I was invisible. You TOLD ME I could do WHATEVER I WANTED!

"I never said there wouldn't be consequences. Besides, what do I know? I'm just a voice inside YOUR head. I'm just you."

I feel sick and numb all at once.

The phone rings and one of the detectives goes into the kitchen to pick it up. He returns a moment later.

"That was forensics," he announces. "We've got a match."

"And?"

"It's the son. They're his prints."

Shit.

The numbness goes away when I feel two hands grab my own firmly from behind, followed by the sensation of cold metal and the clicking sound of handcuffs snapping into place.

"Well look who we found here," says the detective, "hiding in a closet, watching us."

"Dennis Oswald Yerkovich," says the other, "you're under arrest for the murders of Horace Antonovich and Matilda Rawls. You have the right to remain silent. Anything you say can and will be used against you in a court of law. Do you understand the rights I have just read to you?"

I nod.

"Yes or no, boy."

"Yes."

I am convicted as an adult because I'm just a few months short of my 18th birthday and because of the heinousness of my crimes. I am sent to the U.S. Penitentiary in Atwater, where I am assigned to share a cell with another inmate.

He's bigger than I am and has a menacing look about him.

He wears a familiar, devious, satisfied smile as he stares at me silently.

He sees me.

I am not invisible.

It's almost Christmas.

And my life is over.

Sharon Marie Provost

R.I.P.

iles' head was buried in his book, totally engrossed in the story. He moved through the bustling crowd of holiday shoppers as if by instinct because he couldn't be bothered to look up.

He never had enough time to read. Reading was his life, always had been. Then he became an adult and realized people no longer appreciated a voracious reader who spent all their free time in a book. He was expected to work all day, even if there was a lull, and his wife always had a laundry list of honey-do's.

His boss had started docking his paycheck by 10 minutes every time he was caught with a book. He didn't dare fire him because nobody else knew how to perform his job, but he could—and did—make his life miserable just the same. His wife had reached the point where she threw away his precious books if she caught him with one when he had other tasks to do, which was constantly.

He walked toward the busy intersection with careless abandon. He knew the light was about to turn because he could hear the cars ahead slowing as they approached the signal.

He slowed his step a little to time it just right. The plot was at a crucial climax—would Harold win the race?—so he just couldn't stop reading now. He could hear the traffic in front of him idling, so he made the fateful decision to step out into the intersection without looking up first. In his peripheral vision, he caught a blur of movement to his left... the sound of a horn... and then, all was black.

The young man dressed as an elf jumped out of his car and ran over to Niles. He was late for his shift at Santa's Workshop Photography booth. The light turned green, and he immediately made his right turn, failing to notice the pedestrian in the crosswalk. He never thought that the crumpled form now lying in front of him would step out at just that moment.

I... am... dead.

That thought was running through his head when Niles awoke with a start. Well, you can't really say "awoke" so much as "roused." Waking up implies life, and he was obviously very much not alive. He was cold—bone cold—but it didn't feel like the normal chilled feeling so much as a coldness leeching from the very depths of his soul. A quick check confirmed his lack of a heartbeat, or breathing for that matter, as he had suspected.

He was in a very small space, not much larger than the size of his body. A few well-placed hard kicks, and he managed to pop open the lid of what became painfully clear was his casket. It was dark except for a narrow shaft of light shining through the stained-glass window to his right. He looked around the room and realized he was in his family mausoleum in Lafayette Cemetery.

Now that he had ascertained his lack of life, the real question became where was he: heaven, hell, purgatory, somewhere else. Since there was no one there to ask, he was left with no choice but to go exploring. He climbed awkwardly out of his casket and shuffled his way to the door.

Wow, I am really stiff.

He chortled when he realized the irony of his statement.

A real-life stiff noticing that his movements are stiff. Can you imagine that?

With some effort, he managed to jimmy open the door to the mausoleum, and he walked out into the cemetery. He stumbled over the Christmas-colored memorial wreath that had been hung on the door. Leave it to his wife to choose an inappropriate wreath; she only cared about the aesthetics in life. There was no one around, which was not unexpected given the late hour.

He ambled off to find a newspaper that might have an obituary explaining his demise.

But even if I find out how I died, that still doesn't explain why I am walking around. True! True! One step at a time. There must be an explanation for all of this.

He approached the newsstand on the corner and reached into his pockets, looking for his wallet.

But his pockets were empty.

Damn! Of course, I have no wallet. What do the dead need with money? I am sure that was the first personal belonging of mine that Rachel looked for.

"Exxcluuusee mee, sssir. May I loooookk throughh thisss papuh for a mo… mo… momenttt?" Niles slurred as drool slid down his chin.

The newsstand clerk had been watching what sounded like an urgent news brief on his phone, so he was slow to look up. When he did, his eyes grew wide before he screamed for help and ran in the other direction. Niles stood there looking stunned until he looked down at the phone the man had dropped. No wonder he'd been so unnerved. On the screen he saw a news flash about an apparent zombie apocalypse. The recently deceased were rising—a few days after their passing in some cases. Apparently, not everyone who died returned, and no one knew why it was happening or how to predict who might return.

There did not seem to be any reports of violence or cause for concern, other than the shock involved in seeing a dead relative return to the family home. But of course, the public was afraid because they had seen too many horror movies with zombies who fed on the brains of the living.

Fiction has become reality to these twits. God forbid we use a little rational thinking and the scientific method to determine the true nature of these, or should I say us, so-called zombies.

Niles set the phone aside and reached down for a newspaper dated December 22nd to check out the obituary section and see if he could find out his fate. There it was in black and white: He had been hit by a car when crossing the street while reading a book. The driver had been a young kid who failed to yield right-of-way. According to the obituary, Niles' wife hadn't even held a funeral for him, just a private interment.

There was no reason to go home because obviously, she wasn't missing him.

Niles shambled over to the bench to contemplate his next move. Then, to his absolute delight, the thought occurred to him that he no longer had any responsibilities. No job. No need for money to buy food or any other necessity. No wife and, therefore, no honey-do's.

Best of all, he did not need to participate in the clusterfuck known as the Christmas season. He was finally able to do just exactly what the plaque had said on the front of the tomb.

R.I.P.

Niles Johnson

He would not go gentle into this good night. He would *not* rest in peace. He preferred to look at that simple statement in a much more pleasing way. He would finally, **FINALLY**, be able to read in peace. He had all the days of his life... or death... or after death... whatever this was, ahead of him to read without being disturbed. There were no longer any duties of any kind to distract him from his life's dream to read and read and read to his heart's content.

With that thought in mind, he quickly got up and shuffled off toward his home. There were some belongings he needed to collect.

He used the hide-a-key under the front planter to enter his home quietly. He was surprised to find his wife was not at home. No problem... that made this whole matter a lot simpler. He then set about collecting all his favorite books, plus the boxes and boxes of new ones just waiting to be read. He packed those into his car along with his Coleman lantern. He would need more light to read by, after all.

Afterward, he drove his car into the cemetery and parked in front of the mausoleum to make unloading easier. He nearly filled that building to the ceiling, but he was the last family member who would be interred there, so that was of no concern. Once he had completed this task, he returned the car to the house and walked back to his new home.

The ensuing days (and nights) passed by in a blur of blissful reading. He devoured Shakespeare, Tolstoy, Bronte... all the classics. Then he absorbed the writings of Stephen King, Dean Koontz, and Clive Barker. He read travel books. After all, why not? There was no reason he could think of to prevent him from traveling if he so chose. He read every piece of literature, periodical, or reference work he could get his hands on.

But one day, he realized he was straining more to read. It seemed harder and harder to make out the words. He couldn't imagine that a zombie would need reading glasses, but he made his way home again one evening to pick up his old spectacles. When he returned to the mausoleum, he found that they did help to some degree, so he dove back into the books, reading again to his heart's delight.

A few days later though, he realized that he was having still more trouble reading. And further, he noticed smudges of some nasty gook on some of the books he was reading. He examined the mausoleum for any signs of leakage from the groundwater below or rain seeping through a crack in the ceiling, but everything appeared dry and clean.

Later that week, after a stroll through the night air, Niles came back in and picked up his book... and it slipped right out of his hands. It was so slimy that he could barely pick it up without it slipping through his grasp again. After further inspection, Niles was surprised to realize the sliminess was coming from him. All this time, Niles' entire attention had been focused on his books and nothing else—including himself. He had not noticed that his skin was deteriorating into black patches that oozed a thick, dark fluid.

He ran out into the night to inspect his face's reflection from a car window. To his utter horror, he saw that his eyes almost seemed to be melting. They were collapsing in on themselves, and milky fluid oozed from the corners.

No wonder he was having difficulty reading.

Niles racked his brain, desperate to find a solution.

Then an inspiration hit him. He jumped to his feet in excitement... and immediately fell to the ground in a heap. The sharp, rapid motion had dislodged his foot from his leg! Viscous brown fluid dripped from his face as he began to cry.

Carefully, he dragged himself over to the trash can and began to search for anything he might use to improve his situation. Luckily, earlier in the day, a group of convicts performing community service had been in the area picking up and disposing of trash left in the cemetery and a nearby park. He found a broken mop handle, an old blanket left behind by a homeless person, and a long section of plastic wrap from a pallet. He used those items to jerry-rig a splint/sling and reattach his foot securely enough that he could carefully limp on it while leaning on a shopping cart.

In this fashion, he slowly made his way down to the nearby mortuary. He broke into the darkened back side of the building and scooted his way down the hall to the embalming room. There, he found several bottles of formaldehyde, which he safely stowed in a basin to push down the hall to his cart. With that mission accomplished, he made his way back home and immersed himself in the pungent chemical.

He faithfully bathed in that caustic fluid twice daily, but to no avail. With each passing day, his skin began to slough more and more. His joints loosened, then fell apart. One day, he realized he couldn't see out of one eye... and only became aware it had fallen out when he accidentally squished it as he crawled across the floor. Before long, he was not much more than a pile of bones and rotten flesh lying in a pool of primordial ooze. Yet he was still aware, at least for a while.

His last thought, not surprisingly, was a bitter, sarcastic one.

Of fucking course! How arrogant we are to assume that R.I.P. should mean something so peaceful and idyllic as rest in peace. Rest in pieces is more like it!

Stephen H. Provost

Mama's Girls

"How are my girls today?"

Juliette Sweeten opened the door to the basement, and her two girls ran up to meet her, each throwing her arms around one of the woman's legs.

"Mama!" they said in unison.

Juliette nearly lost her balance as they hit her full-force in the doorway to the dingy room, filled as it was with boxes of everything from her wedding dress to old photo albums to a collection of commemorative coins her mother had left her. She had a set from the Bicentennial, one from the 1984 Los Angeles Olympics, even one for each of the Apollo missions. She'd started collecting them after her sister gave her some limited-edition Christmas coins one year: There was one of Santa in his sleigh, one of Rudolph, one of Frosty the Snowman, a Christmas tree, and even coins depicting the Grinch and Krampus!

Her mother had assured her they'd all be worth something someday, but she'd been waiting a long time, and they hadn't increased much in value. Her collection of Hummel figurines was worth even less.

But it didn't matter. She had her girls, Caliope and Rhapsody. They were priceless—and as different as night and day. Caliope wore her platinum blond hair sprouting out to either side in a pair of pigtails. Her crystal blue eyes blinked rarely, as though she were staring right through you, but they always seemed to be smiling.

Rhapsody's raven-black locks flowed out behind her, softer than silk, and her deep brown eyes were soulful rather than smiling. Named for Juliette's favorite song by her favorite band, she fittingly liked to sing, but her voice was usually sad. She was stoic most of the time, except when Juliette arrived each morning with breakfast.

Caliope wore dresses and was always dancing around like a ballerina; Rhapsody was a tomboy.

"Do you want to come out and play for a while?" Juliette asked, and Caliope nodded her head eagerly. Rhapsody didn't bother to respond other than to run past her mother up the stairs and into the living room, where she disappeared behind the couch. Clearly, the game she wanted to play was hide-and-seek.

Caliope was more interested in her mother's attention.

"Pick me up, Mama!" she half pleaded, half demanded, and Juliette obliged, whisking the small girl up into her arms.

She set her down, and they walked up the stairs together.

After a moment, Rhapsody came out from behind the couch

to greet them. "You're no fun," she pouted.

"Tsk-tsk," said Juliette. "Fun is what you make it!"

"It would be fun to go to school," said Caliope. "When can we go to school, Mama? When will we be old enough?"

Juliette tried not to frown at this. She knew the girls didn't like being home-schooled, and even though she would have been happy to oblige, she also knew that neither one of them was disciplined enough to sit still and learn in a classroom setting. Not that she hadn't tried. She was sure they must have ADHD, although she'd never taken them to the doctor for a diagnosis. She didn't trust doctors. She didn't trust them at all.

In fact, she didn't trust outsiders period. That was another reason she home-schooled the girls. She was afraid someone might harm them if she let them out of the house, even just to play in the yard. The neighborhood boys were a bunch of bullies, and she just knew they'd start chasing her two babies. Or they'd get too far away from home and not be able to find their way back. (She didn't dare blame herself for this: If she'd allowed them out before, they might have known their way around.)

Rhapsody had snuck past her once and tried to run away from home. Sure enough, one of the boys had started chasing her, but she'd been able to escape by climbing up a tree in a neighbor's yard. As a tomboy, she took to it naturally. Unfortunately, after spending all of her life indoors, she didn't realize she was afraid of heights until it was too late. Juliette had found her cowering amid the lowest leaves and branches, eyes wide, her arms wrapped tightly around the trunk, afraid to move.

Fortunately, Juliette—who was very tall for a woman at 6 feet and 2 inches—had been able to reach her and bring her down. Rhapsody had clung just as tightly to her as she had to the tree trunk, her fingernails locking painfully into Juliette's skin. But the minute they were home again, she acted like nothing had happened. She was obviously embarrassed, but she was just as clearly too stubborn to show it.

"Well, Mama?" said Rhapsody. "When *do* we get to go to school?"

The girls were trying to gang up on her. Sometimes it worked, like when they got her to let them stay out of the room she'd made for them in the cellar for a few extra hours. But not for something like this.

"I can teach you very capably right here at home," she said haughtily. "You know it's a wild world out there."

Caliope smiled sweetly.

"That smile won't be enough to get you by," Juliette added.

Caliope kept smiling anyway.

Rhapsody just sulked away. "You never let us have any fun," she muttered under her breath.

Juliette whirled on her. "I've had enough of your attitude, young lady." She didn't let herself get angry with the girls too often. Their father had been a surly man with a quick temper who had always wanted a boy but had never managed to father one—and had taken his disappointment out on the girls. He'd even wanted to put them both up for adoption, but Juliette had forbidden it.

"Fine," he'd said. "They're *your* girls. They're *your* problem." The implication was that he hadn't fathered either of them, Juliette knew he was right. But now, all these years later, she'd pushed it so far to the back of her mind that she might as well have forgotten it. What did it matter now, anyway? The man was dead and gone, and good riddance to him. All she needed was her girls.

She immediately regretted being cross with Rhapsody, and

her voice softened. "I'm sorry, sweetheart," she cooed. "Mama's not mad. Not really."

Rhapsody just kept sulking.

"It's OK, Mama," said Caliope. "We like staying home with you. You take good care of us. I *would* like to go to ballet school, though." She twirled around in a circle and bowed.

"I know you would, sweetie. Maybe someday."

She knew there would be no someday. So, she suspected, did Caliope. But she hated to let her down. Delaying the disappointment was better, she tried to convince herself. At least, it was better for her: Juliette couldn't bear the thought that Caliope might take on her sister's more sullen aspect.

Caliope ran over and sat on the couch, and Rhapsody reluctantly followed. As different as they were, the two of them were all but inseparable.

Juliette sat down next to them, and Rhapsody laid her head in her mother's lap. Juliette began stroking her hair, something that always seemed to soothe her, as she found the remote control and turned on *Wheel of Fortune*. Caliope sat up attentively and focused on the screen. It wasn't exactly conventional homeschooling, but it taught the girls spelling and vocabulary. That's how Juliette justified it, anyway.

"I'll buy a vowel," one of the contestants said. "How about an A?"

"No, no, no!" Caliope shouted out. "There's a W up there. I just know it."

"And a C," Rhapsody added.

Vanna White turned over an A in the second letter of the second word in the three-word phrase, which had been introduced as a popular saying.

"Can you solve the puzzle?" Juliette asked them.

Each of the three words was three or four letters, with an

apostrophe in the middle word, so Juliette was confident she wasn't asking too much of them.

"I know! I know!" said Caliope.

"Me, too," said Rhapsody.

"OK, said Juliette. Tell me together, on the count of three. One... two..."

The doorbell rang, interrupting their TV study session, and preventing the two girls from shouting out "The Cat's Meow."

Juliette looked suspiciously at the front door. She wasn't expecting anyone, so she wasn't inclined to answer it, but a few seconds later, the doorbell rang again, followed by an insistent knock and an announcement from the other side: "Department of Child Welfare. We'd like to talk to Juliette Sweeten, if you have a moment."

"Shit!" Juliette cursed under her breath.

"Quick, girls!" she whispered. "Downstairs to your room right away."

They didn't move.

Juliette sighed. She didn't have time for this.

"Now!" she hissed, and jumped at the girls like a trick-or-treater in a sheet popping out from behind a hedge. She didn't do it to be mean: It was playful but serious. Whenever she did it, they knew it was important that they do what they were told immediately.

Juliette breathed a sigh of relief as Rhapsody and Caliope jumped off the couch immediately and scurried down the stairs to the basement, but her heart was still beating fast in her chest. The Department of Child Welfare? What could they want? Were they here to take the girls away from her? To make them go to school? She couldn't let either of those things happen. They were *her* girls, and she was their mama.

Cautiously, she stepped to the door and opened it a crack.

"May I help you?"

A portly man in a dark suit and tie that seemed altogether uncomfortable on a warm autumn day peeked in at her. He was accompanied by a diminutive, freckle-faced woman with medium-length auburn hair carrying a clipboard.

"We're here to check on a complaint, ma'am," the man said. "A neighbor called and said you have children living here who are of school age but aren't enrolled in public school. We have no record that you're homeschooling them..."

"I am," she interrupted them, and immediately regretted it. She would have been better off denying they lived here.

"That's all well and good, ma'am, but we need to see the paperwork authorizing it. The school district says they don't have anything from you—not even your children's names. Do you mind if we come in?

Juliette had a nagging feeling in the pit of her stomach that saying "no" would only make matters worse, so she opened the door and motioned them inside. "You can sit over there on the couch," she said, motioning toward the sofa as she took a seat in the stuffed chair opposite them.

She caught the woman staring at her.

"Is something wrong?"

The woman winced and pursed her lips.

"You think I'm too old to have school-age girls, is that it? Well, I happen to be eighty-seven years young and proud of it." She smiled broadly, displaying a perfect set of dentures. "Now what can I do for you? Would you like a cup of tea?" The words were polite, but the tone was somewhere between annoyance and chastisement.

The woman shifted awkwardly in her seat. "We just want to be sure your girls are getting the proper education," she said. "What are their names, if I may ask?"

"Rhapsody and Caliope."

And how old are they?

"Rhapsody is twelve and Caliope is nine."

The puzzled look crept back onto the woman's face.

"Ever hear of adoption?" Juliette asked, hoping she wouldn't have to produce adoption papers that didn't exist.

The man leaned forward, a serious expression on his face. "Maybe it's best if we just talk to the girls ourselves," he said. "We heard you talking to them as we came up the walkway, so I assume they're here."

Now it was Juliette's turn to shift awkwardly in her seat. "They're... um... in their room."

The man leaned even farther forward and cocked his head, widening his eyes in an expression that said, "And...?"

"It's downstairs," Juliette said. "But I wouldn't go down there if I were you."

Part of her knew that such a statement would only heighten their curiosity and make them more likely to investigate. Another part of her hoped they would. She'd trained her girls about what to do should they feel threatened, and she felt sure they could handle themselves if push came to shove.

Just as she suspected, the two Child Welfare employees took the bait.

"I'm afraid we'll have to check on them," the man said.

Juliette shrugged her shoulders. "Suit yourself. I have nothing to hide."

They started down the stairs, but the woman stopped halfway down and turned back to face Juliette. "Aren't you coming with us?" she asked.

Juliette shook her head. "No need. The girls are well-behaved. Whatever you two might think, I'm a good mom. I've taught them how to act around guests."

The woman hesitated a moment more, then turned back and followed the man down the stairs.

Rhapsody and Caliope sat crouched in one corner of the dark and dingy basement, hoping they wouldn't be noticed. There was no light switch, let alone a light, down here, and just one small window at outside-ground level near the ceiling. The natural light that filtered in through it created more shadows than illumination, especially in the morning when the sun was on the other side of the home.

"Do you think they'll find us?" Caliope whispered, almost gleefully.

"I don't know," said Rhapsody, who was hiding behind a dusty old artificial Christmas tree, several of its limbs missing and an equally dusty star sitting cockeyed at the top. "I'm pretty good at hide-and-seek. It's my favorite game."

"I'll just stick by you then."

The door, which they'd left half-open behind them, creaked as it swung outward, and two silhouettes—one large and the other small—entered the room.

"This is their *bedroom*?" a woman's voice said. "I don't even see a bed."

The other intruder, a man, stumbled over a broom and barely kept from falling as he walked over toward an old dresser. Caliope barely stifled her laughter, and Rhapsody fixed her with a warning look. They didn't want to resort to drastic measures unless they absolutely had to.

The man opened one of the dresser drawers.

"There aren't any girls' clothes in here," he said after he'd gone through all six. "They look like they belong to the mother, and they haven't been worn in years."

"Try the next one," said the woman.

He did and shook his head. "Just a bunch of unopened Christmas gifts. I wonder why she just left them down here."

The woman shook her head. "You know we'll have to report this," she said.

"Ya think?" said the man. "What could possibly live down here?"

He found at least one answer as he brushed aside a spiderweb, not having expected it to still contain the spider that fell onto his neck and skittered down the inside of his shirt. He started jumping and dancing around, trying to shake it out, and stepped on the broom handle again. That sent him tumbling to the floor, a cloud of dust billowing up around him where he'd fallen.

Caliope couldn't contain herself this time. She laughed aloud, and Rhapsody rolled her eyes. "Now you've done it!"

"Oh, stop," said Caliope. "This will be fun."

Rhapsody relaxed and smiled a rare smile in return. "Yes, it will be," she said conspiratorially.

"Who's there?" came the woman's voice. "Girls, are you down here?"

The girls did not appear.

A moment of silence passed, but just a short moment.

Then it happened.

A huge black panther and a sleek white tiger sprang out of the darkness. All teeth and claws and snarls and roars, they pounced toward the startled government workers just the way their mama had taught them—just the way she herself did when she meant business with them. The man, who had barely gotten to his feet, rocked back on his heels and went down again. The woman dashed from the room, screaming like a banshee, and the man screamed even louder as he tried to scurry backward on his hands and buttocks, finally getting to his feet and following her out and up the stairs at a full run.

Neither of them paused to look at Juliette, who was stifling her own laughter, as they flew out the door and made for their car, revving the engine and peeling out on the quiet suburban street.

A few moments later, Caliope and Rhapsody came bounding up the stairs, looking none the worse for wear.

Caliope twirled and bowed before Juliette, quite satisfied with herself, and Rhapsody had a telltale gleam in her eye. "I don't think they'll be back, Mama," Caliope said with a laugh. "No one wants to mess with Bengal Baby and Midnight Felina!"

Rhapsody scowled at her: "I told you, Bengals are orange, not white like you."

"Oh, right."

Juliette was shaking her head. "They'll send Animal Control out for sure."

"Let them come!" Caliope crowed, tilting her head back confidently. "They can't catch us!"

It was Juliette's turn to laugh now. "No, I suppose they can't."

But her expression turned sad as she saw them begin to fade. Why did they have to go so soon? She knew the reason, of course: It took a lot of energy for them to hold their big-cat form—even more than they needed to appear as little girls—and energy was all they were, after all: spirits no longer confined by physical bodies, as they had been when she had adopted them three decades ago.

Juliette had never been able to have any children of her own, thanks to her husband's condition, and when he'd died young, she'd had no interest in marrying again. She was content to live her life with the two fur-babies she had adopted as kittens after finding them alone in her backyard, shivering in the cold, one snowy Christmas Eve. She brushed the snow from their fur, took them into her house, gave them food and milk and all the love they could ever want—the love she'd never gotten from her husband—and they became her girls, like the daughters she could never have,

They were so close to her that when they died at the ages of nine and twelve, they stayed there with her, taking on whatever form they thought she needed. It was the least they could do after how well "Mama" had looked after them all these years. They found they were able to speak to her in her language, or at least translate their own language to hers in her thoughts, something they'd never been able to do in their physical form, and she taught them to behave like the good little girls she always wanted.

When the Animal Control officers came to follow up on a report from Child Welfare of two wild animals being held in the basement of a suburban home in rural Clovis, all they found was the body of an 87-year-old woman who'd died peacefully in her sleep. The basement where the two wild animals had supposedly been kept was empty except for dust, and cobwebs, furniture, old clothing, and those unopened Christmas packages.

They couldn't resist looking inside to see what they contained—and were surprised to find they contained what looked like old cat toys: a little plastic ball with a bell that rolled around inside, a felt-covered play mouse, and a feather dancer.

As they looked further, they also found what looked like a few strands of cat fur drifting along on the afternoon sunbeams.

As they looked more closely, however, they decided they

were mistaken, as those strands appeared to disappear like mist before their eyes.

They left to what they would have sworn was a chorus of distant meows, almost like an echo that went silent as soon as they heard it.

Two kittens and their mama were playing in some far-off field together, chasing butterflies. The wise old cat reveled in her new form as she lounged in the sunshine, watching as one of the kittens twirled like a ballerina while the other scampered up a tree and played hide-and-seek in the shade of its branches. The bank repossessed the house where they'd all lived in a time that now seemed so long ago.

But it didn't matter.

They all were home.

Sharon Marie Provost

Christmas Feast

Pippin arrived home to great pomp and circumstance. As the head elf, he was the only one who was allowed to return from his vacation so late in the year, a mere month before Christmas. The elves at the North Pole worked on toys all year long, but they were especially busy in the month just before Christmas, making presents for all the newly born children and those who had mended their naughty ways... just in the "Nick" of time.

Usually, Pippin was thrilled to start the last-minute rush, but this time he was not feeling well. He loved the cold, wintry weather at the North Pole, but his annual vacation to the warm, wet jungles of Costa Rica always reinvigorated him. This time, however, he had developed a headache and body aches when he was packing for his return. As the day went on, he became overwhelmingly tired and feverish. He nearly slept through his morning alarm, but luckily, he had made it to his departure gate just before they closed the door.

He desperately tried to look happy and prepared for work, but Santa became concerned when he heard from several other elves about Pippin's state.

"Pippin, you know that I am counting on you to run the workshop like a tight ship as we prepare for Christmas night. Do I need to find a replacement?"

Pippin's face showed his dismay at Santa's lack of faith in him. He quickly rolled up his sleeve and held out his arm. "No, Santa. No, sir. Everything will be fine. I was bitten by an animal during a jungle hike, and I think I have a bit of an infection, that's all. I will go directly to the Candy Cane Infirmary and skip the festivities. I am sure Nurse Peppermint can help me."

Nurse Peppermint greeted him with delight; she had always had a crush on him. "Well, how can I help you, Pippin?"

Pippin walked quickly to the exam table and climbed up, displaying his arm immediately. "I need some medicine. I am not feeling well at all, and I believe it is from this wound I sustained from an animal in the jungle. Can you help me? Santa is counting on me tomorrow."

Nurse Peppermint's brow furrowed as she looked down at the reddish-purple, raised bite wound, which was oozing a thick, custard-colored purulent liquid. She didn't recognize the teeth marks. "You look flushed. Let me check your temperature." She popped a thermometer in his mouth as she turned to get lidocaine, antiseptic, bandages, and antibiotics.

When she was done, she removed the thermometer from his mouth with a flourish.

Her face went white. "107! Dear me!" she exclaimed in shock. You must get into that bed over there. I am hospitalizing you immediately."

"No, no, no. You can't do that. Santa's going to check on me after the party to make sure I'm starting to feel better. He is counting on me. I don't have time for this." Pippin jumped off the table quickly but wavered unsteadily on his feet before grabbing the bed to keep from falling. Nurse Peppermint took his arm firmly and guided him over to a hospital bed.

"I promise I will have you out of here faster than Santa delivers toys to all the children of the world. Give me one day, and you will be able to return to your job. I will explain to Santa how sick you are."

Pippin reluctantly climbed into bed and covered up, his body wracked with a severe bout of shivering from the chills that had been descending on him rapidly. Nurse Peppermint placed a cool, wet cloth on his forehead. She gave him an injection of lidocaine around the wound, and then she began squeezing the pus out of his arm. She was horrified at the amount of blood and discharge that emanated from the small holes.

She scrubbed the area thoroughly with Betadine and then wrapped Pippin's arm. She was concerned about the severity of his fever and dehydration, so she inserted an IV to start fluids and IV antibiotics.

Shortly after the nurse had finished his treatment, he surrendered to a deep sleep. He drifted in and out of consciousness and could have sworn he heard Santa come in to talk to the nurse, although he could not recall what he had heard. He finally woke the next morning to a flurry of activity and felt extremely confused. The nurses surrounding him seemed very relieved when they saw him open his eyes.

"Well now, Pippin. You put quite the scare into all of us. How are you feeling?"

Pippin looked around, confused at all the eyes focused on him. "I'mmmmfff oootayyy. Watt izzz olll the fussszzzz?"

He gasped as he heard the slurred words emanating from his mouth. More concerning than the actual words he uttered was how hard he had worked to even come up with that sentence. He felt like he was floating through a fog.

"It is OK, sweetheart. You will be OK. Just relax and let us take care of you," Nurse Jingles cooed before she hurried over to the nurses' desk, where Nurse Peppermint was on the phone. She looked back at him as she animatedly relayed his condition to the head nurse. He heard the words "seizure" and "dysphasia," whatever that meant. Apparently, his fever had soared to a dangerous level, and his blood pressure was bottoming out. He began to shake with fear as an alarm began to blare and his head began to spin again.

Pippin awoke sometime later, unable to see in the darkness—and fully covered by a sheet. He no longer felt sick. Even more concerning, he didn't really feel anything at all. No emotions, no fever or chills, no pain; he felt absolutely nothing except an aching hunger.

But for what?

He pulled the sheet off of him and sat up quickly. He was puzzled to realize that he was in the rarely used morgue. Elves were extremely resilient and long-lived, but they were not immortal. The last time he remembered the morgue being used was during his childhood, nearly 125 years ago.

What am I doing here? I was in the hospital being treated for an infection. I am not nearly old enough to have died. Damn! I am so hungry I can't even think. I will go find food and then figure out if this is an elaborate prank.

Pippin heard another elf in the hallway, singing as she walked in this general direction. His stomach growled more and more as he heard her approach. He climbed off the table and snuck over to peek out the small round window in the door. She was slowly moving this way as she mopped the floor with her back to him.

He licked his lips as his stomach growled more insistently.

He quietly opened the door and crept up behind her. He wrapped his hand around her mouth and dragged her into the morgue. Her fear turned to absolute horror as she realized who was holding her.

"But they said you were dead! Why did you grab me? What is going on here?" she questioned rapidly—her voice rising with each syllable.

Pippin wrapped his hand tightly around her mouth before plunging his teeth into her neck, biting into her jugular vein. He quickly became drenched in her dark red blood as he swallowed great mouthfuls of it. His stomach rolled with pleasure. Her movements slowed and then eventually stopped altogether.

He reached over to the instrument tray nearby and grabbed a scalpel. He carelessly tossed her body onto the autopsy table he had been lying on a short while ago. He slid the blade into her skin and traced a line down from her throat, across the breastbone, and all the way to her groin. He pulled open her abdomen and began cutting out her intestines and other vital organs. He then used the rib cutters to cut all the way up to the top of her ribcage on both sides. He removed the entire ribcage plate so he could access her heart for removal. Finally, he once again used the scalpel to cut the scalp along the hairline and down each side of the head. Then he carefully peeled back the scalp before using the bone saw to remove the top of her skull. Once he had completed that task, he carefully dissected out the brain and placed it in the basin at the end of the table, along with all the other tasty morsels he had acquired.

He peered out the window again to see if the hallway was clear. He then went back to the table to collect his meal before heading out of the morgue and to the side door, exiting into the arctic tundra, taking the scalpel with him.

The North Pole was a harsh environment in which to live, but the elves were well-suited to temperature extremes, especially with their warm, velvet- and fur-draped uniform. Strangely, he felt perfectly fine even though he had only been able to find some rags and bandages with which to cover himself.

Pippin ran across the drifting sheets of ice, deep into the tundra, and found a quiet place to sit and enjoy his meal behind small hills of ice and snow. All was quiet except for the occasional passing of arctic foxes and polar bears. The animals gave him a wide berth, sensing that there was something wrong with him. A short while later, he heard the alarm go off at Santa's compound. It was an alarm that usually signaled a catastrophic shutdown of the toy assembly line, but this time was different.

The next day, he heard a search party go by looking for him —or whoever might have caused the death of the orderly.

"They said he was dead, but where is his body?"

"How could he do that to her? She was so sweet."

"Better yet, HOW could he do that? I was there when he died. No heartbeat, no breathing, cold to the touch... utterly lifeless."

"Maybe it wasn't him. Maybe it was an animal. Maybe someone left the door open, and a polar bear got in."

Pippin couldn't help but laugh. They were totally in the dark. He heard them split up into two-person search parties to investigate different ridges. He buried himself in the snow against the hillside as the first party approached. It was Fred and Marvin, two of the larger, tougher elves. Just when they reached him, he jumped out and knocked them unconscious. Then he bit them to spread the disease and covered the bite marks with some wounds from his scalpel. He left the area quickly before they woke up again.

The next search party was composed of the young twins, Cocoa and Marshmallow. He quickly dispatched them and dragged their bodies into a small cave in the ice, then piled up snow to hide them. They would make a lovely meal over the next few days.

The last search party was made up of Sugar and his grumpy father, Spice. Sugar was afraid of being so far away from the compound. His father quickly left him behind and yelled at him to just return to his room. Sugar turned to head back but was surprised when an arm reached out and grabbed him by the throat. He had mere seconds for surprise and recognition to register on his face before his life-blood ran down him like a river. He dropped to the ground in a heap, and Pippin quickly dragged him to an old fox den in the ice to hide his body.

Spice was just returning to the rendezvous point when he caught sight of Pippin running around a hill. He charged forward, but Pippin tackled him and wrestled him to the ground, knocking him out on the hard ice surface. Spice awoke to a bleeding wound on his forehead that he mistakenly attributed to the sharp ice. He never dreamed that Pippin had infected him while he was unconscious.

The three elves who had survived the attacks finally met up just outside the compound and headed in to make their report to Santa. Santa could not risk any more delays or staff shortages, so he sent them to the infirmary immediately to treat their wounds. Santa then sent out the reindeer to search for the three missing men. Late that night, their bodies were found, once again devoid of their internal organs.

Santa immediately instituted an around-the-clock watch to protect all entrances to the workshop and dormitories. Toy building continued at breakneck speed, even though their workforce numbers slowly but surely dwindled. Every day over the next few weeks, more elves either appeared in the infirmary with mysterious wounds or disappeared from the compound, never to be seen again. Those who came sick to the infirmary became very ill and eventually died. Their bodies were locked up in the morgue, but they too disappeared without a trace.

Nurse Peppermint worked in the infirmary nearly around the clock, caring for all the sick elves. She was desperate to find a cure that worked, determined not to lose one more patient. Early on the morning of Christmas Eve, before it was light, she was cleaning Joy's wound when the infirmary door slammed against the wall. She turned around, and a wide smile dawned on her face as she saw it was Pippin. She still couldn't believe or understand the reports of Pippin being alive when she was the one who had pronounced him dead weeks before. However, there he was in front of her, not looking well at all, but alive just the same.

"Pippppinnnn! I am so happy to see you. Come here at once and get in bed. Let me take care of you, sweetie," Nurse Peppermint exclaimed, blushing. Pippin lumbered toward her menacingly; there was no trace of a smile on his face. She fidgeted with the blankets nervously as he approached and forced herself to keep smiling. She cried out in pain when he grabbed her wrist and twisted it.

"Pippin, stop it! That hurts. Oh no! PLEASE STOP! Hel..."

Her scream was cut off with the swift slash of the knife across her throat. She gurgled, and little bubbles of blood slid down her chin, joining the torrent of blood running from the wide gash in her neck. Pippin quickly finished butchering her body and stowed the tasty bits in a dirty leather satchel tied around his waist. He dragged her body over to the corner, out of sight, and locked the door to the infirmary behind him—after putting up the "Closed for Lunch" sign. He had much more to accomplish in the next few hours, so he could not afford to have anyone raise the alarm just yet.

As Christmas Eve morning dawned, to Santa's great surprise and relief, he found that all the toys were finished, even though he'd been experiencing an unprecedented workforce shortage amid this unexplained emergency. The remaining elves began in earnest to load all the toys into Santa's bag—which can, magically, hold an unlimited number of items. Then they fed and watered the reindeer before harnessing them to the sleigh.

Santa was eating a wonderful meal prepared by Mrs. Claus, when he heard a loud commotion outside.

Suddenly, Pippin and a large group of missing elves burst into the dining hall. They were dressed in tattered, dirty rags. Their eyes were red and stared vacantly at Santa. Pippin was yelling something at them, but Santa found it difficult to understand his words.

"Gith him! Barrr the doorszz."

The group of zombified elves grabbed Santa roughly. Pippin approached him rapidly, wielding a large carving knife he'd grabbed off the table. He slashed violently and deeply into Santa's belly, disemboweling him with a single stroke. The elves holding him dove onto his entrails, slurping and sucking the loops of bowel into their mouths. Pippin jumped onto his shoulder and slashed at his neck, covering himself and the others in a fount of blood. The Christmas feast was ghastly to behold, but only the beginning.

After they finished with Santa, the elves walked out with Pippin as he prepared to leave with the sleigh. He gave them orders to deal with the rest of the elvish employees and to prepare for his return. He took Marvin in the sleigh with him to watch over the reindeer as he slid down the chimneys, completing his mission.

"On Dashur and Dannnser. On Blitzzzed and Coopid. Whateverrr! Let's gooo," Pippin mumbled as he shook the reins. The reindeer, led by Rudolph, flew off into the night, too afraid to even think about refusing. They flew across the sky, taking Pippin from Asia to Europe, to Africa and Australia, and then on to North and South America.

Pippin's mission was simple. He had Santa's lists for all the naughty and nice girls and boys across the world. He guided the reindeer to each and every house. He slid down each chimney and left toys under the tree, but only for those naughty children. Then he crept down the hall to each child's room. At the rooms of the nice children, he would quietly steal in and collect them from their beds. He stuffed each good child into Santa's magical bag and tied it tight. Then he moved on to the rooms of the naughty children and spread the zombie disease.

It was a long night, but he visited the home of each child on the list. Marvin helped him tie the bag shut tight. Then they secured the squealing, crying bag of children securely into the sleigh for the long flight back to the North Pole.

Once again, Pippin arrived back at the compound to great fanfare and adulation. The snow was covered in the blood and body parts of the remaining elves that had been slaughtered. Many of the large tables from the dining hall had been carried out and set up around an enormous bonfire. The atmosphere was electric with excitement about the upcoming ultimate Christmas feast.

Pippin landed near the large cages that had been erected off to the side to hold all the children. The bag was unloaded, and the children were led into the cages, where they were given blankets to keep them from freezing to death... because cold, coagulated blood is foul.

The tables were set with the best Christmas china and large platters were set in the middle with a variety of blades set around them. A small group of children was led to the table, where they were expertly butchered: The chef and his kitchen staff did a masterful job.

The crowd clamored loudly for Pippin to give a speech, and despite some lingering insecurity over his slurred speech, he obliged them.

He climbed onto a chair, raised a blood-filled goblet, and declared loudly, "Merrrry Christmasssszz to allll, and to ollll a good bite."

Stephen H. Provost

Ghostbusted!

Rick Piersall hadn't made his reputation backing away from a challenge, and this certainly was... different. He wanted something special for his annual two-hour "Holiday Haunting" special, and this sure looked like it. His assistant had handed him a letter from a viewer in Mound House, Nevada, named Adolph Sutro, claiming to have knowledge of the "most haunted place in the entire U.S. of A." That was how he'd put it.

That part wasn't different.

Hundreds of places claimed to be the most haunted this or that, and Rick had visited dozens of those since his show, *Haunted Havens*, went on the air six years ago. But this letter wasn't flagging him to some haunted hotel or opera house or abandoned mansion. Instead, it claimed an entire town was haunted—so much so that no one dared live there... or even visit.

Of course, the letter said, some folks might have just left once the cyanide mill closed: It had opened in the early 1920s to process silver, only to close a few years later when the price of the metal fell. Now, the letter claimed, it was totally sealed off to the outside world. The government had made sure of that, supposedly to protect trespassers from the mill's ruins, which had lately been demolished. But it remained a hazard thanks to the number of deep shafts in the area.

That was the government's story. But this mysterious viewer, this Adolph, had a different take: The government wasn't just keeping people out, it—or something—was keeping the ghosts in.

Rick wondered how effective such an effort could be or whether it was even needed. He could have told you that ghosts were often tied to a place anyway—most commonly, their old residence or the place they died. And if they did decide to get out, he didn't see how the government could stop them.

"You can only get to American Flat through my private tunnel, and I am the only person who can grant you access," Adolph had confidently stated in his letter. "If you seek to enter the town through any other means, you may be well assured of failure. What you will find on the other side is, I give you my word, nothing short of astounding, and, I dare say, terrifying."

It was that last word that hooked Rick Piersall. Whoever this Adolph was, he'd obviously seen Haunted Havens, which put a premium on making each locale appear as scary as possible. That's what kept viewers on the edge of their seats.

When Rick has first pitched the show to The Horror Network, he'd played to his strength as an investigative journalist. He'd vowed to place a premium on scientific evidence, supported by credible witnesses. Each episode, as he envisioned it, would conclude with a verdict:

The site in question would be declared either "haunted" or "safe."

THN had liked the concept, in general, but had told him the audience wasn't looking for Scooby-Doo-type ghostbusters. Viewers wanted to be scared. They wanted to believe. And that meant Rick would have to convince them that the places he visited were haunted—or at least very likely could be.

He was "encouraged" to stumble across a number of unexpected surprises during each episode to keep the viewers on the edge of their seats. (These "jump scares," as the network called them, would invariably be edited to occur just prior to commercial breaks.)

"It's just business," the network honchos had told him. "Like in those Scream movies. They're full of jump scares and gotcha scenes, and they always set up a sequel. That's why they work."

"But this is reality TV, not a film script." That had been Rick's argument. Besides, he thought, Scream was part satire, a sendup of horror films. It wasn't meant to be taken seriously. And Rick wanted to be taken seriously.

But they had set him straight: "Who told you reality TV was all real? It's edited like any other show. We show them what we want them to see—and what they want to see.

There's nothing wrong with that."

Rick hadn't liked any of this—not at first. But he figured it was the price for having a show on cable TV. When Haunted Havens became an unqualified hit, he no longer questioned the network's ground rules—especially when the execs allowed him to keep producing the show himself. They obviously knew what they were doing: Who was he to argue with success?

Instead of interviewing skeptics, he confined himself to "true believers." And he learned how to act suitably distressed (read: scared shitless) at a sudden temperature drop in a drafty old mansion. Naturally, the temperature did drop when there was a draft, but Rick knew better than to mention that on camera. And he hyped it up if his EMF meter suddenly picked up a "spectral shadow"—a term he'd coined himself. Or if his flashlight started flickering. Or if there happened to be a sudden noise off-camera.

Skeptics, of course, said the EMF readings weren't ghosts, the flashlight's batteries were loose, and Rick's assistant, Faith Woolridge, was the one who made things go bump in the night.

The network bosses didn't care, and Rick told himself he didn't, either: The skeptics watched, too (so they could try to debunk him) and ratings were ratings. Still, deep down, he always felt a twinge of guilt about playing fast and loose with the facts. That's why, whenever he heard about something that sounded legitimately scary, he jumped at the chance to investigate it. That way, he didn't feel quite so guilty.

This letter from Adolph had that ring of legitimacy to it. Who named their kid Adolph these days, anyway? Even the language of the letter sounded... spooky.

So Rick packed up his equipment and chartered a flight to Reno along with cameraman Cory Ainge, co-producer Skip Hathaway, and on-camera partner Faith, who routinely played the part of "damsel in distress" at the appearance of any grouchy ghoulies.

It was Cory who had given him the letter from Adolph; he and Rick weren't on the best of terms—Cory had made it clear he wanted more time in front of the camera and that he thought Rick was a control freak—but the show was a success, and

Rick was the boss, so he stayed in line. He even brought Rick show ideas from time to time.

Mostly, Rick just tossed them, and Cory wasn't happy about that either. So it was natural that he seemed especially pleased at his boss's response to the Adolph letter.

The flight to Reno was uneventful—with one exception. When the plane hit some pretty bad turbulence in its descent to RNO, Rick found himself wondering if the ghosts from American Flat had sent a welcoming committee. But Faith (who'd grown up down the road in Verdi) said this was typical.

"If you don't like wind, you won't like Nevada," she told him.

Even with her reassurance, Rick didn't breathe easy until the plane landed safely at the airport, where they picked up their rental car for the drive to Mound House, a small town just east of Carson City, a little more than half an hour away where letter-writer Adolph had said he'd be waiting.

Mostly, it was known for its four legal brothels.

Adolph met them just outside one of them: the Moonlite BunnyRanch just off Highway 50. Adolph hadn't mentioned the brothel in the directions he'd sent; he'd just asked Rick and his team to meet him at "the old Pony Express stop"—which happened to be on the brothel property. When he greeted them, he ignored the brothel entirely, although Rick suspected the man was a regular. Attired in a double-breasted suit and decorative cowboy hat, he looked very much like the kind of gentleman who would find something he liked on the BunnyRanch "sex menu," even if his overgrown mutton chops made him seem a little old-fashioned.

Okay, a lot old-fashioned.

The way he talked only confirmed that impression.

"Good day, sirs and madam," he said, extending a hand. "I trust this day finds you well. I see you have brought with you one of Mr. Edison's Kinetographs. Grand! They certainly have advanced further than I suspected. You will want to record this for posterity!"

"Kinetograph?" Faith said, puzzled.

Adolph pointed at Rick's video camera, which he was using to film the exchange.

"Ah," she said, not looking any more at ease with her new knowledge.

Rick looked at her and shook his head slightly. Whoever this man was, he was obviously playing a role. He'd heard about Chautauqua performers taking on the personas of historical figures in nearby Virginia City—site of the biggest strike in mining history—and he felt sure that Adolph was doing just that. Rick just couldn't figure out who he was supposed to be.

It probably didn't matter.

He climbed in their rental car, and they drove him toward the private tunnel he had referred to in his letter, which was less than ten miles up the highway. Once they reached the property, he directed them past a fence and onto a dirt road that wound up toward a low line of hills. At the end of the road lay the tunnel, framed by brick covered in white plaster. The wide entrance was surmounted by a signboard shaped suspiciously like a headstone that read "Sutro Tunnel" along with the date 1888. It had been commissioned, the signboard revealed, on October 19, 1869, which meant it must have taken a long time to complete.

The Sutro name sounded vaguely familiar, so Rick got out his smartphone and tried to google it. Unfortunately, however, he had no reception this far out.

"What's that contraption?" Adolph inquired.

He certainly was playing the part of the 19th century gentleman.

"I've heard that name somewhere," Rick said, pointing above the tunnel. "I was just trying to figure out how I knew it."

Adolph chuckled. "Of course you have, my friend," he said. "Sutro's my name. Adolph Sutro. I told you it was my tunnel in the missive I sent you. I finished it just before I went back to Frisco. I'm the mayor there now, you know. Just on a little sabbatical this weekend. It's a shame my old friend Samuel no longer lives in these parts. I would have liked to tip a glass with him."

"Samuel?" Skip asked.

"Clemens," Adolph said. "Goes by Mark Twain these days. A genuine chucklehead coffee boiler if ever there was one. Once tried to joke about a friend of mine being bald." He tipped his cap, revealing his own hairless pate. "That was taking things a little far, especially since the man in question was not bald. His name was Ball. He thought that was funny. But when I refused to laugh as he expected, he had the gumption to label me as 'insensible to the more delicate touches of American wit.' In the press, if you can believe that. But I eventually forgave him. He's more famous than I am these days, and funnier now than he was then, so how could I not?"

Skip just stared at Rick, as if to say, "Is this guy for real?" But he and Cory both ignored him. This was great stuff. Either this Adolph guy was acting—and doing a great job of it—or he'd gone round the bend more times than a NASCAR driver. Whichever it was, it made for great TV.

"So," Rick said, adopting his serious TV ghosthunter voice, "if we go straight through this tunnel of yours, we'll reach the ghost town you told us about, American Flat."

Adolph nodded. "That's what the letter said, did it not?

Well, I suppose that it isn't entirely accurate. The tunnel goes to Virginia City.

That's what I built it for: to drain water out of the mines up there. But there's a side tunnel about halfway up that goes off to the left. That will take you to American Flat."

"You'll show us this tunnel when we get there?"

He shook his head vigorously, looking both determined and a little scared. "Me? Go back there?" He acted as though it was self-evident why he would want to avoid doing so, but the team's puzzled looks persuaded him to explain. "Most of us ghosts never get out of American Flat. Those of us fortunate enough to do so are most definitely not going back. I'll never set foot in that tunnel again."

"You're saying you're a ghost?" Faith said.

"Quite so, I'm afraid."

The man was certainly not a ghost, Rick felt sure. He was obviously an actor—probably planted by The Horror Network to spice things up. Without bothering to tell Rick, which was taking things a little far. Rick was fine with playing the part of the spooked spook-hunter, but he didn't like being played for a fool or wasting his time on a wild ghost chase. So he did what any veteran ghost-hunter would do: He sought confirmation the whole thing wasn't a hoax.

Pulling out his temperature gauge, he waved it in the air a few inches from Adolph's face.

"What in tarnation...?" Adolph leaned back abruptly, taken by surprise, but Rick still got his ambient thermometer close enough for a reading.

It was well over 80 degrees outside, it being summertime in the Nevada desert (they always filmed their *Holiday Haunts* episode months in advance), but to Rick's surprise, the thermometer read 42.

Forty-two!

Any ghost investigator will tell you that a sudden, highly localized drop in temperature indicated the likely presence of a ghost.

Rick did a double-take, but he wasn't convinced. Still, whatever trick this Sutro character—or whoever he was—had pulled made for great TV. Rick shot a glance at Cory to be sure he was getting the footage, and a quick nod confirmed that he was.

Rick hammed it up, stepping back and opening his mouth wide for effect.

"O... kay...," he stammered, feigning the kind of fear he manufactured every week for the camera. "We... believe you. Just tell us where to go, and we'll be on our way."

Adolph shook his head. "In through there. I told you," he said, pointing at the tunnel. "Just watch for that side passage I told you about."

Rick nodded, still pretending to be scared out of his wits as he backed up toward the tunnel.

"You'll be wanting these," Adolph said, producing four lighted mining helmets, as if from out of nowhere. Rick had been counting on the lighting from Cory's video camera to help them navigate the tunnel, but he made a show of accepting the helmets anyway and having everyone strap them on. It heightened the sense of theater. Frankly, he wished he'd thought of it.

"Be careful," Adolph added. "Time's a funny thing in there."

The four of them made a show of moving quickly toward the tunnel, with Rick taking the lead, followed by Faith and Cory, and Skip bringing up the rear. Skip's schtick was to scream at the appropriate time to remind the audience just how dangerous ghost hunting was, even though the team never seemed to "discover" why he'd raised the alarm.

Sure enough, they'd only gone a few steps into the tunnel when Skip let out a scream: one that sounded much more intense and heartfelt than usual. It wasn't just a cry of fear, but of pain.

"Fuck!" he shouted, and Rick uttered his own silent curse because they'd have to edit that out.

"Watch the language." Rick said, but as he turned back toward Skip, he saw the man writhing on the ground, wincing in the shadows near the cave mouth as he grasped his ankle with both hands. Rick's questioning look was met with more cursing.

"Snakebite, you asshole! Fucking rattler. Where's the med kit?"

Rick froze.

He looked helplessly at Cory, then at Faith, but he knew the answer before he saw them shake their heads.

"What the fuck?" Skip half-shouted, half-whined. "We're in fuckin' Nevada and you didn't bring a snakebite kit?!?"

"We'd better go back," Faith said.

Rick knew she was right, but something in his head was making him hesitate, pulling at him to go deeper into the tunnel.

"Rick!" Faith shouted.

"She's right," said Cory. "We need to go back."

But it was Adolph who spoke next, his tone oddly cheerful and detached considering the circumstances. "I've got a snakebite kit right here," he said. "I always have one handy. It is Nevada, after all."

The quip wasn't lost on Rick, but the pull of the tunnel was still just as strong. He looked at Adolph, then back into the blackness.

"Never you worry," Adolph said. "Go on ahead. I'll have him fixed up in no time."

That was all the encouragement Rick needed. "Thanks," he shouted back, then turned to Faith and Cory. "Come on. We should get through this tunnel while there's still enough daylight left to film."

"But...," Faith began to protest.

"Who's in charge here?" Rick snapped, surprised to hear the impatience in his own voice. Then, more softly: "C'mon, guys. Skip's in good hands." He was trying to convince himself of this, but the pull of the tunnel was stronger than his level of reassurance about Adolph. Hell, he didn't even know the guy. But why would he say he had a med kit unless he really did? Besides, he was right: This was Nevada. Everyone here had one. Except Rick and his team.

He could tell Cory and Faith were reluctant to leave Skip, but they knew who the boss was, and they followed his lead. It was a good thing too. The tunnel turned out to be longer than he'd expected: nearly two miles before they reached the side passage Adolph had told them about. Covering those two miles took a lot longer than Rick would've thought; he told himself it was because they were moving more slowly through the darkness, with only the camera light and helmet lamps to guide them. But Adolph's warning kept echoing through his head: "Time's a funny thing in there." Had he been referring to the tunnel or the ghost town... or both?

The drip-drip-drip of water and the trickle of a stream through the tunnel heightened the sense that their journey was interminable, like Chinese water torture.

Rick tried to calm himself: It always seemed to take longer to get to a place—especially when you didn't know the way—than it did to come back. But his nerves weren't having it.

It was a relief when the three of them finally stepped out into sunlight, which blinded them

for a moment before their eyes adjusted to the unexpected scene before them. They hadn't expected to find much in American Flat, if anything. The city itself was long-since gone, and even the cyanide mill had been razed nearly a decade ago. But what they saw flew in the face of everything they knew or expected.

There before them was a bustling town, filled with buildings in various stages of completion. None of the ones that were complete looked to be more than a year old; most were constructed of wood or, in a few cases, brick and mortar. Dozens of people were out in the streets, hurrying this way and that, but there wasn't a car in sight: just a number of horse-drawn wagons and carriages.

A sign on one of the buildings read "American City Hotel," while another proclaimed itself the Eureka Hotel, "Theodore Gosse, proprietor." Both were hubs of activity, but neither more so than Brown's Exchange Saloon, where a sign promised that the "best quality of wines, liquors etc" was "always on hand." From the number of customers entering the place, and leaving in various stages of inebriation, Rick surmised that living up to that promise might be a challenge.

It wasn't the only watering hole, either. The Willows Saloon looked just as popular—perhaps even more so, since it advertised having a race track out back.

Faith pulled Rick close and whispered in his ear: "We must have come out in Virginia City. That's where Adolph said the tunnel led."

Rick shook his head. He'd been to Virginia City for an early episode of Haunted Havens, before Faith joined the team, to investigate the haunted Washoe Club there. He knew this place looked nothing like Virginia City.

Come to think of it, though, Faith should've known too. Shouldn't she? She'd grown up in Nevada, barely an hour away from here. There wasn't anything to indicate that they were standing in Virginia City. Besides, there were plenty of signs that said "American Flat" or "American City."

"It's a movie set," Cory offered, not bothering to whisper.

But Rick didn't think it was that, either. He'd never seen a movie set so elaborate that it went on for blocks in every direction.

They were still trying to get their bearings when a man wearing a bowler hat ran up to them and thrust a piece of paper in Rick's face. "You gentlemen look like you know a good opportunity when you see one. Get in on the ground floor, my friends. Invest now, and you'll make a killing. It's the new Virginia City! It's bigger than Aurora!"

"And you are...?" Rick asked.

"Buddy McGursky, at your service," the man said, tipping his hat. "Representing William Hunt, broker and mining secretary of six mining concerns, hereabouts. But I'm sure you know the name. He's on the level, I assure you."

"Hey," said Cory, looking at Faith. "Weren't you a Hunt before you married...?"

She scowled at him, a reminder that she didn't lije to discuss her former husband. She'd only kept the name because she'd started doing the show when she was still married, and Rick had insisted she keep it. If it had been her show...

Cory shrugged. "Maybe this William guy's your great-great-something-or-other."

She wasn't any less irritated at this. "It's a common name," she spat.

Rick ignored their exchange and took the flyer. "We'll keep

it in mind," he said in a polite tone that failed to mask his suspicion.

"You do! You do!" said McGursky before quickly hopping on down the road to accost another pedestrian.

Rick noticed Faith shivering.

"Cold?"

"Aren't you?" she answered.

Come to think of it, he was. The sun was still high in the sky, and the dust on the streets made it clear that the place hadn't seen rain in some time. He looked around at the people coming and going: Some were dressed in summer attire, and the rest looked very uncomfortable in their formal clothing. There wasn't a wool coat or a pair of gloves to be seen. It didn't make sense, unless...

Rick pulled out his ambient thermometer and began walking around, staring at it the whole time. He was nearly knocked off his feet by a horse-drawn carriage, whose driver shouted at him: "Somebody steal your rudder, ya half-wit?" But he was too fascinated by what he was seeing to care. The thermometer wasn't fluctuating wildly, as it did when you encountered a spirit. It was steady. But the reading was too low.

In fact, the reading was 42—the same temperature it had shown when he'd waved it near Adolph.

"What? Is it broken?" Cory asked.

Rick stuck it under his armpit to be sure, and when he removed it, it was close to his normal body temperature. He shook his head. "Take a look." But as he held it out in front of him, the reading began to drop rapidly until it settled once again at 42.

"Huh. Jackie Robinson's number," said Cory.

"Or," Rick offered, "the answer to the ultimate question of

life, the universe, and everything."

Cory just laughed. "More questions here than answers."

"You can say that again," said Rick.

But Faith was shaking her head in exasperation. "Sports. Science fiction," she said dismissively. "The answer is obvious: Adolph's a ghost, just like he said he was. And everyone here's a ghost too. This isn't just a ghost town. The entire town is a ghost."

Adolph had said the entire town was haunted. That had been part of what intrigued Rick in the first place.

It made sense in a twisted sort of way, but it also seemed absurd. Rick remembered reading a quote from Sherlock Holmes: "Once you eliminate the impossible, whatever remains, no matter how improbable, must be the truth." But Holmes was a fictional character, and this situation was very real. Far from eliminating the impossible, Faith seemed to be suggesting the impossible. And they hadn't eliminated everything else. Not yet.

"Maybe," he said, unconvinced. "Where do you think we can find some answers around here?"

Cory shrugged and pointed to the Willows Saloon across the street. "Bartenders know pretty much everything that goes on in a town," he suggested. "And what they don't know, you can get from one of the customers if you buy him a drink."

That sounded reasonable to Rick, who lost no time in making his way across the street to the Willows, which advertised itself as "a place of resort, amusement and refreshment." There weren't any tables available, and there was just one open space at the bar.

He turned to Faith and Cory: "You two wait outside," he said, adding under his breath to Cory, "Whatever you do, don't stop filming. Zoom in through that window there." He pointed. "And keep the mic boom pointed straight at me. With luck, you'll be able to pick up what's being said." He wasn't sure of this last: The saloon was filled with boisterous cussing, hooting, and the sound of glasses being slammed down on the tables. Rick was surprised he hadn't heard a gunshot.

He was even more surprised that no one had said anything about the videocam, although it stuck out like a sore thumb. Even Adolph had remarked on it back on the other side of the tunnel. But here, it was as though it didn't exist.

Cory nodded, and Rick claimed the open seat, next to a man who sat hunched over a mug of beer. His shoulders rose and fell with his heavy breathing, and his cowboy hat was pulled down over his face.

"What'll ya have?" said the bartender, adding, "and drink it down quick or make way for someone who will."

Before Rick could answer, the man next to him wheezed, "He'll have the special, J.T. I'm buyin'." The voice sounded familiar, but Rick couldn't place it behind the wheezing and sputtering of the man's obvious drunkenness. Besides, who would he know in this place?

"Thanks," he said, turning to the man.

The cowboy didn't look up.

The bartender, a tall but wiry man with a big shock of golden hair, stepped to the back shelf and pulled down a dusty, unmarked bottle. He opened it and sloshed some of its contents into a shot glass, then set it on the counter in front of Rick.

"Down the hatch," he said with a humorless smile. "I'll get you another if ya want it, but ya won't need it. It's powerful stuff."

Rick stared at the shot glass for a minute, then decided he'd better do what he was told if he wanted time to ask his questions. He put the shot glass to his lips, threw his head back, and downed it in one swallow, wondering what it was. It tasted like shit, the way he imagined turpentine or motor oil or formaldehyde might taste. Not like any whiskey, rum, or bourbon he'd ever tasted.

He made a face and looked up. "Tell me...," he started to ask the bartender, but J.T. was gone.

"He won't say shit," wheezed the stranger sitting next to him.

Rick turned to look at him, but the man was staring down at his beer from underneath the wide brim of his hat. Yes, he seemed drunk, but he hadn't touched his drink since Rick had come in.

"How long have you been here?" Rick asked him.

"Just got here." The voice did sound familiar, but it was clipped and his breathing was labored, and he wasn't saying enough for Rick to place it. Yet. He told himself to listen more closely and tried to ask a question that would get more out of the man.

"Where from?"

"Sutro."

That was no help.

"And this is American Flat?"

He shrugged. "Signs say."

"Who all lives here?"

For the first time, the stranger said more than a few short words: "Nobody lives here, Rick. Nobody's lived here for 100 years. They're all dead. So am I, now, thanks to you."

The man knew his name. And the voice... It couldn't be...

The stranger finally turned to him, raising the brim of his hat to reveal his face. "That's right, Rick. It's me. Skip."

Rick felt his chest pounding. He was having difficulty breathing. "God, it's good to see you're okay. How'd you get here ahead of us? Where'd you get those clothes?"

Skip curled his lip up in a smirk. "The town gave 'em to me. The town provides."

Rick had no idea what that meant. Skip couldn't have been here long enough to change clothes, let alone get drunk.

"Shouldn't you be resting?" he suggested, not knowing what else to say.

But Skip ignored him and slammed his hand down on the bar. "Another for my friend here, J.T.!" he shouted at the bartender.

The saloonkeeper reappeared and hurried over to refill Rick's glass.

"Drink it!" Skip demanded.

The bartender nodded. "Now. Or clear the seat."

Rick downed the shot.

"Good man," Skip said. "But you weren't listening, Rick. I'm not okay. I'm dead." He growled the last word. "You didn't bother to listen to Adolph before you left me behind back there. He told you he'd never set foot in that tunnel again."

"You mean he didn't get the snakebite kit?"

"There never was a snakebite kit. He said he wanted me to die. No, he needed it, because he needed someone in here to take his place. If he hadn't, he would have been forced to go back. American City must have a stable population. Exact numbers. The population as it stood on this exact date in 1864. When Adolph escaped, he had to send someone back. To be a ghost here in this ghost of a town. That someone was me."

"What about the government? Adolph said..."

"Crock of bull," Skip said. "The government has nothing to do with it. It's just the rules of the game. The way things operate. An eye for an eye, a tooth for a tooth... a life for a life."

Rick's breathing was becoming more labored, and he could tell it wasn't just at the shock of what Skip was saying. His head was pounding, and his hands were shaking. The room was spinning, and when he looked up at the ceiling to gain his bearings, that was spinning, too. He retched, but nothing came up.

"J.T.!" Skip shouted. "Another! That should do him!"

J.T. refilled Rick's shot glass again, but he shoved it away from him and off the back of the bar.

"That's bad manners, Rick," said Skip.

"Get your ass outta here!" J.T. yelled. "Now!"

Rick had never wanted to vomit, but he was trying to puke now. Desperately. But his body wouldn't cooperate.

He turned to Skip and tried to stand, putting out a hand to steady himself on the barstool. "What's in that shit?" His voice sounded to his own ears like a gurgling whisper. He felt like his heart was about to go through his chest.

Skip grinned. "Didn't you hear Adolph talking about the cyanide mill?"

Rick's body convulsed, and he fell to the floor.

"Now you'll be the ghost, but there'll be one too many. Which means I can go back! I'll still be dead, but I won't be stuck forever in this godforsaken hellhole." No sooner had he said this than he made a beeline for the door, with several other people in the bar sprinting after him, throwing down chairs and knocking over tables as they tried to beat Skip to what they all craved.

Freedom.

There could be only one.

Rick looked frantically toward the window for Cory and Faith, but they were nowhere to be seen. He wondered how cyanide from a mill built in the 1920s had made its way into a drink served in 1864. Or did it just seem like 1864? Was it really 2023 after all?

"Time's a funny thing in there."

The echo of Adolph's words was the last thing Rick ever heard.

Before he died, that is.

Cory and Faith made it back safely to The Horror Network's studios in New York, where they presented the videotape of their experiences to the producers. They looked shocked to discover that the tape was mostly blank. The only thing on it was a brief scene showing Rick Piersall's body lying on the bare earth of American Flat.

A forensics team found the corpse at that very spot.

An autopsy revealed that Rick had died after ingesting cyanide, and investigators suspected foul play. Skip's body, meanwhile, was found just inside the entrance to Sutro Tunnel, where he died as the result of a rattlesnake bite. Investigators questioned Cory and Faith in connection with both deaths before releasing them. Cory, however, was taken into custody a week later after police searched his email and found an incriminating exchange with Skip. The pair had apparently been plotting to take control of the show and force Rick out. "By any means necessary," one of the emails said.

Was this evidence of a murder plot? Investigators thought so, but with Skip deceased and his death ruled accidental, there was no one to corroborate their theory. They went looking for Adolph but came up empty. It was as though he had never existed.

They couldn't even find the tunnel to American Flat that Cory and Faith both swore they'd taken.

So the charges were ultimately dropped, and the episode, such as it was, never aired. A *Holiday Haunts* rerun investigating the former Field Lane Ragged School, which inspired Charles Dickens' *A Christmas Carol* and which still exists in London. The investigative team claimed to have found the real-life Ghost of Christmas Past haunting its halls, and it had been the top-rated episode of all time.

After that, *Haunted Havens* continued to be seen in reruns, and The Horror Network recently announced that new shows will be produced to air this fall, under the revised title *Haunted Havens with Faith Hunt*.

BROWN'S
EXCHANGE SALOON,
AMERICAN FLAT.

BEST QUALITY OF WINES, LIQUORS ETC, ALWAYS ON HAND.

"You will find Brown as snug as a Bug in a rug,
And snugger than any other Bug-ger."

Historical background: Adolph Sutro really was the mayor of San Francisco and really did build the Sutro Tunnel to drain water from the mines at Virginia City. His lack of wit was the subject of a letter by Mark Twain published in the Virginia City Territorial Enterprise during the winter of 1863-64. American Flat was a real boomtown in 1864, and the businesses mentioned in this story really did operate there; the business slogans were taken from the 1864 city directory. J.T. Keepers was the proprietor, with his partner Barton Lee, of the Willows Saloon. American Flat experienced a brief revival in the 1920s when a cyanide mill known as the United Comstock Merger Mill operated there, but the government razed the abandoned mill in 2014 and subsequently restricted access to the area.

Sharon Marie Provost

Justice Gone Wrong

He had entered the house hours ago to prepare before her return from work at precisely 6 p.m. She got home every day at the exact same time. He had never seen someone so precise in all their activities. That's what had piqued his interest in her when he had seen her eating at a local restaurant last month.

He had followed her home that evening and begun a detailed surveillance to determine her viability as his next victim. Over the next month, he found that she fit the bill perfectly: She lived alone, rarely had visitors and her schedule was very consistent.

She entered the house—her arms full of groceries and the messenger bag she used to bring work home to review before the next day. She put the groceries away methodically: first the frozen items, then the refrigerated items, and finished up with the cabinets and then the pantry items. She seemed to have a routine that she never deviated from for everything she did. As expected, she next went to her bedroom to change into her stretch pants and a loose T-shirt.

That's where he was waiting for her. As she passed the bedroom door, he silently slid out from behind it and pressed a cloth soaked in chloroform to her mouth. A few gasping breaths of panic, then she crumpled into his arms. He picked her up and carried her into her office, where he had carefully prepared for the evening's activities.

He had learned how to prepare a kill room from his job as a forensic investigator and, most importantly, his favorite TV show, *Dexter*. But his impulse toward cruelty dated back much further. Michael had grown up from a young age with a desire to scare and hurt other living creatures. It started with the rather benign torture of bugs, typical of many young boys, by lighting them on fire with his magnifying glass or pulling off their legs. However, that quickly progressed to setting small fires in the woods near school or behind the local grocery store.

It wasn't long before he moved on to the wholesale torture and murder of stray animals and then local pets, even those owned by friends or neighbors.

Then, when he was 14, as his hormones really began to rage, he found he wanted to hurt people, especially girls. However, he was smart and cautious enough to hold his impulses in check—at least for the time being—because he did not want to go prison.

Luckily—for him at least—the year was 2006, the year a new show premiered on Showtime... *Dexter*. Everybody was talking about the novel premise of this show: that a forensic investigator was a serial killer (albeit of other serial killers or vile criminals who had escaped justice) who carefully cleaned up his crime scenes to prevent his capture.

This seemed like the perfect life for Michael. He loved science. He loved to watch true crime shows to get off on the grisly details of murders perpetrated by others. He watched them reverently, with as much attention to detail as he paid to all his homework.

A perfectionist by nature, he never wanted to fail at anything he tried. A career as a forensic investigator would let him see crime scenes up close and personal and maybe even learn a few things. Even better, he would have a chance to prevent the collection of evidence at his own future crime scenes if, God forbid, he should ever accidentally leave something behind. But Michael had one important and unfortunate desire that was different than Dexter's. What fun was it to kill fellow criminals? It was a lot more fun to find innocent, good people and make sure their worst day in life was also their last.

He carried Claire—that was her name, he had found out after looking her up at work—into the office that he had covered in plastic. He placed her sitting up in her desk chair and tightly wound duct tape around her wrists and the arms of the chair, so she couldn't move or fall out of the seat. He was dressed in plastic coveralls, like those worn in labs or by people spraying toxic chemicals, as well as gloves and a paper bonnet over his hair. He then sat on the edge of the desk in front of her and waited for her to wake. When she began to stir, he stood up with a large, sharp knife in his hand.

Claire awoke with a start, madly looking around the room in confusion, before her eyes fell on the terrifying sight in front of her. She began to whimper and beg for her life as tears streamed down her face.

"P... P... Please! Please don't hurt me. I am a good person. I have never hurt anybody. I won't tell anybody you were here. Just leave, and neither one of us will think or speak about this again."

Michael smiled and began to chuckle.

"I can't do that. What would be the fun in that? I didn't come here to just scare you. I have no fear of being caught. I will leave when I am done with you... not one moment before."

He grabbed the front of her shirt and pulled it taut to make slicing it open easier. He knew most women felt more off-guard when their bodies were exposed. As he had hoped, her whimpering increased, and she tried to scrunch her body forward to cover herself. He dragged the knife lightly down the skin of her chest, applying just enough pressure to cause a couple of shallow lines to appear and blood to slowly seep out. The sight of blood made her face blanch, and she began to hyperventilate.

"Hmmmm... are we afraid of the sight of blood? Those are mere drops. Maybe we should try some more. What do you think?"

Claire opened her mouth to scream, but he saw it coming and covered her mouth with his hand tightly before she could. With his other hand, he reached over to grab another piece of duct tape that he had prepared for just this moment. After placing it over her mouth, he used the knife to slice a deep cut in her forehead. Head wounds bleed profusely, and therefore it would create the sense of terror he craved. Her eyes grew wide, and her respirations increased rapidly when the blood dripped past her eyes.

She struggled against the tape to no avail.

"Now you see how serious I am. This is not a game—at least not for you. There is nothing you can do to stop what is about to happen. It is best that you just accept your fate.

"Are you ready?"

Claire shook her head vehemently, pleading with her eyes for mercy. But there was no mercy coming for her today… or ever again. Michael raised the knife and plunged it deep into her chest, right into her heart. She felt an intense, searing pain as the blood pumped rapidly from her body, and she moaned and exhaled loudly through her nose. Within a few moments, she slumped forward in the chair, unconscious. Another moment later, she breathed her last as Michael watched intently.

Over the next two hours, he carefully mopped up the excess blood with towels he had brought, so that none of the blood would drip anywhere in the house once he rolled up the plastic sheeting. He examined her body fully to make sure no stray hairs or fibers from his person were sticking to her skin or clothing. He carefully wiped down the back door handle and all the other surfaces he had touched to make sure he did not leave any fingerprints. After all, you couldn't exactly show up at a crime scene wearing latex gloves without potentially drawing unwanted attention.

Next, he removed her bloodstained clothing and wiped off all the blood on her skin before he re-dressed her in a fresh, clean outfit. He used Goof Off to remove the tape residue from the arms of the chair, and then moved her body to her bed. He left no sign to show where or why or by whom she had been killed. Now he could leave and wait for the call to investigate the scene.

The call came two days later after her employer called the police to report their concerns. She was their most reliable employee and never missed work. She never even showed up five minutes late without informing her employer promptly.

Her only emergency contact, a sister who lived across the country, had not heard from her in weeks. Clearly, they were not close—but that was not surprising to anyone who knew Claire's loner nature.

Michael and his least favorite co-worker, Barry, were called in to investigate after patrol cops had been dispatched for a welfare check and seen her body through the open bedroom curtain. At first, the patrolmen had called it in as a potential suicide. But then they entered the home and got close enough to see the baffling, gaping knife wound in her chest, with not a drop of blood spilled anywhere in the house.

Not surprisingly, the investigation yielded no evidence. Not a single drop of blood, strand of hair, unknown fiber, or fingerprint was found anywhere in the house. The woman's time of death was narrowed down to within an hour and a half after she completed her workday. However, there was nothing to indicate whether she had been killed in her own home or slain elsewhere and then left there. No one in the neighborhood reported seeing any suspicious persons, activity, or vehicles in the area that evening. Her receipt from the market was found in the trash, but no one at the store had seen anyone following her in the store or when she left the parking lot.

If Barry had been the lone investigator on this scene, nothing would have been found—even if it had existed. He was truly inept at his job. Further, he was by far the laziest person

Michael had ever met when it came to working or doing anything worthwhile. All he cared about was his extracurricular activities.

Barry was a loner, suspicious of the government and banks. He frequently went on vacations deep into the wilderness, far from civilization, to hunt whatever game was in season. He usually went on these trips with all the supplies he might need, purchased from a store near his home run by people he, for the most part, trusted. If he had to get something unexpected, he always carried cash and was so unobtrusive that few people remembered ever having seen him in large groups.

But his weird demeanor did stick out when he was in smaller groups.

Luckily, Barry's skills and dedication to his work—or lack thereof—didn't matter because Michael had left nothing behind for him to discover. He was sure because he had gone over the scene himself with a fine-tooth comb, as any forensic investigator should.

Michael should have been happy, but he just found himself annoyed watching Barry do little to nothing as he prattled on about his next trip, coming up on the weekend.

Yet that wasn't the worst of it.

He found himself bothered that this murder had not been as enjoyable as he had hoped.

He was simply *too good* at hiding his crimes. He no longer felt any thrill or spark of fear that he may be caught. He had been trying to up the ante by spending more time surveilling the potential victim; more time in the home preparing before the kill and then terrifying them beforehand. He had even started committing more messy, gruesome murders. But it just wasn't enough.

He decided that maybe he should leave behind some evidence after all: carefully cultivated evidence that wouldn't lead back to him. Evidence that would not be immediately obvious, but—if the investigator was doing their job—would be found. Evidence that would be confounding to the investigative team. Maybe he could even create a string of evidence from several crimes leading them to the conclusion that there *was* a serial killer, but not the identity of that killer.

At least, not the real killer.

Michael found his next victim while working out at the gym. She hid herself in the back corner of the room, using whatever equipment was farthest away from the other members. When he tried talking to her, she blushed bright red and excused herself politely but quickly.

One evening, he saw her outside in the parking lot, standing by her car and looking flustered over a flat tire. He offered to help, but she politely declined.

He wasn't about to give up, though. When he asked if she had a cell phone to call anyone else, she admitted that she neither had a phone nor anyone to call. However, she said she would use the phone in the gym.

Michael had an answer for this as well. He told her the gym owner never allowed anyone to use the phone, and he once again offered to call a tow truck for her instead.

This time, she accepted his offer.

Michael offered to stay with her while she waited for the truck, but she told him she would be fine. Michael acquiesced and left the lot—going far enough to be out of her eyesight but staying close enough to keep tabs so he could follow her home later.

Thus began the surveillance of his next potential victim. She already seemed to be the perfect match, but he had to make sure she truly did not have anyone who regularly visited, and he could determine her schedule.

A few weeks into his surveillance, he decided it was time to carry out his next murder plot, but this time was going to be different. While hiding outside her house, observing her, he overheard that she had a repairman coming on Friday. So, on Thursday night, he quickly entered her home an hour before she was due to arrive.

Searching the garage, he found a lead pipe that would be perfect for caving in her skull. Then, he donned his usual protective garments, so as not to leave any evidence that could be tied back to him.

Michael brought along some hairs that he had collected from Barry's chair that did not have roots attached. Traces of maternal DNA could be collected from the strand itself, but they would not be able to tie them back directly to Barry since none of his family had ever had their DNA entered into CODIS, the Combined DNA Index System. He also brought with him some fibers from fabric, furniture, and curtains he had obtained in various locations around town. This time, he had no intention of using plastic sheeting to prevent bloodstains. However, he did have towels and bleach on hand. Now it was time to enact his plan—if only she would hurry up and get home.

She came into the house nearly on time, carrying takeout, which explained her slight delay in getting home. She sat at the table and read the newspaper quietly while she ate her meal. Then she headed back to her room to take her shower before climbing into bed and watching her favorite TV show, *America's*

Got Talent. By the time she got to her bedroom, he was hiding in her closet, waiting for her to get in the shower.

He quietly stole out of the closet and entered the bathroom, lead pipe in hand. He rapidly slid open the curtain and hit her on the back of the head, and she slumped into the tub instantly.

He knew one well-placed blow to the head could kill someone, and the forensic rule of thumb was "the first blow is free." The person's head will, of course, bleed, but there will be no castoff blood spatter showing directionality. But he didn't want it to be that easy this time. He leaned her over the edge of the tub and hit her once more in the same location. This time, blood squirted out of the back of her head and then was cast off from the pipe as he raised his hand from the backswing.

This time, his cleanup process was different. He washed all the blood off the back of the shower wall using the removable shower head attachment, but he did not use bleach to completely remove all traces: just what was visible to the naked eye. He did, however, use the bleach to thoroughly remove the large pool of blood in front of the tub. He knew it would be baffling for investigators to find no blood on the floor given the nature of her injuries, which would be immediately apparent. When they used luminol to look for latent blood, they would see the glowing blood-splatter spray pattern. The luminol—which causes trace amounts of blood to emit a blue glow—would also react to the bleach, revealing a smeared pooling mark over a large swath of floor that had clearly recently been cleaned with bleach. It would make the investigators question why someone would so thoroughly clean part of the scene but not the rest.

Michael checked the body and areas of the home he had inhabited thoroughly to make sure he had left no hairs or fibers of his own. Then he carefully went about leaving select traces of the hairs and fibers he had brought with him in the bedroom, on the back door jamb and her clothing. He even left a smudged fingerprint on the back door handle that he made sure could not be identified. He had used his victim's computer printer to write a note, which he attached to the front door, telling the repairman she was working in the back of the house and to just come in and find her. Once the scene was ready, he unlocked the front door and then slipped out unnoticed through the backyard.

Now he just had to wait for the repair man to find her the following afternoon. He was off work the next two days, but Barry and Thomas were on the schedule to work forensic investigations. He couldn't wait to see if they would find all his clues and what they would make of them. He drove home feeling truly excited again, much like he had after his first kills. He had only killed 12 people all told, but it is amazing how humdrum and boring it had become.

A story on the news the next night revealed that a body had been found under "potentially suspicious circumstances."

Potentially suspicious??

He'd left a deep depression in her head from the two blows!

When he returned Tuesday, he looked up the case as soon as he had a free moment

He could not believe his eyes.

There was no mention of blood spatter having been found. There was some discussion involving the severity of the head wound, but investigators surmised she might have hit her head on the porcelain soap tray on the shower wall and then on the edge of the tub itself. They didn't even seem concerned by the questionable way her body had been found draped over the edge of the tub. They simply concluded she might have briefly regained consciousness and tried to climb out. Not only was there no mention of a blood-spatter pattern that had been cleaned up being found on the shower wall, there was not even any mention of the mysterious lack of blood where it *should* have been found on the floor and in the tub.

How could this be? Is this whole department inept? Why weren't the upper brass questioning these bizarre findings—or more accurately, lack of findings?

A quick look at the investigator logs explained everything quickly. Apparently, Barry had investigated the scene alone. Thomas had called in sick.

That abominable, lazy asshole! He doesn't even try... the quick way out is all he cares about. He ruined my whole game. Now no one even knows that there has been a murder, let alone started trying to ponder why someone covered it up and who they may be. Clearly, I need to make sure I investigate these scenes, so I can find the evidence. And someone needs to teach that asshole a lesson.

Michael was in such a foul mood that he couldn't even manage to bring himself to be civil to Barry when he saw him later that day. The last thing he wanted to hear about was that asshole getting another Christmas off to go hunting... again. The holiday itself didn't really matter to Michael, but it was always so busy around the holidays. Somebody besides him should have to deal with all the craziness, especially when that someone was the laziest person on the force. Usually, he could feign interest in Barry's plans for his next hunting trip, but this time he just tuned him out. Then Barry uttered one word that couldn't help but draw his attention...

Hampton.

Usually, Michael hunted for victims closer to home, but he had found an interesting prospect the previous weekend at the mall. The young woman seemed to fit his usual profile of an organized loner ideally. He was immediately drawn to her, so he'd followed her home. As she drove farther out into the forest, he had become concerned that she would be outside his jurisdiction, but he was pleasantly surprised to find she lived just within the county lines.

In Hampton, to be exact.

A quick look in the system, on Barry's computer of course, gave him her identity, Meredith Hanson. She was single... perfect.

This may be just what I need. I can time it so that I can investigate and so that a certain asshole just happens to be in the area at the same time. Normally, he flies under the radar, but maybe I can set it up so that someone notices him.

Michael forced himself to listen and ask a few safe questions about Barry's trip. He found out that it was a little more than five weeks away. He was leaving the day before Christmas Eve in fact. That would give him enough time to prepare with his usual surveillance. As usual, Barry was going alone and staying in the forest, rather than a campground. It would take some work to find a way to make sure someone noticed Barry, but Michael had faith in his skills. It helped that Barry really wasn't going to be all that far from where his target lived.

The next few weeks went by in a blur of planning and investigation. Michael once again collected hairs off Barry's chair and jacket when he left the room. This time, he found a couple that still had the roots attached so that DNA could be extracted. Barry rarely remembered to lock his car, so Michael collected some fibers from the seat and carpeting as well. He even retrieved a discarded glove from the trash that would surely have Barry's fingerprint inside.

He carefully watched the woman on his days off and in the evening when he got off work. He quickly learned her schedule was very regimented, just as he had expected. She came home directly from work each day at 6 p.m., changed into overalls to do a little gardening, took a shower, and put on sweats, before making herself dinner. Then a little TV watching, and she was off to bed by 9. The only person he had seen visiting her house was a neighbor once, and his target seemed to work quickly to dispatch the visitor after getting the cup of sugar she had come to borrow. The timeframe was going to be tight though. She apparently did see her sister once a year at Christmastime. He had overheard her on the phone, and her sister was arriving at 3 p.m. on Christmas Eve.

Luckily, her location was ideal. She lived in a small cluster of homes with long driveways that were about half a mile apart, all off a single road. Early in the surveillance process, he had walked down that road bundled up with a hat and scarf to obscure his features so he could gauge how observant the neighbors might be. He did notice an old man with a neighborhood watch sign in his yard who did seem to keep track of all the comings and goings. He was frequently outside decorating his home for Christmas, like Clark Griswold. This made his surveillance a little more difficult because he did not want to become known himself. However, he quickly found a side road about a mile up the highway that led into the forest. From there, it was only a short walk through the trees up to the back of his target's home. He could easily observe her without being seen.

Finally, the big day of Barry's trip arrived. He would be driving out to Hampton that night after work. Barry's paranoia and secrecy about his life extended even to his employers. Therefore, he never parked his car in the precinct lot but instead a few blocks away. This gave Michael the opportunity to visit Barry's car on lunch and remove the large hunting knife he always took with him to skin and butcher his big-game kills. Michael would be using this knife for his own game tomorrow. Plus, Barry would be forced to go into town to the small market that served as a bait and tackle/hunting/convenience store to get a new one when he found it missing.

That night, Michael left work excited for the next day's big adventure. He had the next day off since he was scheduled for Christmas Eve and Christmas Day. He had carefully packed all the supplies he would need into a large, camouflage canvas duffle bag. He had procured a camo outfit to wear on his walk into the woman's neighborhood to both obscure his identity and catch the attention of the nosy old man. He went home and fell into a fitful sleep, dreaming about the next day's big plans.

The next day, in the late afternoon, he drove out to the side road he had found and carefully secreted his car deep in the woods. He walked back up the highway and turned down the road to her home. He made sure to walk past the old man's home and then out of sight before turning off into the woods to approach her home from the back. He had one hour to get into her home and prepare for her arrival.

He used a lock pick to enter her back door and carefully laid out some plastic sheeting on the floor. He stood on that as he changed out of the camo suit and into his protective coveralls, gloves, and bonnet. Then he carefully packed the camo outfit into a plastic bag and stowed it in the side pocket of the duffle bag to avoid any cross-contamination of hairs or fibers. Once this was done, he carefully stowed the bag in the hall closet after removing the knife and duct tape.

Michael then decided to have a little fun. He wanted to see if he could make her nervous with a few carefully placed clues that might suggest all was not right in her home. He started by leaving her bedroom door open a crack—because she always closed it upon exiting in the morning. Then he left the kitchen window behind the sink unlatched and partially open. He took joy in carefully rearranging her ornaments on the Christmas tree, placing the angels in compromising poses with each other. Finally, he went back to the sewing room to await her arrival.

She came in promptly at 6 as usual and left her purse, keys, and cellphone on the end table near the front door. Then she headed back to her room to change before heading out to the garden. He heard her pause outside the door, mumbling to herself, "How did that get open?"

Once she had changed, she headed out back. While she gardened, Michael carefully snuck out of the sewing room and moved her cell phone from the end table to the kitchen counter. She came into the house and immediately went to retrieve her cell phone before heading back to the shower.

"What in the Sam Hill? I could have sworn...,"she cursed under her breath as she looked for the phone. Her brow furrowed in consternation as she looked around. Relief flooded her face as she finally noticed it lying on the kitchen counter, but that look quickly gave way to a frown and a look of puzzlement. She sighed loudly, then grabbed the phone before heading back to her room. She started the shower and scrolled through Facebook as she waited for the water to warm up. She purposely set her phone down on the edge of the sink and looked back at it before climbing into the shower. When she emerged from her room a short while later, she seemed more at ease. She was even whistling as she made her way into the kitchen to make dinner.

She filled a pot with water and put it on the burner to begin heating. Then she started cooking the hamburger for the pasta sauce. After retrieving the pasta from the pantry, she fanned her face because the kitchen had become a bit stuffy with the food cooking away. She reached up to turn the latch on the window and realized it was unlocked and open a smidge. She jumped back a step… right into his waiting arms. She inhaled with a gasp and felt a sharp jab in her back.

She opened her mouth to scream.

"Don't you make a fucking sound!"

She considered her options and then slowly closed her mouth. "I… I won't. I promise."

Using one arm, Michael locked her arms behind her back and poked the tip of the knife into her skin, drawing a drop of blood. She whimpered in pain, and tears streamed down her face as she felt that single drop slowly slide down her skin. As she realized he was pushing her toward the bedroom, she began to struggle.

In vain.

"Wait. Please! Please don't do this to me."

"No worries, my dear. I have no intention of ravaging your fine body. At least not sexually."

He twisted her arms up farther behind her back until she winced in pain, and pushed her forward roughly into the room. He let go just as she cried out in pain, and she fell onto the bed roughly.

He saw the scream coming and punched her in the face—hard—just before she could emit any sound. Her legs hung limply over the side as her vision blurred and she lost consciousness. She awoke with a start a short time later. Duct tape covered her mouth. Her hands and feet were taped together as well. He sat in the corner of the room, a wry smile on his face.

"Game time!" he exclaimed with a laugh. "Now this is what I call 'big game.' Let's see what I have learned about butchery these last few weeks. Step one, in theory: I am supposed to go for a clean shot; I must prevent unsightly damage to the carcass and keep my prey from running off and hiding. Step two... well I guess the other steps don't really matter to you. You won't be alive for those."

The woman struggled mightily against her bonds and attempted a muffled scream, but to no avail. Her pupils dilated and her breathing increased as she contemplated what Michael had said. Snot bubbled out of her nose and mixed with the flow of tears down her face. She desperately tried to pull her hands free from the tape as he slowly stood up and approached her, the knife held out menacingly in front of him. She kicked her legs out at him as he reached over her, landing them squarely in his stomach.

"Oooffff! Damn, that hurt," he wheezed. He pushed down on her abdomen hard, pinning her in place. Then he placed the tip of the blade over her heart and started slowly pushing it into her chest. Blood bloomed around the blade and streamed down her chest. Her eyes grew ever wider as she hyperventilated and tried desperately to scream. He climbed onto the bed and pinned her legs underneath him as he held her arms down on her stomach. He watched her breathing become more ragged. He marveled at the way the blade literally pulsed with the beat of her heart, emitting a new fount of blood with every successively slower beat. Her struggles lessened with time, so he slowly extracted the blade to watch the last gush of blood flow forth as the light faded from her eyes.

Now it was time for the hard work. He inserted the blade just below her sternum and slowly began to flay open her abdomen. He walked out to the closet to retrieve his duffel bag of supplies. He retrieved a smaller knife that was better suited for cutting the bits of tissue and sinew holding her entrails in place. Setting aside the pitcher, he took hold of the antique porcelain wash basin on the bureau. Then he pulled her intestines out in one giant loop and laid them inside.

He carefully stacked the rest of the organs around them, ringing the edge of basin before filling the porcelain pitcher with blood pooled in her chest and abdomen. He used the large knife to open her chest further and began the painstaking process of removing the lungs and heart, which, once he had accomplished this, he placed in a large glass vase that had been sitting next to the basin.

After he finished gutting her, he returned to the large hunting knife, which he used to remove her head. He mounted it on a wooden plaque he had brought with him. Then he removed the painting that hung above her bed and put the new "trophy" mount up in its place, carefully affixing a big red bow to her forehead. Then he carefully severed her hands at the wrist, placing them in the two stockings she had hung on the mantel out in the living room.

His task complete, he rinsed the blood off the knife and placed it in a plastic bag. Then he set about searching the place carefully to make sure he had left no trace evidence or fingerprints belonging to him. He closed the kitchen window and returned her phone to its normal location by her purse. He carefully placed the hairs and fibers linked to Barry that he had obtained in various locations around the house: putting hairs on her bed and body, fibers on her clothing and in the chair where he had sat while waiting in the sewing room.

He packed up all his belongings in his duffel bag once more and headed outside. He carefully changed out of his coveralls, wrapped them up in the plastic sheeting he had brought with him, and carefully stowed them in the bag as well, taking care not to transfer any blood to his street clothes.

One last step was needed, and that was the planting of the glove with Barry's fingerprint in the woods a short distance from the back door, as if it had been carelessly dropped. He then locked the back door and crept through the woods to where he had parked his car.

Michael took the long way home so as not to backtrack through any of the areas he had driven through earlier in the day. He felt simultaneously electric with the energy from such an exciting kill and exhausted from the exertion it had required. Now he just needed to go to bed and wait. He was scheduled to work for the next five days, and he knew the call would come soon. But he had to wait for Barry to return to complete the one last step in his plan.

He rose the next day early, eager to get to work. The call did not come, but that was fine because he had the suspicious death of a vagrant in the park to investigate. He was puzzled as to why he didn't hear anything though. A quick look at the airline scheduled showed the sister's flight had been delayed yesterday and was rescheduled for Christmas morning. However, at midday the following day, the call he had been waiting for finally arrived. He fought hard to cover his excitement when he rode out to the scene with Thomas and Andy. The gruesome nature of this crime had prompted an all-hands-on-deck call for the crime scene investigation unit. They had even tried to call in Barry, but he had not answered his cell. Not even the most senior detectives remembered such a horrific crime in the area during the twenty-odd years they had worked at the precinct.

The three forensic investigators worked in tandem, methodically poring over the scene. Thankfully, these co-workers knew their job, so all the evidence was collected this time. In fact, Michael was not even involved in the collection of the hairs, fibers, or the glove he had left behind. He kept himself busy dusting for fingerprints all over the house, searching for signs of forced entry, and bagging and tagging the organs. Ten exhausting hours later, they finally sealed up the house and left with all the evidence they'd collected bound for the lab.

The investigators had pored over the neighborhood along with patrol cops, questioning all the neighbors regarding anything they knew about the victim or any suspicious activity they might have seen in the area. The old man and a kid riding his bike in the area reported seeing a "hunter" in camo walking through the area that afternoon. Neither of them could give a clear description of the man though, and no cars had been seen in the area. A bulletin on the news that night asked for any information regarding the case and whether anyone knew the identity of the mysterious man in camo.

Barry returned to work the next day as expected. He was full of stories about the wonderful time he'd had slaughtering woodland creatures. And he complained about how he'd needed to replace his favorite hunting knife because it was missing from his car. He hadn't liked the way the owner had stared at him when he was shopping.

"He acted like he had never seen anyone walking around in camo before, even though he owns a hunting and fishing shop. I tell you, I don't like to patronize places I don't know and trust. If I hadn't been in the middle of nowhere, I would have never set foot in there."

Michael smiled and nodded like he understood Barry's feelings.

Perfect!

Now it was time to place the last piece of evidence. On the way back from testifying in court on another case, Michael walked over to Barry's car and switched out the hunting knife he had used at the crime with the one that Barry had purchased. Not surprisingly, the knife was nearly, if not exactly identical.

Leave it to paranoid Barry to only buy the tried and true, rather than try something new.

His task complete, Michael headed back into the precinct to finish out his day. The evidence was still being processed, but the results were expected back at any moment. He walked in to find the place abuzz with activity. Apparently, the family of his previous victim had raised enough of a stink that the brass had agreed to look at the evidence and scene again. Thomas and Andy had been sent out to work the woman's house again once investigators noticed that Barry had not mentioned seeing any blood at the scene of a quite serious head wound. The coroner, when questioned, had agreed there should have been quite a lot of blood—especially since it did appear that the victim had hit her head twice in the "fall."

Thomas worked on the bathroom while Andy searched the rest of the house. When Thomas sprayed the luminol and shut the bathroom door, the room was literally aglow between the spray pattern on the back shower wall and what appeared to have been a large pool of blood that had been cleaned up, probably with bleach.

Thomas began to collect swabs from the wall, the floor, and the seams along the tub.

Further testing confirmed that it was definitely blood.

Now that they knew the blood had been cleaned up, investigators ordered a thorough second forensic evaluation of the scene in order to collect any further evidence. This time, the unknown hairs and fibers were collected and sent to the lab. Another medical examiner evaluated the autopsy findings, after which the victim's manner of death was changed to homicide and the cause of death to bludgeoning.

The smudged fingerprint Michael had left was found, but of course could not be identified.

Michael could not believe his luck. *Thank God for small favors.* Finally, someone could admire his handiwork.

Barry had been called into the chief's office along with the head of the forensics department to be questioned about his incompetent processing of the scene. He was put on administrative leave pending an official inquiry into his fitness for duty.

Later that day, all hell broke loose when the fingerprint in the glove from the brutal dismemberment case came back.

There was a match!

The fingerprint belonged to none other than Barry Adams.

A short while later, the DNA evidence from the roots on the hairs found came back with the same match. Every Police Department employee's DNA and fingerprints were in CODIS and AFIS. No one wanted to believe that the killer could be one of their own, but Barry had been "on vacation"—hunting in the woods, no less—when the crime had occurred. The department had attempted to call him in to help work the case, but he had been mysteriously unreachable.

The police chief reached out to the district attorney, and a warrant was obtained to search Barry's apartment and car. The homicide detectives presented Barry with the warrant and picked him up to be interrogated. Barry, of course, denied any knowledge of the victim or the crime. He claimed that he had been deep in the forest just outside Hampton the whole weekend.

They questioned him about his activities over that weekend. He told them about the rabbit and deer meat they would find in his chest freezer from his kills. He denied seeing anybody the whole weekend… until they confronted him with the information that had just come in on the tip line. The owner of the hunting shop had seen the news and called to report the odd man who had bought a hunting knife there the day of the murder. He even had security camera footage that clearly showed Barry in the store buying a knife that precisely matched the wounds inflicted on the victim.

Barry claimed to have forgotten about the encounter.

The interrogation went on for hours as evidence was collected from Barry's home and car: fibers from furniture, carpeting in his home and car, car seats, and clothing. Investigators brought in the knife, camo suit, and other hunting supplies that Barry stored in his car. The knife was swabbed for traces of blood and sent to the lab for stat processing along with all the other evidence.

As the day progressed, the blood found on the knife came back as a match to the victim's.

The array of evidence against Barry soon became staggering. Over the ensuing days, fibers from Barry's car were found to match those found in the home. At the same time, results started coming in from the bludgeoning case as well. The fibers were not currently traceable to anyone. However, maternal DNA from the hair had been obtained… and it was a match to Barry.

Now he was linked to two different brutal murders.

The case against Barry was overwhelming. The only person who could definitively identify him was the man who had sold him the very kind of knife used in the crime and described him as odd and disturbing. Traces of both a maternal and full DNA from both scenes matched Barry's. He could not explain why he'd missed evidence showing the first case was a murder, other than to admit his laziness and lack expertise when it came to forensic investigations. Pure and simple, he had no defense, so the cases were a slam dunk.

Barry finally stood trial for the two murders late the next year. He could not afford an adequate defense attorney—not that it would have made a difference. He had zero proof that he had not been involved in the crimes. He was found guilty of murder in the first degree in both cases and sentenced to death by lethal injection.

Michael could not believe his luck... no, *skill.* This could not have gone any better. The bludgeoning had not been nearly as satisfying as he had hoped, but the dismemberment had exceeded his wildest dreams. The fear and pain he had seen in her eyes still gave him a thrill when he thought about it. And better yet, he had perfectly committed both crimes while leaving nothing to tie him to them.

Best of all, he had rid himself of that slovenly fool, Barry. That added an entirely new dimension to his pleasure, because he had a third victim that no one even knew WAS a victim.

Now... how should I set up my next spree?

Stephen H. Provost

The Santa Syndicate

Follow the evidence wherever it leads. That's how we operate at LAPD. It's about integrity. Yeah, there are some crooked cops, but not me. I spent 18 years at the department, first on the beat and then as a detective. But what do I get for following the evidence? A pink slip, that's what. And on Christmas Eve, no less.

I know what you're thinking. I crossed the thin blue line

and ratted out a fellow cop.

Nope.

The evidence led me to someone even more untouchable. I've investigated everyone from Mexican cartel kingpins to corporate crooks. All the big "families" make it their business to insulate their godfathers from the law, making their cronies take the fall, laundering their funds and doing deals to keep themselves looking squeaky clean.

But I've never seen an operation with this kind of scope. It's not national or regional, it's worldwide. It penetrates every neighborhood of every major city, even into backwoods pot grows and moonshine stills in Appalachia.

It doesn't deal in drugs, though. It's all about human trafficking and using kids as sweatshop labor. I thought operations like this had gone underground since they passed all those child labor laws back at the turn of the 20th century. I was wrong. This one's bigger than anything I've ever heard of, and it's got the best front possible... which is why no one believes me.

But I swear it's true, because I followed the evidence, and this is where it leads.

At first, I thought it was bullshit. One of my informants told me that kids had been disappearing downtown. It's a bad neighborhood with a lot of people, so no one notices when someone goes missing—at least when that someone's a street kid with no ties and nowhere to stay.

But Frankie J. noticed because I have a deal with him to be my eyes and ears down there. He mentioned it in passing once, not expecting me to care because I was out on a narcotics sting. I did care, though, because I've got a 9-year-old kid of my own, so I started asking him about it whenever I went down there, and nearly every time, he said some other kid had disappeared.

Then one day, *Frankie* disappeared. No one knew—or admitted knowing—what had happened to him. I assumed he'd run afoul of Danny Boy DiCarlo, who'd consolidated most of downtown as his territory.

I knew DiCarlo, so I arranged a meeting and asked him. As I expected, he claimed to know nothing. But he didn't tell me to fuck off, which wasn't like him. Instead, he gave me some info on the latest kid who'd gone missing.

"What do you care about some kid?" I asked him.

He shrugged. "Normally, I wouldn't. But Gino was my top lookout. I don't take kindly to someone tryin' to horn in on me, ya know."

I nodded. "Vukovich Cartel?" They'd been making a play for downtown for a while now, but Danny Boy shook his head. "I know all their people. This guy wasn't one of them. He was one of those bell-ringing Santas with the kettles. Louie was making the rounds when he saw the guy give Gino something. Then he just lost them. Haven't seen Gino since."

"I'll keep an eye out," I told him, and I did.

I started staking out sidewalk Santas, and I started to notice them enticing kids with candy or trinkets or even bigger toys—always when they thought no one was looking, and always kids who were by themselves, wearing dirty, torn clothes.

I'd try to follow at a safe distance, but they always disappeared around a corner with the kid.

I was determined to get to the bottom of it, but my CO somehow got wind of it. When he called me in, I was expecting a slap on the wrist and his typical "keep your nose clean and do your job" speech.

Instead, he asked for my gun and my badge and told me I was being suspended.

"Suspended? For what?"

"It's an IA matter now. Dismissed."

"On Christmas Eve?"

"I said, dismissed!"

So I went. From his tone, I could tell someone had gotten to him. He was scared, and no one scared Captain J.T. Mulroney.

On my way home, I dropped in at Walgreen to pick up a boombox and a Batman Lego set for my kid. Jonah was spending this Christmas with me (the ex and me alternated holidays), and I had to get him something more than the Nerf football I'd picked up earlier. The boombox was as much for my ex as for Jonah: I knew all that loud music would annoy the shit out of her.

I grabbed some KFC, picked him up from J.C.'s Afterschool Care, and we went home to settle in for a *Star Wars* marathon. (He'd never seen any of the movies before, and he asked things like why the effects on Episode 1 looked so much better than Episode 4, and whether Darth Vader needed an inhaler for his asthma.)

Somewhere between Jabba the Hutt and the Ewoks, we both fell asleep, and I awoke with a start around midnight to the sound of a bat caught in the chimney. Except it wasn't a bat. It was some guy in a Santa suit crawling out of my fireplace, holding a Glock 43 and pointing it at Jonah.

I recognized him. He was the kettle Santa from downtown, but what was he doing here?

"No sudden moves, asshole," he growled. "The kid comes with me."

He lunged forward and grabbed Jonah, who was just waking up, and shouted, "Hey!"

"Shut up!" the intruder shouted. "Your dad here's been naughty this year, so you're coming with me."

"Who the hell are you?" I demanded.

"Who do I look like, Einstein? Just think of me as Child Protective Services. Gotta hand it to ya: No one's ever got this close before. That's why I'm collecting a little insurance, man, so ya don't go off on your own after I took your badge."

"You...?"

He laughed, and it sounded nothing like ho-ho-ho. More like "ha-ha, fuck you."

"I know you're packing your own piece, so slide it across the floor to me." When I hesitated, he cuffed Jonah on the side of the head so hard a trickle of blood rolled out of his ear.

I surrendered my weapon.

He smiled the kind of smile I'd seen on Danny Boy and Ivan Vukovich and Left-Eye Patrillo when they knew they had you. And he had me all right, but he wanted to be sure, so he aimed his Glock at my right kneecap and fired.

Bullseye.

I crumpled to the ground, writhing in pain and watched through wincing eyes as he took out some rope and tied Jonah securely to him, dangling down as he threw up a grappling hook and disappeared up the chimney.

I've got a big chimney and the guy, despite the Santa suit, was pretty skinny, so I wasn't too surprised he fit. Still, it seemed a bit theatrical. What, did he have a helicopter hovering over the house?

I was in no shape to get up and check. All I could do was pull my cellphone out of my pocket and try to see well enough through the haze of pain to dial 911.

As far as the police were concerned, it was just a home invasion and kidnapping. I never said anything about the Santa suit. It was suspicious enough that they'd kidnapped a kid, never sent a ransom note, and left no sign of forced entry through any of the locked doors or windows.

My ex accused me of orchestrating the whole thing to "steal" Jonah from her, and she got the cops to believe her, so my suspension became termination—even though they never found any direct evidence against me. They didn't have enough to charge me, but they had enough to fire me—or so they said. And so, they did.

Fortunately, my insurance lasted long enough to cover treatment on my shattered kneecap. I got a replacement, went through rehab... and then it was time to find my son.

You might think that would have been difficult, and it should have been except for one thing: I'd embedded a very small tracking device in the handle of the gun I'd surrendered, so I knew exactly where the weapon was: Just off the coast of Ellesmere Island in the Arctic Ocean north of Canada. Either it was a malfunction or Kettle Santa had gone to absurd lengths to dispose of it in literally the middle of nowhere.

I'd earned my pilot's license some years back and had managed to keep it current by making brief flights every few months in Captain Mulroney's Cessna: He'd thought it wasn't a bad idea to keep me qualified, in case I ever needed to fly. Considering my terminated status with the department now, that clearly wasn't an option. I'd have to fend for myself... which wouldn't be cheap. It cost $200 to rent a plane, easy—and that was just for an hour. It might take me a couple of days to get where I was going (a Cessna ain't no 747 when it comes to airspeed), and that didn't account for the cost of fuel, so I was looking at ponying up several thousand bucks.

That second mortgage I'd taken out to add a game room onto my house? That would be put to a different use now. I had enough left over to pick up an M16 assault rifle, a parka, mummy bag, heavy-duty tent, lantern, portable stove, survival kit, a Ka-Bar combat knife, and three weeks' worth of supplies, among other things. I didn't expect to find Jonah where my tracker was, but in the event I did, I was going in prepared for war.

This is my kid we're talking about.

As it happened, though, I wasn't prepared at all—not by a long shot.

Ellesmere Island is about as far north as you can go without hitting the ocean that spans the top of the world between Canada and Siberia. Right now, it's the site of the magnetic north pole, which (unlike the geographic pole) moves around from place to place. Wherever it was, I didn't expect to find anyone there, just a clue to where Kettle Santa might have taken my kid.

Boy, was I wrong.

The northeastern edge of Ellesmere Island was certainly isolated, but that didn't mean it was barren. Thankfully, the weather was clear, so I had a bird's-eye view of the frozen land below. I found myself approaching what looked like a wide, paved runway, in the middle of what looked to all the world like a full-fledged military installation. This was crazy. I was over Canadian territory, but the Canadian military didn't have anything like this. Was the U.S. leasing this land for a secret base, and, if so, to what purpose? To prevent a Russian attack? I couldn't fathom the Russians mounting any kind of offensive from the north, and attacking Canada would start World War III anyway.

"Cessna 172, please identify yourself. State your flight clearance code and intentions. Please be advised you have entered restricted airspace. Failure to comply will bring an immediate military response. Do you copy?"

Shit.

"Canadian government, this is Cessna 172 Skyhawk SP, serial number 172S1163 out of Los Angeles, California, requesting permission to land."

"This is Delta Dancer, Skyhawk. You are not in Canadian jurisdiction. You have entered restricted airspace governed by the sovereign state of Alfaria. I say again, please state your clearance course and intentions."

The accent was strange. I didn't recognize it. It didn't sound Canadian or Russian... or anything.

Whoever was on the other end of this transmission, they trusted me about as much as I trusted them. I was obviously going to have to improvise.

"Off course and low on fuel, request immediate permission to land for refueling."

There was a brief silence, then crackling on the channel, and finally, "Skyhawk, granting provisional clearance to land for refueling. Please follow the lights on the runway to your destination. You will be met by an escort upon landing. You are not to exit your plane, but will wait for us to complete refueling. Then you will be expected to depart. Is that clear?"

"10-4." Now that was hardly a friendly welcome.

What was this place?

Beyond the hangars and control tower, I could see a settlement of some kind, consisting mostly of industrial-looking buildings with smokestacks belching streams of gray-black soot into the air. Whoever lived in Alfaria, they certainly didn't seem too concerned about climate change.

My mind started to race. I'd come this far without any real plan, expecting to be met with snowdrifts and barren waste. I hadn't counted on this... They said I'd be met by "an escort" and wouldn't be allowed to leave the plane.

Like hell.

I was going to get out, and I was going to find my son, period.

Figuring I was almost certain to be outgunned by whoever was there to greet me on the ground, I decided to try a friendly approach. "Delta Dancer, requesting information on Jonah McBride. I have reason to believe an international fugitive may be holding him somewhere in the Arctic Circle against his will. Do you copy?"

There was another moment of silence and more crackling. Then, to my shock, came the answer. "Affirmative, Skyhawk. The minor in question is in our custody."

My heart leapt. I wondered what had happened to Kettle Santa, but it hardly mattered: Jonah was safe.

"I'm his father," I blurted out. "I'm here to take him home."

More silence.

"Hello?"

No answer. This couldn't be good.

I felt the wheels touch the ground, and I began taxiing toward the refueling station. Fortunately, the runway wasn't iced over. I hadn't thought to worry about that until that last minute, when it was too late to wonder whether I'd just go skidding off the end.

Through the window, I saw what looked like a line of four Jeeps coming toward me, each carrying a pair of armed men in parkas.

I had an M16.

So did each of them.

They pulled up in front of me, short of the refueling station. I had no choice but to stop and open the door to a cold blast of wind.

I opened the door and was greeted by eight men holding automatic weapons, all of them trained on me.

"You will accompany us to the factory," the first one said in a clipped voice.

"But, I thought..."

"You want to see your son, right?"

I nodded, apprehensive.

"Then you will allow us to blindfold and cuff you, and we will take you to him."

I didn't seem to have much choice in the matter. I was outnumbered and outgunned—to such an extent that I'd left the M16 in the Cessna. I still had my knife and a Saturday Night Special tucked away out of sight, but I doubted they'd do me much good unless I had the element of surprise... which I clearly did *not* have at the moment. These men were on high alert against anything suspicious. Fortunately, they didn't think to frisk me, or didn't think it necessary when I submitted to being bound and blindfolded.

It was an unsettling experience, but nothing compared to what I saw when we reached our destination and they removed my blindfold.

Before me was a massive factory, bigger than any I'd ever seen, with workers by the thousands, even tens of thousands, creating... it couldn't be... creating *toys*. It was like I'd stumbled into Santa's Workshop, but the workers weren't elves—there are no such things as elves, right?—they were children, some as young as 6 years old. My eyes widened as it dawned on me: Jonah must be one of them, being put to work as slave labor here for... for what?

I was about to say something when I saw him. Not Jonah, but a thin figure in a red suit with a long but scruffy gray-white beard and a look in his eye that I'd seen before.

It was Kettle Santa, the guy who'd kidnapped my son and, apparently, all these other kids.

"Well, look who it is!" he exclaimed as he strode forward, hand extended. "I never thought I'd see *you* again."

I didn't take his hand, but I couldn't anyway: My own hands were still cuffed.

"Who are you supposed to be? Some sorry excuse for a Santa?"

He looked wounded, but not sincerely so. It was the kind of expression a sociopath wears to disarm his target. I'd seen it before in criminals, and I recognized it on him. "Not 'supposed to be,' man. I am. The genuine article. Though most people around here call me Nicky. But being in law enforcement, you've probably heard of me as Nicky the Saint."

I did a double-take. Nicky the Saint was reputed to run the largest crime family in the world, but no one had ever seen him—at least no one had ever seen him and lived to tell about it. He was like a myth. Most people weren't even sure he existed. The captain had said something about him once; had called him a figurehead for the Comet Crime Front, a rallying point to ensure loyalty who his followers believed in but never saw. This might be Nicky the Saint, or it might just be someone using that name to his own ends. At this point, it hardly mattered.

I tried to gather my composure. "I'd like to see my son. I'm assuming there's a ransom."

The man laughed. "We don't hold kids for ransom. We train 'em to be productive citizens. No video games. No TV. No social media. Just good hard work 16 hours a day, seven days a week, with no time off for holidays."

"Not even Christmas."

"Hey, if I gotta work Christmas, so do they. Just setting an example."

"But why all this? What do you do with all these toys?"

Nicky laughed again. It was that ha-ha-ha, fuck-you laugh of his. "We sell them, man. You know Realmart, toy stores, online sites..."

"You sell them to those places?"

"Fuck no, man. How stupid do you think I am? Those places are just fronts for our organization. We've got a monopoly, bruh. We sell direct and mark up the prices because people *think* there's a middleman. But there's not. It's just us. It's all us, baby!"

My shoulders slumped. I looked back at the plane and saw some of Nicky's henchmen removing my M16. Two more of them stepped forward, and now they *were* frisking me. They took the gun. They took the knife.

"You're not going to let me take my son home, are you?"

"Ha-ha-ha! Now why would I do *that*? No one sees Nicky the Saint and lives to tell about it—no adult, anyway. Your son's still alive, but he doesn't even remember being your son. He's mine now. Young minds are so easily molded, right? I can make them into whoever, whatever I want. But we older folks are stuck in our ways. You can't change me, I can't change you. You can't kill me, but... oh, that's right, I *can* kill you. I'm afraid I can't let you expose me. You've come too close already."

He nodded toward one of his henchmen, the one to his right and closest to me.

"Allow me to introduce Roger Taylor," he said. "He's been here with me since he was 5. He follows my orders without question. Jonah's getting there too."

He nodded again, and I felt a sinking feeling in the pit of my stomach, followed by a stabbing pain in my gut as the man plunged the knife he'd confiscated from me into my flesh. He twisted it, thrust it further in, and twisted it some more until the pain was so excruciating I felt myself blacking out.

When I came to... well, I never did come to.

I wouldn't be able to tell you this story. But you wouldn't believe me anyway.

Sharon Marie Provost

Nine Lives

The voluptuous, raven-haired beauty walked briskly through the airport as she headed toward the customs area. She carried only a small backpack, a cat carrier, and a smile on her face.

She was excited to start her new life in America, unencumbered by the beliefs and judgments of the townspeople in the small Scottish village from which she hailed.

But first, she had an errand to complete...

Sometimes, pet rescue adoptions fail because the animal is unruly and untrainable. Other times, the animal is placed in the wrong home with other pets, children, or those who do not have the time to care for them. And unfortunately, sometimes they are placed into neglectful homes. But sometimes... sometimes those adoption failures are deliberate.

On the animal's part.

Sometimes those pets *want* to come back to be placed... into the home of their next unwitting victim.

Elspeth, better known as Ellie when she is up for adoption, is one of those cats that returns to different shelters repeatedly. An adorable, chubby, black cat with a white spot on her chest, she knows how to sit at the front of her cage, playfully pawing at the air, begging for attention—just like the adorable kittens down the way do. She caresses the bars with her face, just asking for a soft scratch on her velvet head. Now who can resist that?

It's no surprise that, inevitably, she is always adopted again—and quickly.

Everything always goes well in her new home at first. She endears herself to her new owners and seems to know exactly what they need to make them love and trust her. Some like her to sit in their laps for hours on end, where she allows them to pet her and, in so doing, to reduce their own stress level. Others just like the occasional rub against the leg to let them know there is some company in the house with them.

Whatever their need, Ellie meets it... at first. She eats her food promptly when fed. She never makes a mess outside her litterbox. If let outside, she stays nearby and returns instantly when called—she never sneaks out of the house for those who want her to be an indoor kitty.

Then one day, everything changes. Ellie becomes bored with playing the perfect little house kitty. Once her owners trust her, there is no longer any need to engender their goodwill. That's when Ellie starts thinking about her move to the next home. Planning is involved because she never wants to make the same exit twice; after all, there is no need to create suspicion. More importantly, it isn't any fun to repeat her crimes.

No one can say Ellie lacks creativity.

Her first home was with an old man who had lost his wife the year before. He was lonely and only needed someone else in the house with him. Occasionally, he would pet her or spoil her with a little milk in a saucer or a bite of tuna when he made his sandwich each day for lunch.

"Here you go, *liebchen*," he would coo to her as he set down the saucer.

His own health was failing, so he rarely left the house. He never strayed far from his bottle of nitroglycerin pills, which he kept on the kitchen counter next to the dish drainer. It seemed that his heart was giving him issues more often lately, so that seemed like the perfect place for Ellie to start.

One day, after carrying the trash out to the can at the curb, he came back to the house holding his heart and breathing heavily. He headed straight for his medication and opened the bottle, setting it down on the counter as he reached for the water glass he kept in the drainer. He didn't notice that Ellie had jumped up on the counter behind him.

Carefully, she slithered up next to him— and knocked the bottle of pills into the sink when he turned on the water, promptly washing them all down the drain. He cried out in dismay as he shut off the water and desperately scrambled to find any remaining pills. The more desperate he became, the more he clutched his chest in pain.

After only a few moments, he dropped to the floor, and his breathing slowed, then stopped. His caregiver found him the next day upon arriving to take him to his doctor's appointment. Faithful Ellie was found lying next to him. No one in the family wanted a pet, so they returned her to the shelter later that week.

"That poor dear cat. Mr. Walters had just called me two weeks ago and thanked me for our efforts in getting him such a sweet cat to provide him with company," Miss Edwards, the shelter director, told the staff when Ellie was returned.

So dear Ellie, the shelter favorite, was placed back up for adoption immediately. Everyone felt sorry for her and made sure she was accepted on the local morning news as the "Pet of the Week" just in time for the Christmas adoption season. They were always very selective around the holidays about adopting pets because so many people returned them. They would make sure this time that she found just the right home.

It wasn't long before that perfect situation presented itself: A young, single mom came to adopt her. She had recently had a baby and wanted her own child to grow up with a young pet, just as she had. Christmas was the perfect time for her child and her new pet to start their life together making memories, starting with a Santa picture at Petsmart. Plus, she herself was lonely, since her boyfriend had left when she refused to put the baby up for adoption. The adoption center checked her references and found that Melissa had been a responsible pet owner in the past, according to her veterinarian.

Ellie ingratiated herself with the young mom, sitting on her lap and quietly letting her pet her until she fell asleep when the baby was napping. She would wake to find Ellie curled up next to the baby in her crib. Everything was going just as the woman had wanted, and her life felt complete.

"You are a godsend, sweet Ellie. I am so glad I brought you to our home. April will grow up with you as her best friend, just as I did with Juniper, " Melissa whispered to Ellie, as she looked in on April peacefully sleeping in her crib with Ellie lying at her feet.

Ellie could see how happy she was, so it was time to figure out her next plan of departure. On Christmas Eve, the baby fell asleep early, so the young mom took advantage of the opportunity and went to bed early herself. Tomorrow would be a big day. She was so excited to celebrate Christmas with her new little family. Ellie quietly climbed off the bed and made her way down the hall past the Christmas tree to April's room. She jumped into the crib softly, so as not to wake the baby. She carefully walked up to the baby and lay down on her chest, placing her paw over the baby's nose and mouth, stealing her breath. It didn't take long before the baby started to struggle, coughing and trying to cry. Ellie then pressed down tighter to stifle the noises. When she was sure the child was gone, Ellie walked back down the hall and climbed into bed with Melissa.

The next morning, Melissa was shocked to realize that the baby had not woken her during the night. She walked into her room, expecting to find her slowly rousing, but all she saw was her lying there, unnaturally still. She ran to the crib and picked her up quickly, checking her breathing—even as she realized her infant daughter was cold and stiff. She broke down sobbing as she ran to find her cell phone to call for help.

The ambulance arrived quickly, but nothing could be done. Melissa was devastated at the loss and decided to move home, where her parents could console her. But her mother and father did not want the cat in their home because of her younger sister's allergies, so she regretfully turned Ellie over to the shelter once again.

The shelter workers felt so bad for Ellie that they were even more determined to find just the right home for her. This time, they found a young woman named Rebecca who had property out in the country and loved animals. She had horses, a goat, a small herd of dairy cattle, and one cattle dog that had been raised around cats. They had tested Ellie early on, and she did not seem bothered by the presence of cat-friendly dogs. Still, they made the young woman bring in her dog; when they interacted appropriately, the adoption was carried out.

Ellie arrived at her new home and was pleasantly surprised. She discovered it had a cat door that let her go outside into a protected "catio" decorated with cat trees; shelves for climbing bolted securely into the wall; patches of cat grass growing in the dirt plot; and plenty of hanging toys for batting. Even better, because she was in the country, an assortment of wildlife visited her there: mice, squirrels, small birds, and other animals that were small enough to enter her enclosure.

"Look, my little kiki, at the beautiful home I have designed for you. I think you will be very happy here, " Rebecca said to Ellie as she watched her explore her new enclosure.

Life progressed comfortably enough for quite some time. Ellie spent her days outside on the catio capturing prey and torturing it. She would bat mice and squirrels around, then let them start to run away, only to grab them brutally in her mouth once again. Her evenings were spent in the house torturing the dog when Rebecca's back was turned. She loved to hide around corners and bat him on the nose when he walked by. Rebecca just couldn't understand why he never interacted with her since he had always loved cats. But it didn't matter, she figured, because they didn't seem unhappy with each other.

Ellie spent many evenings in Rebecca's lap as they watched television. She had everything a cat could desire at her disposal. But once again, Ellie became bored, and besides, it was time.

Now, just how would she successfully navigate this death without causing suspicion? This was the question uppermost in her mind.

Then, finally, it came to her.

A few weeks later, Rebecca awoke with a fever, chills, muscle weakness and pain, headache, and swollen lymph nodes. She thought she had come down with the flu after attending the rodeo a few days earlier, but she kept working. She didn't think too much of it because she had contracted the flu several times throughout her life, and she thought of herself as one tough cookie. Then the flu progressed to coughing, and breathing became difficult. She had never been one to visit the doctor, so she tried self-care at home by resting, drinking fluids, and taking Ibuprofen and Dayquil Cold and Flu.

None of it had any effect.

The symptoms rapidly progressed to the point that she could no longer get out of bed. She couldn't even make it to the one phone in the house out in the kitchen.

She had a cell phone, but it rarely worked so far out there in the country, so there was no way to call for help.

Little did she realize help was what she desperately needed.

She was found deceased a few days later when her hay delivery arrived. The delivery driver, a longtime friend, became concerned when he heard a ruckus coming from the barn and field: a cacophony of barking, whinnying, bleating and screaming from the goats, mooing and other panicked sounds caused by all the starving, dehydrated animals who'd been left without anyone to feed or water them.

The driver entered the unlocked back door and found his friend lying in bed dead with her mucus membranes—her nose, eyelids, and lips—chewed off. The dog was lying on the floor beside her, but the cat was nowhere to be found. The cause of death was ruled to be pneumonic plague, the facial wounds having presumably been caused by her starving dog and cat.

It was well known that she had loved to feed the local wildlife, so it was believed she had contracted the plague from a bite by an infected flea on one of the squirrels or mice that visited her home. Little did they know that the rodents with the fleas had been brought into the house by Ellie. The catio was found with a hole dug under the chain-link fence, so the cat was presumed to have been attacked and eaten by a coyote.

In actuality, Ellie had slowly made her way back to town and been picked up by the local humane society truck.

Time to start at a different shelter.

Naturally, Ellie won over the new shelter's staff quickly, so they put every effort into finding her a good home. She had put on her best show of being an affectionate, affable cat who enjoyed the company of humans and other pets alike.

A young, quiet man came looking for a cat to introduce to his first apartment. After an introductory visit and a home inspection, Bryan's request to adopt her was approved quickly.

Bryan took her home after making a stop at the pet store to buy her a litterbox, bed, food, treats, and toys, and she settled in quickly in her new home. Not much was expected of her except for some occasional nuzzles against his leg, and that she sleep in her own kitty cot on the floor next to his bed.

Ellie quickly lost all interest in this new home.

Further, she had decided it was time to explore some more interesting extraction methods.

One day as she was lazing around the house pondering what to do, the perfect opportunity presented itself. The young man worked an IT job from home. He had the bad habit of starting to cook food, then walking away to the computer for a moment.

Unfortunately, that moment far too often led to the food being burned.

This time, the meal was completely inedible, so he began to scrape it into the sink and down the garbage disposal. The sink quickly became plugged from the clumpy, burned mess, so he turned it off to remove the clog by reaching down into it with his hand.

Ellie seized this opportunity to jump onto the counter, where she nuzzled her cheek against the garbage disposal switch—when the unfortunate Bryan's hand was still deep in the drain. He began to scream and panic as the blade tore up his hand. As he struggled, he got his hand stuck as he tried to back up and pull it out at an angle.

Finally, he managed to free his mangled hand as blood poured from the wound and down his arm. Three fingers had been completely severed; the other two hung from bits of flesh and sinew. His palm had been flayed open, so muscle and bone were both visible. Combined with the excruciating pain of his injury, the horrific sight of it was just too much. As he turned away from the sink and saw his hand mangled and spewing blood, he passed out, striking his temple on the countertop as he fell.

Ellie sat in the kitchen next to his body, watching with delight as the blood slowly pumped out of his destroyed hand. She was startled when his body began to convulse in a seizure from the head injury he had sustained.

Later that day, Bryan's mother came by to check on him after he failed to answer her repeated phone calls. Ellie ran out the door when his mother opened it and began screaming in terror when she saw her son lying in a pool of blood on the kitchen floor.

Ellie walked down the street and over to a young woman sitting on a bench eating her lunch in the park. The woman looked very lonely, so Ellie put on her full adorable kitty charm. She started by rubbing her face softly on the woman's leg. When the woman smiled down at her, she jumped up onto the bench next to her and sat down. She gingerly leaned forward and tentatively sniffed at the lunchmeat in her sandwich, then quietly meowed.

The woman began laughing.

"You look and sound hungry there, darling. Here you go," she said gaily as she pulled the turkey lunchmeat out of her sandwich.

Ellie slowly ate the bites of meat she was offered; then she nuzzled the woman's hand, purring when she was finished. The woman began to pet her head, so Ellie climbed into her lap and lay down in a tight knot. The two of them sat there happily for the next hour. Finally, the woman had to return to her work. She picked up Ellie and placed her on the ground and set off walking toward her home office. Ellie began to follow her home, and the woman was surprised to see her close behind when she looked back to check on her.

"Baby, don't you have a home? Go home, sweetie. Go home."

Ellie sat down and stared at her as she told her to go home. When the woman started to walk away again, she resumed following her. The woman looked back and saw that she still had a stalker.

"Let's see where you live. Let me look at your collar," she cooed as she gently reached down to part the fur looking for a collar. "I don't see one. Are you a stray? Is that why you were so hungry?"

Ellie nuzzled her hand once again and looked up at her with her most adoring gaze. That was all it took. The young woman picked her up and began walking home again.

"I will call the pound when I get home and, if nothing else, place an ad in the newspaper to make sure no one is looking for you. In the meantime, let's go get you settled."

When they returned home, the woman placed Ellie in the bathroom while she ran out to get some supplies for her. A quick call to the pound in an attempt to find her owner proved fruitless, so she got online and placed an ad before resuming her work on the blueprints for the new shopping mall. She never heard back from the ad she ran for one week, so she decided to keep Ellie. Working at home was lonely, so she could certainly use the company.

Ellie settled in well initially because she was fed well, had free reign in the house, including the woman's bed, and better yet, she was let out each day to explore the neighborhood. She quickly learned the young woman was friends with the older woman next door when she came home to find them sitting outside on the patio. The older woman thought of her young neighbor almost as a daughter, and she visited so often it was like a second home to her.

The older woman jumped up the minute Ellie appeared.

"I... I have to go home. I am extremely allergic to cats. I can't take a chance. I'll talk to you later," she stammered quickly as she began to walk toward the gate. Her breathing had quickened as her stress level rose when she couldn't find her asthma inhaler.

The young woman called out a quick goodbye before turning to Ellie.

"Well, let's get inside and see to dinner."

Ellie followed her into the house and settled in on the couch. The routine was starting to be a little *too* routine, and it was getting to be time again. After dinner, she followed the young woman into her office and jumped up on the table in the corner, then up onto the filing cabinet next to it. The perfect idea struck her as she looked up at the shelves right behind the young woman's desk. There she saw architecture books, architecture plaques, and trophies, as well as some family pictures.

She climbed silently across onto the second shelf, where the trophies were. Then she crossed the shelf carefully so as not to knock anything down, until she reached a heavy, sharp glass trophy in the shape of a narrow pyramid. When the young woman leaned back in her chair to stretch, as she often did, Ellie pushed the top of the trophy off the edge, so that it fell point-first.

The trophy landed directly on the top of the woman's head, impaling her.

She began to moan unintelligibly and twitch as the blood poured from the top of her head. Before long, her movements and breathing ceased.

Ellie knew she had one more step to take before her evening mission was complete. The young woman had made plans earlier for her neighbor to meet her at the house so they could go out to a movie. She had made note of this and made sure to prepare for her arrival. First, Ellie ran into the kitchen and knocked the neighbor's spare emergency asthma inhaler off the counter—where the young woman kept it in case there was an emergency when the neighbor visited. (The young woman vacuumed the couch and locked Ellie in a room in the back when the neighbor visited, in an effort to prevent an allergic reaction.) Ellie then nosed the spray under the storage cabinet across the kitchen, where it couldn't be seen. Then she ran to the back of the house to hide before the older woman's arrival.

A short while later, there came repeated knocking at the door—which, of course, went unanswered. The neighbor tentatively opened the door and called inside, trying to garner further attention. When her "hello" went unanswered as well, she started to walk down the hall, looking for the young woman.

At last, she came to the young woman's home office, where she found her friend slumped over in her chair and covered in blood, with the trophy protruding from the top of her head. As the grim reality of what she was seeing set in, she began to hyperventilate and then screamed loudly. She ran over to check on the young woman, and her breathing turned to harsh wheezes and gasps when she felt no pulse.

She braced herself against the wall and slowly turned to make her way down the hall to find her spare asthma spray. She had left hers in her purse in the car parked out front. She was beginning to weave as she reached the counter and found no spray in sight. As her panic increased, her breathing turned to small gasps, and the color began fading from her face. She felt lightheaded and slumped to the ground. As her head hit the tile floor, for an instant she saw the spray lying under the storage cabinet, just out of reach, and Elspeth sitting right next to the cabinet twitching her tail happily.

At that very moment, she breathed her last.

After checking on her handiwork, Ellie walked out the open front door and headed out to find her next home.

Ronnie and Samuel had spent eight weeks investigating a rash of odd deaths—which seemed even more peculiar because a cat was mentioned in several cases. Being seasoned demon hunters, they suspected the cat was either a demon or a witch's familiar performing her dirty deeds.

The case had gone cold for the past month, until one day when they heard a supposedly heartwarming story on the news: The director at a local nursing home owned a beautiful black-and-white cat that visited all the patients in the home. They all loved her, but she seemed to know when patients were about to pass. She would situate herself on their bed, keeping them company in their final hours.

This was just the lead they had been looking for, and they knew there was no time to waste.

Ronnie and Samuel showed up at the nursing home the next day with a blanket and a cage. They talked their way past the front desk by claiming to be family members of the director who had come to pick up the cat for its annual exam at the veterinarian. They talked soothingly to the cat as they gently picked her up and placed her in the cage, covering it with a blanket sprayed with Feliway to keep her calm and obstruct her view. (They didn't want to tip her off to their motivations because it could be dangerous to do so—or give her a chance to escape.)

Upon returning to the motel where they were staying on the edge of town, they carried her directly to the demon trap they had drawn on the floor of their room.

Once in the trap, she could neither escape nor do them harm.

When everything was prepared, Samuel removed the demon dagger from his bag under the bed and carefully approached the cage. Then, like a magician ripping a tablecloth out from under a table of place settings, Ronnie rapidly removed the blanket, and Samuel leapt forward and plunged the knife directly into the cat's heart.

When they were sure the demon cat was dead, they carried the cage back out to the car and drove out into the forest to burn the body with salts and herbs, making sure that all the evil had been destroyed. They returned to the motel to get a good night's sleep before taking on another case.

That night, however, they were alarmed to see a story on the local news: They'd been caught on videotape removing the cat from the senior home. Police were investigating the catnapping, and the public was outraged. Clearly, they would need to leave first thing in the morning to avoid any legal fallout, so they began packing up.

Then, at 6 a.m., they arose and hurriedly packed the car before heading down to the office to check out.

"Excuse me!" Elspeth said with a cheeky smile as she brushed against Ronnie and Samuel when she entered the motel lobby. They held the door open for her and then continued on their way to the car. Clearly, the stupid Americans did not recognize her as the evil entity they had been seeking.

Elspeth had come to the New World from the Scottish Highlands, where she was simply too well known.

It had become too difficult there to steal the souls of the dead by passing over their bodies after death, as was her custom. As of late, the villagers had developed methods of distracting Cat-Sith such as Elspeth and keeping them away from bodies.

In truth, the Cat-Sith weren't cats at all—at least, not all the time. Actually, they were witches who could transform themselves, taking on the form of a cat. But there was a catch: They could only do so nine times. The ninth time they transformed, they couldn't come back: They'd be stuck in the form of a cat until the end of their days.

Elspeth had transformed back into her witch form for the sixth time to make the journey to America. Upon arriving and realizing that no one knew about the Celtic legend of the Cat-Sith here, she found that it was both easier and more fun to steal souls from the bodies of the dead by inflicting the mortal blows herself.

Having settled in a new home, she'd happened to see the story on the news about Ronnie and Samuel, the world-famous demon hunters. Apparently, they had stolen and killed a poor, innocent housecat.

She'd become concerned that they might realize their mistake at some point and come after her. So Elspeth had transformed herself back into a witch for a seventh time and had gone to the lonely motel just outside of town herself to lay low for a few days while she plotted her next move. She never imagined she would run into the demon hunters themselves, but clearly, she had little to worry about.

She excused herself when the desk clerk asked if she had a reservation, then exited the lobby and headed over to a car in the back of the lot. With a flick of her wrist, she unlocked the car and started the engine, then climbed in and drove away, headed for parts unknown. This country was her oyster. Maybe she would explore the Central Coast of California... maybe the South... Who knew? She was free to go wherever she liked. She just needed to be a little more subtle in her soul-stealing murders and allow a little more time between acquisitions.

God forbid she had to do any more transformations—and end up stuck as a helpless cat for life.

Stephen H. Provost

Thirteenth Friday

"Step on a crack, break your mother's back!"

"Step on a crack, break your mother's back!"

"Step on a crack, break your mother's back!"

"Step on a crack, break your mother's back!"

Their taunting rang in Freddie's ears as he sat in the hospital lobby, waiting to hear news of his mother. His father sat next to him, nervously running his hands through the dark brown hair that remained on both sides of his head as he rocked back and forth slightly in his chair.

Freddie rocked, too. He had picked up the habit from his father. He rocked to the cadence of their sing-song teasing. They'd formed a line along both edges of the sidewalk as he'd walked the gantlet toward the bus stop, just as they did every day. They waited for him outside the house, then lined up like poorly trained boot camp soldiers ready to do their duty and harass him.

Freddie never knew the exact reason they'd chosen him to pick on. Oh, there were many excuses. He was tall and gangly, but so were several of the other kids. No one ever bothered them. Maybe it was his name: Digby Mudge. He hated it. The kids used it as an excuse to call him "Little Dicky" as they pointed at him, then laughed hysterically the moment it was out of their mouths. That's why he went by Freddie. He didn't like his middle name, Frederick, particularly, either. But it was better than Digby. Anything was better than Digby.

He'd always been so careful not to give them an excuse to laugh at him more by stepping on a crack. But that particular morning, he'd missed one: a new one from the day before, which had apparently been caused by a tree root having grown just enough beneath the concrete to crack the sidewalk. He'd tried to continue walking as though nothing was wrong, hoping they wouldn't notice. But of course they did.

"Oh, no!" Jenny Martin called out.

"He's done it now!" hooted Jimmy Malone.

"Mom's a goner for sure!" said Lamont Patrick.

None of them had weird names.

"Poor Little Dickie!"

"He's sure to wet his bed!"

Everyone broke into laughter, pointing at him and hopping up and down.

Maybe they'll pee their own pants, he thought. *Stupid kids. Stepping on a crack won't do anything. What do they know?*

Plenty, it turned out.

His father had pulled him out of school at lunch that day. His mother had fallen down the stairs outside their apartment building, where they lived on the second floor. She was unconscious at first, and when she woke up, she couldn't move. They had to load her onto a gurney and into an ambulance, which whisked her away to St. Matthew's Hospital.

It's all my fault, Freddie kept telling himself over and over as he sat there in the waiting room. His father had pulled him off into the hospital chapel and told him to light a candle and pray for his mother, but he knew that praying would do no good. He had jinxed her by stepping on that crack. Those kids had been right. They knew something he didn't know about life. *That* was why they made fun of him, he was sure.

They knew.

He didn't.

He really *was* a freak.

Freddie's mom recovered, but she never walked again. She never blamed him for the accident: She had been trying to balance two bags of groceries and had fallen backward when trying to catch one of them as it slipped out of her hand. But he blamed himself, because he knew the truth. And his father blamed him too. He had made the mistake of telling him about what he'd done on the sidewalk—what a mistake *that* had been! Before, his father had always been patient with him when he'd told him about the bullies, and he'd called him "Freddie" even though he'd named him Digby after his own father.

He never called him Freddie anymore.

Or even Digby.

It was worse. He'd taken to calling him Dickie, just like the bullies—when he spoke to him at all, which was only to make him do some chore or remind him of what he'd done to his mother

"She was out buying groceries for us on her day off," he

would tell him. "Now she can't work at all anymore. It's all your fault we had to move into a smaller apartment. I won't hear you complaining about not getting a PlayStation for Christmas or having to go to a new school or sharing a room with your little brother."

Not that he ever *had* complained. He hadn't. He had learned to keep his mouth shut and just accept his fate, even though his little brother was always shouting at him and stealing his toys. As for the PlayStation, he liked reading better anyway, which gave his father an excuse to call him a nerd—and not in a playful or complimentary way. He'd been excited about the idea of changing schools at first, eager to get away from the bullies who had harassed him so mercilessly at Yorktown Grammar School. But the kids at his new school, Farragut Elementary, were even worse. Kids were like sharks: They smelled blood. And Freddie's entire body was covered in the invisible blood of shyness and insecurity.

He waited for them to dare him to step on a crack on the way to the bus stop, ready to come back at them by saying his mother's back was already broken. *So take that!*

But they didn't tease him about that.

They didn't even bother him on the way to the bus stop. But once he was there, they cut in front of him in line. When he tried to stand his ground, Billy Marker pulled a pin out of his pocket and held it up in front of his eye, jabbing toward it threateningly until he backed down. But giving them what they wanted didn't help either. Even when he let them in front of him, they would push his notebook out of his hands so all the papers went flying out onto the ground. Sometimes, his homework assignments wound up soaked in a puddle, and if they managed to escape that fate, the bullies would snatch them up before he could and smear mud all over them.

"Dog eat your homework?" they'd say.

Then they'd tear it up in front of him and throw the pieces skyward, to be carried away on the wind.

Of course, the bullies never lost *their* place in line.

Meanwhile, Freddie's grades suffered, in part because of what happened to his homework so often at the bus stop, and in part because he was so afraid of the bullies he started to feign sickness so he could stay home from school. His father finally took him to the doctor, who prescribed a medication that was "sure to make him better." But it turned out to be a placebo, so when he dutifully got "well," his father accused him of faking to avoid doing any work.

He was assigned more chores as a result.

At Christmas, Freddie didn't get a PlayStation. Instead, his mother bought him a little grey cat named Rhiannon.

She told him that Santa had kept her as a pet at the North Pole, but that she had been too cold there, so he had wanted to find a new home for her. He just knew that Freddie would take good care of her, so he had left her in his care.

Freddie still believed in Santa, and he was convinced that he had left Rhiannon for him because of the kindness he had shown in leaving milk and chocolate chip cookies out for Santa the night before.

His father had been against the idea of letting Freddie have Rhiannon, but who could argue with Santa? He had relented and allowed her to stay as long as Freddie promised to clean the litter box every day and use his allowance to pay for the cat food. This actually made Freddie very happy. Maybe now, he thought, he could prove to his father that he could be responsible. Besides, he loved Rhiannon. He smiled at the way she purred as she circled around his feet, and how she would jump into his lap and nuzzle up against him. She didn't do that with anyone else in the house. Only him. It made him feel special.

He dutifully cleaned Rhiannon's litter box and bought food for her, making sure she was fed and watered every day. Meanwhile, he worked hard to improve his grades, which he was able to do despite the bullying because he was actually a very smart boy. But his father never gave him any credit for taking care of Rhiannon ("You're just doing what's expected"), and even when a school-sponsored IQ test measured him at near-genius level, his father refused to believe it. He just scoffed at Freddie and accused him of cheating—even though it wasn't the kind of test you could cheat on.

Rhiannon became Freddie's best and only friend... until the day before Halloween of the next year.

On his way to school, Freddie saw Billy Marker carrying a sack in his arms. The sack was moving, which Freddie thought was odd.

Freddie knew better than to say anything to Billy or any of the other bullies at Farragut, but this time, his curiosity got the best of him.

"What's in the bag?" he asked, regretting the words the moment they left his mouth.

"Come and see."

Freddie approached cautiously and peered down into the bag when Billy opened it for him. Then, quick as a flash, out jumped a ball of fur amidst a chorus of howling and hissing. For an instant, he thought Billy had somehow gotten hold of Rhiannon and made her panic so badly that she'd run away. But this wasn't Rhiannon. Rhiannon would never act like that toward him. Besides, it was the wrong color.

The black cat jumped at Freddie, clawed desperately at his

arm, tearing his shirt sleeve, then landed feet-first on the sidewalk and darted away in a blur, right in front of Freddie.

"Ha!" Billy said in a self-satisfied tone. "Black cat crossed your path. You're cursed!"

"That's not what it means!"

Billy nodded knowingly. "You'll see." And he sauntered away like the king of the world.

Freddie looked at his arm and found it was bleeding where the cat had clawed him, then tried to dust off the black fur that clung to his now-torn shirt, but it clung to him tenaciously. He told himself he didn't believe all that nonsense about black cats. He was, after all, a smart boy. But then, in the back of his mind, he kept hearing it...

"Step on a crack, break your mother's back!"

"Step on a crack, break your mother's back!"

"Step on a crack, break your mother's back!"

"Step on a crack, break your mother's back!"

He already knew he was cursed. He didn't need a poor innocent black cat that had been forced into a bag by mean old Billy Marker to tell him that!

But what he didn't know was what would happen next.

When he got home, Rhiannon didn't come out to greet him as usual. When he asked his mom where Rhiannon was, she said she hadn't seen her.

Freddie looked all over the house before he finally found her crouched under his parents' bed. When he tried to call her out, she hissed at him. He couldn't get her to come.

"It's probably that other cat's hair on your shirt," his mother told him. "She's just jealous."

His mom couldn't get her to come out from under the bed either, which was no surprise: Rhiannon had never come to anyone but Freddie before. But that's when she made the mistake of telling his father about the problem, which of course made him curse Freddie and accuse him of abusing Rhiannon. He then muttered a string of bad words (which he had told Freddie never to use) under his breath as he headed for the pantry, returning a minute later with a broom.

"This will get your stupid cat out of there," he declared, then stooped down on the floor and began swinging the broom wildly from side to side under the bed.

There was a "mrrrrowwwwwl!" and a skittering, and presently Rhiannon came dashing out from under the bed like the Tasmanian Devil, flying toward the window and, finding it open, leapt to freedom.

"Dad!" Freddie yelled.

"Oh, shut up," his father told him. "Just let her go. Or stop bitching and go find her. I don't care."

Freddie searched and searched, but he never did—find her, that is. Every Christmas, he stayed up as late as he could, sitting by the fireplace, waiting for Santa to come down the chimney with Rhiannon tucked safely in his arms. But he always fell asleep before midnight, and the milk and cookies he'd left were untouched when he awoke. He was convinced it was all his fault that Rhiannon had disappeared, and that Santa hadn't brought her back. He must have been on the naughty list.

And from then on, he knew that Billy Marker had been right: He always heard the bully's voice in the back of his head, announcing, "You're cursed!" But he pictured it coming from Santa's mouth.

Poor Rhiannon.

Freddie never got another cat after that. His grades got worse again because he stopped caring. He didn't even care about the bullies anymore. All he cared about was staying inside and avoiding anything that might make his miserable life even worse than it was.

He grew up, got a job at a fast-food restaurant that paid minimum wage, and collected aluminum cans for extra money—not because he liked doing any of it, but because if he didn't, he wouldn't have any place to call home. His father had kicked him out when he turned 18. He was sure his mother would have objected, but she'd died a year earlier, and his father didn't want Freddie around to "cramp his style" when he "put himself back on the market."

He managed to scrape together enough cash to buy an ancient Dodge Dart that barely ran so he could get to and from work, and to rent a dingy studio apartment in a neighborhood with shoes tossed over power lines and syringes discarded in the gutters.

Yes, Freddie had grown up, but he'd never outgrown his fear of the bullies who had harassed him throughout his childhood. He had good reason for this: They had grown up too, and they hadn't changed one bit. Billy Marker moved away, but Freddie's boss at Taco Hell (his name for the place where he worked), Janice Goodling, was harder on him than Billy ever had been. She never gave him regular hours, so going to college wasn't an option. And she scheduled him for the graveyard shift one day and the morning shift the next, so he'd be too exhausted to enjoy his time off.

One day, when he got off work, he was in a relatively good mood because it was a Friday and he'd just received his paycheck. So, as he drove out of the parking lot, he mustered every ounce of hope he had left, defiantly proclaimed, "Things will get better. They have to!"

Then he panicked.

In the back of his head, he heard the bullies from childhood warn him, "Better knock on wood!"

They'd never actually said that, but somehow he knew they would if they were there now.

Frantically, he began looking around for wood to knock on. But the car was just metal and plastic: There was no wood to be found at all!

Unfortunately, his sudden dismay had distracted him from the road in front of him, and from the traffic light that had just turned red facing his direction. His car glided at a leisurely pace into the intersection, where it was hit broadside by a sedan—whose owner jumped out of the car and began cursing up a storm, calling him every name in the book as well as a few he hadn't heard before.

His car was totaled, but that didn't really matter considering the price of his insurance doubled and he couldn't afford to pay it. He received a citation, which cost him all the money he had, and he lost his job because he had no way to get there to work graveyards because public transportation didn't run that late. Assuming he could afford that, which he couldn't. All because he hadn't knocked on wood.

He was sure of it.

He looked at the calendar and, knowing it was Friday near the middle of the month, was sure he would find out it was also the 13th.

Somehow, though, it wasn't.

But from then on, he wouldn't be taking any chances. He wouldn't go out at all on any Friday the 13th, he wouldn't walk under ladders, he would avoid any places where he was likely to see cats, and he would always knock on wood. He'd find a way to beat his curse. Somehow. Some way.

One day, Freddie found a four-leaf clover sticking up,

ironically, through a crack in the sidewalk. He plucked it up and stuck it carefully in his shirt pocket.

From that moment forward, things started looking up.

He enrolled in night school, earned his associate's degree, and did so well that he earned a partial scholarship to the local state university. When that was combined with state grants, his entire education was covered.

He met a girl named Phoebe who reminded him a lot of his mother: kind-hearted and understanding. Not bad to look at, either. She even had a cat named Persephone, who curled herself around his legs and purred like a motorboat. Freddie liked to tell himself she was the reincarnation of Rhiannon.

Phoebe let him stay at her place while he studied to earn a degree in engineering while she worked at the hospital in admissions. It was a modest life, but a pleasant one, which was all Freddie had ever wanted.

If Phoebe thought his superstitions were silly, she never let on. She never questioned when he stepped around ladders or skipped class on Friday the 13th. He was a good enough student that it didn't matter, and in a stroke of good fortune, his instructors never gave exams on a Friday the 13th anyway.

As he reached the final week of classes before graduation, Freddie was carrying a perfect 4.0 GPA and poised to graduate summa cum laude. Because his school operated on a trimester system, the school year ended in late March, and a clear day with a cool breeze greeted him as he stepped out the door for his last day of school, confident that he would ace his final exam in advanced engineering design.

It was a Friday, but it was not the 13th.

The stars were aligned.

Almost as an afterthought, he patted his shirt pocket as he walked into the classroom… and froze.

Where was his lucky four-leaf clover?

He had left it at home!

Did he have enough time to retrieve it?

He always made sure to be early to class, so he might have just enough time.

Running back down the stairs that led to Briney Auditorium, he sprinted to his 10-speed bike and began pedaling like a madman back toward his apartment. Halfway there, he began panting. Yes, he was exerting himself, but he shouldn't be this out of breath. He felt his heart pound against his ribcage, as if in protest, and something told him he should slow down, turn back. His good luck charm wasn't worth it. He knew the material. He would ace the test anyway.

But maybe he was feeling out of breath *because* he didn't have the clover. Maybe once he got it, everything would be fine again.

He kept going, but each time his foot pressed down on one of the pedals, he felt a little worse. If this kept going, he wouldn't be *able* to turn back. Where was the point of no return? He didn't know.

He had to stop.

His body wouldn't let him keep going.

Yet he had to.

If he failed this test, he'd still graduate, but without that perfect GPA. And he had to be perfect, or everything would collapse.

He felt dizzy.

But he kept pushing.

Until...

The world spun and turned black. He vaguely felt his knee crack against the sidewalk, but feeling, sensation... everything was fading.

And.

Gone.

Paramedics arrived to find Freddie's lifeless body lying on the sidewalk next to his crumpled bike.

They found a four-leaf clover in one of his shirt pockets—the one he hadn't checked.

Time of death was listed as 1:45 p.m. Friday, March 26.

It was the 13th Friday of 1993.

Sharon Marie Provost

The Shining Night

In a quaint Bavarian village in the German Alps there lived a boy named Gunter... Gunter das Monster (Gunter the Monster), as he was known to the townspeople. He had earned that nickname through his wicked ways, which he had displayed since the young age of seven.

Gunter was difficult, to say the least. He was disruptive in class, a bully to all the other children, and destructive with school equipment. It seemed like nothing was safe from Gunter.

He would either break, vandalize, or steal every item he encountered.

Gunter's mother had to work multiple jobs to pay the school back for all the damage he caused. Worse still, she had to degrade herself by begging the school regularly to keep them from expelling him. Gunter's mother was a proud woman, whose self-worth was determined by her reputation amongst the townspeople as a hard-working Christian. She tried to pretend her heart was not hurt every time she heard the other women in town judge her parenting skills or seemingly threaten her precious son.

"Someday that boy will pay for what he has done, and it will be an awful sight to behold."

"She is so high and mighty, but someone needs to tell her how to raise a child properly."

Gunter heard them talk about him and his mother, but he couldn't be bothered to care what they said. He loved to torture the townspeople—young and old alike. He scared younger children with stories of monsters and ghosts, especially tales from local folklore, and threatened them with violence if they refused his demands. He knew these stories well because his own mother had used them for years to torment him for refusing to do his chores.

Gunter's mother doted on him. However, the stories she told him always warned that some evil entity—such as a witch, a wolf, or her favorites, Frau Perchta, or Krampus—would make him pay for his misdeeds.

Those warnings, however, had little effect.

Gunter still enjoyed tormenting every person he met, and more than anything, he enjoyed making his mother's life difficult. He knew she was a God-fearing woman, and that she worried about his soul. Yet he always managed to sneak away rather than attend church with her—to her great dismay. He never cleaned his room and rarely even attended to his own basic bathing and grooming. She often lamented that the barnyard animals in the village smelled better than he did, comparing his behavior to that of his "drunkard slob of a father," who had not been an influence, good or bad, in his life. The man had gone off one day into the mountains—drunk, as usual—to hunt. He had gone missing and was presumed dead when he never returned.

But his mother's dismay at Gunter's actions and her admonitions only irritated the boy.

Most annoying to him were her superstitious ways. She didn't just try to scare him with fairytales, she actually believed them: especially the local Christmas folklore regarding Krampus and Frau Perchta. To Gunter's utter embarrassment, she would stand outside church during the Yule season, admonishing the villagers—and especially children—to be kind and well-mannered, and reminding them of how important it was to keep their homes clean and their chores done. She even had a needlework decoration hanging in their home with the warning:

When Christmas draws near,
Kind, well-behaved children need not fear.
When slovenly, naughty children abound,
Krampus and Frau Perchta come round.

The Christmas season was Gunter's favorite time of year for two important reasons. The first was because he received many presents from his doting mother—both because she was afraid of him, and because he was her whole world. The second (and most fun for him) was because it gave him the chance to scare the other children and townsfolk.

On December 5th, better known as Krampusnacht or Krampus Night, he would run around town encouraging other children to misbehave with him, stealing food from the street fair, scaring old widows and spinsters, and vandalizing other villagers' homes.

His favorite malicious act was perpetrated on unsuspecting old ladies: He would knock on their door and run away around the corner so he could watch their reaction to finding a flaming bag of excrement he'd left upon their porch steps. When they screamed for help, fearing their homes might go up in flames, he would run back around and offer his own assistance... for a small fee. When they paid him, he would urinate on the bag to put out the flames and then stomp on it, spreading the mess across their meticulously cleaned porches before running off laughing.

After he had corrupted the other children with these misdeeds, he would terrify them by spewing stories of the terror, pain, and even death that Krampus and Frau Perchta could inflict upon them—the very same stories his mother used to torture him. He told them how Krampus, the horned half-goat, half-demon creature, would visit children that night with St. Nicholas and beat the naughty ones with birch rods. Sometimes, Krampus even took the worst children to hell with him or ate them.

Upon hearing Gunter's stories, many a child would run home on Krampusnacht, crying to their parents, confessing their wrongdoings while desperately looking for a way to repent.

Of course, Gunter's mother believed those stories too. She desperately tried to make him stay home and behave during the season to prevent Krampus from stealing her precious boy. But she was even more worried about Frau Perchta. Between Christmas and when Twelfth Night arrived on January 6th, she tried to ensure that the house was meticulously cleaned, that the flax was obtained and spun, and that a traditional bowl of porridge was left out for the Frau on that last night.

She tried to enlist Gunter's help in making sure the household chores were done to the Frau's satisfaction.

Gunter, however, delighted in evading all her efforts to protect him. Worse still, he even sought to undo what he viewed as her ridiculous attempts at saving them from Perchta's wrath.

Life in the village had shown him that there was no reason to worry about such "stupid" beliefs. Gunter never faced any consequences for any of his actions. On the contrary, his mother would still shower him with whatever gifts she could afford, especially at his birthday or Christmas.

Gunter's Uncle Otto—his mother's brother and the only other family he knew—was less understanding. He had come to the house for an overnight visit one evening before Christmas the previous year, and of course, he found Gunter up to his usual ways. The boy arrived late to dinner, even though he knew company was expected. He demanded his dinner as soon as he entered, without even saying hello to his weary mother or his uncle. When his uncle chided him for his bad behavior, he simply ignored the gruff old man and announced he was going to his room, without being properly excused from the table.

He did not, however, go to his bedroom.

Instead, he sneaked into *his uncle's* room, intent on finding some form of mischief to engage in as payback for his uncle's meddling. Rummaging through his uncle's bag by the bed, he found the man's most prized possession: a pocket watch from his dear departed wife. Gunter promptly threw it on the floor and ground it under his heel before picking it up again and carefully placing it back into the bag.

Later that night, he heard an angry cry when his uncle went to his room and found it. Moments later, the man stormed into his room and demanded that he confess to breaking it. But of course, Gunter lied straight to his face. He even had the guts to laugh at his uncle's reaction.

His uncle grabbed him by the scruff of the neck, prepared to "give him a beating he would never forget." As Gunter expected, he was saved when his mother ran in and begged her brother not to hurt him. She promised that Gunter would be properly punished the next day.

"Someday, you will get what's coming to you," his red-faced uncle had promised, warning him that Krampus would come for "evil little boys like him."

To his mother's dismay, his uncle immediately packed his belongings and swore he would never return to his sister's home again so long as "the devil's spawn" remained. As he stormed out of the house, he repeated his warning threateningly.

"Boy, one day you will go too far, and your mother will not be there to save you. You will rue the day you were born."

The year since then had gone as every other year had for Gunter, who was never held back in school, even though he barely passed any of his classes.

This time, he failed all of them—except for physical education. He liked to exercise and play. But even more to his liking, this particular class afforded him an opportunity to "accidentally" hurt other children in his zeal during games.

Yet despite his poor marks and violent behavior, he was promoted to the next grade as usual at the end of the year. His mother had overheard other parents discussing their theory that the school just pushed him through each year in an effort to be rid of him.

His instructors had tried everything they could think of to get him to behave, but they were not any more successful than his mother. At the start of the year, they had given him detention as punishment when he was caught doctoring another student's sandwich. Gunter hated Timmy because he was a "goody goody" who followed all the rules. He was the one kid Gunter could not convince to perform wicked pranks on other people. Gunter had been sent to the corner of the classroom to work alone after he was found berating Timmy during recess. Later, his instructor noticed him missing from his desk and found him putting Ex-Lax in Timmy's sandwich.

He went to the first two days of detention—just to see what problems he could cause—and, as usual, he was so disruptive and abusive that the teacher in charge finally threw up her hands and told him to go home. Nobody said anything when he did not return to the detention hall after that.

Gunter quickly learned that the harder he worked to make people hate him, the more he was shunned. And the more he was shunned, the more freedom he had to cause trouble. He had successfully alienated almost the entire town, and best of all, his meddlesome uncle had not returned to visit them since the previous year, just as he had promised. Not that he would have noticed, since he scarcely spent any time at home anymore.

One Sunday morning, however, he returned home and snuck in briefly to retrieve his slingshot, which he used to target store windows, other children, and small animals. He arrived to find his mother singing to herself as she busily cleaned their home.

As usual, she was off-key as she sang that ridiculous, oft-repeated tune. He'd heard it from her for as long as he could remember—although he had never heard anyone else sing it—and it always made him laugh:

Through wintertide we don our cloak
And toil beneath the wizened oak

Day by day and into night
When daystar yields to pale light

Inch by inch and speck by speck
We scour ev'ry niche and crack

In hearth and home we render clean
The shadowed places in between

Unfortunately for Gunter, on this occasion, he laughed just a bit too loud, and when his mother caught him, she dragged him to Sunday school. However, he was determined that he would not be forced to stay there. After hitting the Sunday school teacher, making multiple young girls cry, and tearing up a Bible, he was sent home. His mother was "advised" that, in the future, he should perform Sunday school Bible readings on his own at home.

Once again, the Christmas season arrived with a flourish.

Gunter was up to his usual tricks and faced no repercussions. Krampusnacht passed with no sign of Krampus there to punish him. Instead, St. Nicholas left him small gifts, nuts, and other goodies stuffed in his shoes, which he had left by the window. On December 24th, his mother bestowed upon him many wonderful presents, as she did every year.

Of course, he did not reciprocate or even bother to thank her.

Instead of being grateful for her generosity, he grew more and more irritated with what he considered her constant nagging. Each year, as he got older, she demanded that he do a bigger share of the household chores in preparation for Twelfth Night, warning him more fervently than ever about what Frau Perchta would do to him if he refused.

But Gunter had reached his breaking point when it came to his mother's absurd superstitions. He *knew* that Frau Perchta was just a story parents told their children, trying to instill a strong work ethic in them—or so they said. He was sure that parents really wanted an excuse to be lazy and get their children to do all the work for them! And he was even more sure that *no one* was going to punish him or anyone else on the "Shining Night" when the star of Bethlehem shone down.

This year, Gunter decided, her lies had to end. He was not going to do her bidding now... or ever. It was high time she realized that. This year, he would do everything in his power to end this farce once and for all.

If he couldn't make her stop, he would avoid his mother altogether. He left the house each morning before she rose and returned after she went to bed; in between, he spent his time causing trouble or playing in the hills.

He did no work at the house to clean it.

He did not help his mother prepare or spin their allotted flax.

He did not go shopping in the village so she could prepare the Twelfth Night porridge for Frau Perchta.

The day before the Frau was to arrive, he peeked in through the window at his mother and saw that she had nearly completed her cleaning. Having grown hungry from a day of mischief-making, he decided it was safe to go home for dinner that night.

Since she was finishing the last of the day's chores, there was no need to avoid her notice by sneaking past her, so he came in with a clatter, tracking mud in as he headed to the table. The stew was ready, piping hot on the hearth, so he helped himself without waiting for her to join him. As expected, she was singing that dreaded song of hers as she swept and dusted the last of the dirt from the shelves and baseboards, but this time, he noticed, there was something different.

Inch by inch and speck by speck
We scour ev'ry niche and crack

In heart and home we render clean
The shadowed places in between

"You sang it wrong. You said 'heart,'" Gunter called out to his mother with a sneer on his face.

"Mmm hmm." She didn't even look at him as she focused on her mopping.

The next day, Gunter's mother begrudgingly and fretfully completed all the remaining tasks, ensuring that nothing was out of place. She hoped if the house were sparkling clean, the porridge hot and delicious, and the flax spun perfectly down to the last straw, that maybe, just maybe the Frau would skip their house.

Gunter did not lift a finger to help her.

He was gone as usual.

And at the end of the night, she went to bed full of fear because he had not yet returned home.

It was near midnight when Gunter quietly stole into the house—and immediately set out to undo everything his mother had done to prepare for the night. He "forgot" to wipe his shoes and tracked more dirt into the house, which, of course, he didn't bother to sweep up. He burned all the spinning his mother had done. He disposed of the porridge promptly. (It was certainly delicious.) He put the bowl in the sink, caked in dried porridge, and splashed water on the counter as he poured himself a drink. He sprinkled flour all over the counters. In short, he did everything he could to dirty the immaculate house his mother had painstakingly cleaned.

He wanted to show her once and for all that the Frau was just a figment of her warped imagination. Besides, it was fun!

When he had done his worst, he prepared for bed, exhausted, and fell into a fitful sleep nearly instantly.

About an hour later, Gunter awoke to a rumbling like thunder and the sound of the wind wailing around the house. This seemed quite bizarre because the weather had been perfect when he went to bed a short time earlier. He shook his head and turned over, throwing a pillow over his head, and he had finally started to drift back to sleep when he heard a rustling sound... inside the house.

His mother never got up in the middle of the night.

For a moment, he was concerned. Then he chuckled quietly and decided it must be a rodent enjoying the fruits of his labor.

Or was it?

A moment later, he jumped and sat up straight in bed: He was sure he heard his name quietly whispered—no, hissed—in the hallway. That was no rodent, and it did not sound like his mother's voice. Once again, he suppressed the fear that was trying to creep up on him, allowing himself to lean back on his pillow. Surely, this must be one of his so-called friends (who were really his reluctant minions), trying to get back at him.

As he lay there, forcing himself to calm his breathing, he saw the doorknob start to turn.

His apprehension faded, turning to anger.

SOMEBODY dared to come into HIS room. This was really just too far. Who did they think they were? He would show them!

Gunter jumped up, ready to pound them into submission. He ran to the door and yanked it open, expecting to confront some neighborhood boy who'd snuck in to spook him. But he saw before him someone—a creature; an old hag in tattered rags with stringy black hair and a pale complexion that made her look barely human. She stared out at him through laughing, vacant eyes over a hooked nose as she balanced herself easily on the uneven floor, even though one foot was obviously larger than the other.

Gunter couldn't believe his eyes. Surely, he must be dreaming. It couldn't possibly be! Yet, it must be... it had to be! There, standing in front of him, was the exact image of Frau Perchta, just as he had heard her described so many times by his mother and others in the village.

She grinned at him threateningly.

Gunter backed away, tripping and falling back onto his bed.

The Frau lurched menacingly toward him. "You... you are the evil little boy I have heard so much about these past few years," she hissed.

Gunter stammered unintelligible guttural sounds as he shook his head back and forth vehemently.

"No! No, it is not me. I am a good boy," he whined.

"Then who made the mess in the kitchen and all through the house?" she demanded. "Who ate the hot, delicious porridge that your mother made for me? Why do I find ashes in the hearth, instead of freshly spun flax?"

"I didn't mean... I didn't know. I'm sorry. I won't do it again. I will be a good boy from now on. I will go clean..."

"Stop! I don't want to hear it! Lies... it is all lies," Frau Perchta declared.

She advanced on him menacingly, brandishing a long, sharp blade as Gunter mewled hopelessly. He rocked back and forth like a toddler as his eyes glazed over, realizing his fate was sealed. The neighbors later recalled hearing grunts and cries of pain issuing forth from the house, but they were much too afraid to investigate. Everyone knew this was the night that the Christmas witch Frau Perchta rode through the skies, so they barred their doors and stayed inside.

A short while later, the rumbling and wailing winds receded, and the oppressive darkness that had surrounded the home lifted.

It was early the next morning when Gunter's mother crept down the hall to her son's room. She was sure Frau Perchta had paid them a visit, yet she herself had escaped the Frau's wrath. She could envision in her mind's eye what terrors the Frau might have visited on her beloved son.

But any horrors one might have imagined could not compare to the sight she beheld when she opened the door to his room. There, propped up on the bed, was her beautiful boy. His now-lifeless body had been disemboweled; his organs and entrails lay spread out across the bed. In their place, the night visitor had stuffed his abdomen with straw and small pebbles, leaving it open for the world to see the intruder's frightful handiwork. His hand clutched a small note with a single word written across the top: "Slovenliness." Scrawled at the bottom was the signature of Frau Perchta, along with a short postscript: "Krampus sends his regards as well."

Gunter's mother ran to the door, and the whole village heard her cry out for help. Women ran to her side as she broke down sobbing and told them her worst fears had been realized.

"Why didn't he listen? Why?" she sobbed as they took her into their arms.

She had warned him so many times. She had done everything she could to keep him on the proper path; to dissuade him from the evildoing that could only have ended the way it did... just as it had for his father.

The men in the village helped remove Gunter's body and took him to be prepared for burial.

Once they had carted him away, his mother's demeanor immediately calmed, and she began to re-tidy her home. She started a fresh pot of porridge on the hearth as she worked, humming her familiar tune. The villagers in the town were bewildered by her stoic behavior, but they chalked it up to shock. They left her in the capable arms of her brother, who had just arrived unexpectedly.

Everyone in the village learned a lesson that year, especially the children. No one wanted to be the next victim of Krampus or Frau Perchta. Likewise, though, no one mourned the loss of young Gunter, except for his mother.

Or did she?

Stephen H. Provost

Let's Make a Deal

Andrea Beecher sat in an uncomfortable chair that she didn't notice was uncomfortable. Her full attention was on the hospital bed next to her, and the prone body of her husband Mark, motionless except for the slow rise and fall of his chest. That sight, together with the sound of the heart monitor's rhythmic beeping, gave her an excuse to hope. A poor excuse, but an excuse nonetheless. Hope against hope.

It was the night before Christmas, and if you couldn't have hope at Christmas, when could you?

But this certainly was not how she envisioned spending Christmas: hoping against hope and crying. She felt guilty about the crying, because she was supposed to be staying strong in her faith for Mark. She owed him that much, and she owed it to the Lord. Mark had been her first love, and despite their problems on and off over the years, she still loved him with the love of the Lord—and with the desperation of someone who didn't know what she would do without him.

He'd been the breadwinner, the head of the household under the Lord.

But now she looked over at him, and he seemed so different. So meek. So helpless. Mark had been in a coma for nearly three weeks now since the accident. He'd fallen off a ladder working on a power line in the foothills north of Fresno, and he'd somehow managed to survive. But his head had been caved in, and the doctors had detected only minimal brain activity.

Piped-in Christmas music wafted in over the hospital speakers. She recognized the tune: "Blue Christmas" by Elvis Presley, but this instrumental version didn't do it justice. It wasn't the same without the King's voice. "...without you..."

She looked up at the man in the white robes. His nametag read Dr. Bernie Singh. She hadn't seen him before—he just happened to be the one making the evening rounds this night, when her regular doctor was home carving up ham for his family at Christmas Eve dinner. But Singh was just like her regular doctor, and just like all the rest: a man of little faith. Or none.

"So he's not brain dead," she told him.

Singh shifted his weight uncomfortably from one foot to the other. "Well... not technically, but..."

"That's all I need to know. He's going to be fine. The Lord said it, and I'm claiming it!"

"I'm sorry, ma'am, but I have to be honest: Keeping him alive isn't doing him any good at this point. He won't come out of it. There's just no way he's going to survive. The respirator is doing all the work for him. It's just as alive as he is at this point."

"Miracles can happen. Remember the Christmas star?"

"We deal in science, Mrs. Beecher."

"Well, I deal in love. This man is the love of my life." Her voice rose. "He's the only man I've ever loved. God brought us together, and I'm not letting you kill him."

Dr. Singh, shook his head and muttered something he didn't think she could hear under his breath. But she had good ears.

"He's already dead."

"No, he's not."

The voice wasn't Andrea Beecher's. It came from somewhere behind Dr. Singh, but Andrea couldn't see anyone there, and Singh himself didn't respond to it.

"He can't hear me. This is only for you."

Andrea craned her neck, trying to look past Dr. Singh. All she could see was the plastic green wreath, decorated with just-as-plastic red holly berries, that stood over the doorway.

"I'm sorry," Dr. Singh was saying. "The decision is yours. We'll check back on him again in 12 hours."

Of course, the decision is mine. I'm his WIFE!

But she chastened herself at the thought. The decision wasn't hers, it was God's. And God had told her he would live.

Singh turned and left the room, tapping his pen against a clipboard in an annoying fashion. He was just the doctor on duty; Andrea had never even seen him before. *How dare he tell me my husband is dead. He's still breathing. His heart is still beating. And that heart belongs to me!*

Andrea was about to turn around when she caught sight of a movement where the doctor had been. Then the movement coalesced in her vision, becoming the form of a tall man dressed anachronistically in a top hat and long, black flowing robe with tails. He wore a set of old-fashioned pince nez spectacles—the kind that clipped onto his nose, holding them in place without the benefit of ear extensions. A pale yellow tinge ringed his dark eyes, as though he had jaundice. But otherwise, he looked perfectly healthy. His chin was free of whiskers, but his face was framed by mutton chops that were full but failed to distract from the impression that he was impeccably groomed.

And he had an odor of lavender about him.

He wore a long black coat with tails and carried a dark brown cane with a white tip on the end that made it look like a cigarette—a resemblance that repelled her. She hated cancer sticks, as she called them. They had killed her mother. And smoking was a sin. She scowled at that, but part of her almost wanted to laugh: The character in front of her reminded her of the snack-food mascot, Mr. Peanut.

She shoved both thoughts from her mind and focused as she sat up straighter and folded her hands in her lap, gripping one tightly in the other.

"Excuse me? Who are you and what are you doing here?"

Visiting hours were over, and she herself had only been allowed to stay because of her husband's dire condition. The hospital staff were sure they could persuade her to "pull the plug," and they wanted to act like they cared enough to let her be there when the curtain fell. That's what she surmised, anyway.

The man tapped his cane against the side of Mark's bed, and she thought she saw him jump.

Just my imagination, she assured herself.

He bowed slowly, as though savoring the motion. *Odd*. "My name is Luke," he said in a clipped voice that told her he wasn't interested in sharing his surname. "As to what I am doing here, I have come to save your husband's life—if you will allow me."

Her heart jumped in spite of her. Could this mysterious man be an angel of God? Like the archangel who told Mary she was pregnant, or announced Jesus' birth to the shepherds near Bethlehem.

But that was impossible... wasn't it?

"Are you a doctor?"

Luke chuckled, "No, my dear. No. He is beyond the reach of medicine. The good Dr. Singh admitted so himself. It is an admirable thing for a human to know his own shortcomings."

Or give up.

She chastened herself again and remembered the words of Jesus: "O ye of little faith." She had to have faith. She HAD to. She'd been reciting Bible verses in her head, trying to remind herself of God's mercy; that with him, all things were possible, but she found herself wavering despite all that. *Lord, I believe; help my unbelief.*

"One must know when to give up," Luke said, opening his palms outward. Was the gesture an apology or an invitation?

"I am not giving up," Andrea declared. How had he known what she was thinking?

"Nor am I," Luke said cheerfully—too cheerfully considering the circumstances. "As I said, I have come to save your husband's life. I'd hardly call that giving up."

Andrea let out a sigh. He was talking in circles, and she had no time for it. She wasn't giving up, but she wasn't about to let the man give her false hope that *he*, in particular, could help her. That was God's place. Unless he was an angel sent by God, she didn't see how he could help her. Then again... maybe he knew someone who could. Maybe that's what he was getting at.

She fixed him with a piercing glare through narrowed eyes. "How?"

He answered his question with one of his own. "May I sit?"

She said nothing, but he did anyway, fetching the other chair in the room and pulling it up next to her, rather too close for her liking. She also didn't appreciate the fact that she had to look at him sidelong, rather than directly in the eyes. As a woman of discernment (her pastor had told her she had this gift), she prided herself on her ability to read people—and she preferred to have those people in front of her.

Luke rested his hand on hers, and despite her initial revulsion, she didn't pull away. Could a touch be both comforting and disturbing at the same time?

His was.

Like an angel's.

"Who are you?" she asked again.

He smiled. "Have you ever read Dickens? 'A Christmas Carol'?"

"Yes..." What was he getting at?

"You might perhaps know me as the Ghost of Christmas Yet to Come. I show people... possibilities. The way things will be if they continue in a certain way, and how they can be if the right decision is made."

"A ghost? Or a demon?" Andrea eyed him warily. She had been taught to believe that ghosts were merely Satan's minions in disguise, sent to tempt the living into sin.

"You believe in the Holy Ghost."

She nodded.

"Well, there is a ghost with a grand reputation!"

She had to admit he had a point, but the Holy Ghost wasn't exactly *that* kind of ghost.

Luke was tapping his cane on the railing of Mark's bed in a hypnotic rhythm, and when she looked back over at Mark, she would have sworn she saw him twitch again.

"Despite your faith, you are worried your husband will die. Admit it." Luke tapped his cane abruptly on the hospital floor; it struck with a CRACK! and produced an echo that circled the room.

She didn't answer.

"I have faith," he continued. "I can show you a different future than the one you fear—one in which your husband will live, just as the Lord intends. I am, if you will, the instrument of the Lord in this matter."

She still didn't say anything. He was confusing her now. Was he a ghost? Or an angel? Or something else entirely?

"Tell me," Luke said, looking straight ahead as he sat alongside her, "would you give your life to save your husband's?" He said it casually, as though he were asking her what her favorite cocktail was.

She didn't hesitate. "Of course." How could she say anything else? She was terrified of death, and Mark had always insisted that she couldn't live without him—that if he were to die before him, her life would become meaningless. She knew he meant it. They were *that* close—or he was that controlling.

Satan, get behind me! Mark said that because he loves me! We are meant to be together, as God has ordained.

She balled both fists up. She was a warrior of God.

But still she questioned... Whatever Mark had intended, people said things they meant in the moment and later came to regret because time or changing circumstances made them think differently. People did get divorced... though they weren't supposed to.

She clenched her fists tighter. *What God has joined together...*

But regardless of any of this, she *had* to say she'd die for Mark. It was the socially expected response to say you would die for your spouse, especially when you were talking to a stranger... and Luke certainly was strange.

"I can make that happen," he said matter-of-factly.

She turned to him, "Excuse me?"

"I can save Mark's life if you allow me to take yours."

She just stared at him. "You want to kill me?"

He laughed. "It is not what *I* want that matters, but what *you* want. If you want your husband to live, the price must be paid. 'Thine eye shall not pity, but life shall go for life.' So it is written."

"So you can't just have pity on him and save his life?"

"Correct."

"Says who? That's in the Old Testament. What about what Jesus did? He healed the lepers and made the blind to see without ever requiring anything of them."

"Except their faith."

She didn't know what to say to that. She was too embarrassed about her own lack of faith, and now that he'd said that, it worried her even more.

"You believe in God. Believe also in me," Luke said. She recognized he was quoting Jesus, but applying it to himself. That was either blasphemy, or...

"Why should I?"

"Because I'm your only hope."

She looked at him, unsure, trying to read his eyes. But it was as though she were looking right through him.

"God gave his own firstborn son for you. Abraham offered up his only son on Mount Moriah. Will you not, in this same way, give yourself as an offering for your husband?"

She considered.

"OK," she said at last. "If you bring Mark back and the doctors give him a clean bill of health, *then* you can kill me." She looked at him expectantly, certain she knew what he would say. And sure enough, he said it.

"It doesn't work like that. *You* would have to die *first*. The universal life force must be replenished before it can be drawn from anew."

What kind of mumbo-jumbo was that? "Universal life

force?" That certainly was *not* in the Scripture.

She pulled her hand away. "How convenient for you. I wouldn't be around to see that you followed through on your end of the bargain... which, of course, you won't because you can't. Get behind me, Satan. I won't be gaslit by some sadistic bastard." She clapped her hand to her mouth. She *never* swore. But she was angry, and she didn't like being played.

Luke stood up and bowed to her. "As you wish," he said, then took two steps to the door.

The piped-in music changed to "Grandma Got Run Over By a Reindeer."

"Good riddance," she said under her breath and turned back to look at Mark. His chest was still rising and falling. The heart monitor was still beeping in regular time. She must have imagined that he'd moved earlier when the stranger had tapped his cane against the railing on his bed.

But then, she heard the stranger's voice again. "There *is* another way."

She stood and spun around to face him, her hands balled up into fists. "If you don't leave right now, I'll call security."

He laughed that easy laugh of his and said, "Go ahead. If that's what you really want to do."

This was getting exhausting. Andrea hadn't slept in nearly 20 hours, and she had no energy for further confrontation. Despite herself, she found herself asking him, "OK, *Luke*. What's your alternative?"

"I can take someone else's life instead."

She did a double-take. Was he serious? Murder was a sin.

Still, she asked: "Whose?"

"Does it matter?" he said. "Someone who has crossed me in the past and whose life I would like to end. A sinner."

Andrea crossed her arms in front of her. "We're all sinners,

Luke."

There was a beep, and a voice came over the intercom. "Code blue. Doctor Nye to ICU, stat."

At that very instant, an idea came to her. Andrea pointed. "There." She said. "Whoever that is is probably going to die. You can take that one and save my husband."

"It doesn't work that way."

"Of course it doesn't." She smiled ruefully. "You just want an excuse to kill someone so you can implicate me if they catch you. Either that or you're just an agent of the devil trying to play with my mind." She wasn't honestly sure which it was.

But nothing she said seemed to faze him.

"They won't catch me," he said. "And I won't leave a shred of evidence tying anything to you. You have my word."

She shook her head slowly, and he shrugged.

"Suit yourself. I will leave you in peace and leave your husband to die."

He said it so nonchalantly that it was a shock when, for the first time since she'd been standing watch over Mark, the heart monitor skipped a beat. The beeping turned irregular. Mark's body shuddered, then convulsed so violently that the breathing tube was jarred loose.

He began gasping for breath as though he were drowning.

Andrea gasped herself—in panic.

"Doctor! Nurse!" she yelled. She pressed frantically on the help button at the end of the cord wrapped around the bed railing, then ran out into the hallway; fortunately, several members of the medical staff were passing by, and they all changed course to rush through the door ahead of her and attend to Mark. They didn't seem to notice the formally attired stranger in the center of the room who... suddenly wasn't there.

Andrea didn't have time to wonder where he'd gone. Her

entire attention was focused on Mark as she stood straight, her back pressed hard against the far wall.

"Oxygen!"

"Get that tube back in."

"He's not responding."

"Keep trying."

"We're losing him..."

Andrea heard a snap, and everything froze. The doctors. The heart monitor. Mark's chest. Everything. It was like someone had hit the pause button on reality.

But her eyes could still move. She shifted them to one side and saw Luke standing there, nodding. Somehow, he wasn't affected.

"Now is the time to choose," he said. "Ten seconds from now, your husband will be dead. Unless you act. Unless you do what I have asked of you and give your consent for me to end another's life. Then his will be saved. I give you just one warning: While I will leave no evidence to link you to my deed, I must inform the victim's family that you were responsible for his... or her death."

What if they decide to come after me?

She couldn't move her mouth. It was just a thought. But he answered her: "You told me before that you would gladly die for Mark. Were you lying?"

No.

"Then you have nothing to fear, now, do you?" He smiled at her restless anxiety. "But rest easy, my dear. I won't allow anyone to touch you."

How could he possibly give her such an assurance? She didn't know, but she did know that he had somehow stopped time to present her with this option. Horrible as it was, it was her only hope of saving Mark.

She had to take it.

"OK," she said, "but..."

Luke vanished, and time resumed. The heart monitor started beeping again—regularly. And before the doctors could insert the breathing tube again. Mark's chest was rising and falling again, and rising. And rising... *My God! He's sitting up!*

His eyes were open, blinking, and he was looking around, awake and alert. The doctors stepped back from the bed in shock. "It's a miracle," one of them whispered.

Mark ignored them, his eyes searching until he found Andrea, still pressed against the far wall. He lowered the bed railing and swung his legs out over the edge to stand in a single fluid motion. Then he rushed over to her and took her in his arms, kissing her gratefully as he stroked her hair.

"God, I thought I'd lost you," he said, his voice filled with relief.

She just laughed an exhausted laugh of disbelief. "I think that's my line."

She took his face in her hands and kissed him back.

The guard entered the cell with a banana split and a large slice of white cake, topped with heavy cream frosting. It wasn't the typical prison meal, but this wasn't the typical occasion. Prisoners awaiting execution got to choose their final meal, and Andrea Juliet Beecher, convicted murderer, had chosen this one.

She'd been sentenced to death because the case had been clearcut and the crime especially heinous. Mark Beecher's mistress, Samantha Duncan, had been found butchered and mutilated in her own bed—a picture of her and her lover naked in a lewd embrace clutched in her hands. Those hands, it was true, had been severed from the arms and placed on the dresser across the room. Her head was propped up in the bathroom sink, eyes gouged out, vacant holes staring straight forward.

Her feet were in the doorway.

Her intestines had been pulled out and lain on top of her torso.

Samantha Duncan, ten years younger than her paramour, had met him by chance at a bus stop in Midtown after work one Thursday afternoon. Andrea had been away on her annual "girls' night sleepover" with her friends from high school, who got together once every year, and Mark had taken the opportunity to have a sleepover of his own. He'd seduced Samantha, or maybe it was the other way around, with margaritas and flattery before they'd done the deed in the first of what became many rendezvouses over the course of the next six months.

Andrea never knew a thing about it. She said so on the witness stand, but under cross-examination, she'd confessed she didn't remember where she'd been on the night of the murder. It was the truth, but it didn't sound good. There'd been a reason her lawyer had advised her not to testify. But she knew she'd be acquitted. There wasn't any evidence. Luke had assured her there wouldn't be, and she'd believed him. After the way he'd brought Mark back from the dead, how could she not?

But there *had* been evidence: enough to convict and then some.

"You lied to me," she told the guard, resigned.

Luke just smiled back at her. "I did no such thing."

"You told me you wouldn't leave any evidence tying me to the crime; that you wouldn't allow them to touch me."

He nodded patiently. "And that was the truth. They never did touch you, did they? And I didn't leave any evidence. He did."

"Who?"

"The killer, of course."

"But I thought you..."

"Come now, my dear, do you really think I'm stupid enough to do such a thing myself? True, they couldn't hold me, but it's fun to see what you can get away with, don't you think?"

She shuddered and began sobbing. She'd entered into this sick agreement to save a man she thought she loved, but who had betrayed her in the worst of ways. And now she was paying the ultimate price for it.

Where was God in all this? Where was his justice? Where was his mercy?

Luke sat next to her and put an arm around her. It felt cold. She was too shaken and defeated to care. "There, there, dear. You said you would give your life for him, and that's exactly what you are doing. You should be happy. Mark is alive because of you. You saved his life, and that vile bitch Samantha Duncan is the only one who was sacrificed. You can't pretend you're sorry she's dead."

Andrea started crying harder. It came in waves.

She felt sick.

She retched and vomited—right into the banana split. She didn't care. She couldn't eat it anyway. She picked up the slice of cake and threw it at Luke, but it splattered against the wall of the cell and slid down to the floor, leaving a trail of white frosting on the wall. Luke was gone. Had he ever even been there? Did it even really matter?

Postscript: Andrea Beecher died the next day of lethal injection, unaware that the real murderer had been caught. He was tried and convicted a few months later, and received the same fate as she had. Samantha Duncan had tried to blackmail him with a nude picture of them together in a compromising position, and he had responded by butchering her.

His final meal was steak and potatoes. The same guard who had brought Andrea her cake and ice cream took it to him on the night before his death. He didn't know the man and was puzzled to see his face pressed against the glass of the execution chamber, smiling at him as he breathed his last.

Mark Anthony Beecher died a year to the day after he was supposed to, on the night before Christmas. They didn't usually conduct executions on Christmas Eve, but they made an exception in his case: The crime he'd been convicted of was so heinous, the man who administered the lethal injection—a Southern Baptist—insisted on doing so "as a service to God and his people.

Luke smiled to himself as he saw the needle prick the man's skin. Sometimes it was worth the wait, he thought to himself. An eye for an eye was fine for people who believed in God, but he was no believer—and certainly no angel. To his way of thinking, it was better when you got a twofer.

He could have asked for no more satisfying gift at Christmas.

Sharon Marie Provost

The Last Train to Clarksville

Sabrina rubbed her temples as she stared out the window of her room at the bed and breakfast, trying to understand what she was feeling. This was supposed to be a simple vacation to unwind and have fun before her life got more complicated. Instead, her life—her feelings—had become just that: more complicated than ever.

Sabrina had had her life all planned out since she was ten years old. To say she was dedicated and hardworking—one might even say single-minded in her determination—was an understatement. She'd had her career picked out by the time she was ten, and she dove into her pursuit of that dream headfirst. She didn't spend her time socializing with other children, and she did not have time for frivolous dates in her teenage years.

Boys were just a distraction. The only extracurricular activities she pursued after her schoolwork were those she thought would help her get into the perfect undergrad program… and then the right medical school.

Her mom had been diagnosed with stomach cancer when Sabrina was only five. She didn't have a fun-loving, playful, cookie-baking mother like the other young girls at school. That's not to say that her mother didn't love her and spend endless hours of quality time with her: They read books together, watched educational TV shows, discussed Sabrina's future, and delved into all her little girl dreams, some silly and others surprisingly focused.

Her mom was often tired, nauseated, and in pain. She just didn't have the energy to do all the physical activities that most mothers did, but that was fine with Sabrina because she loved their discussions. It made her feel like an adult, mature and wise, when they talked about life.

All that changed though, when her mother passed away shortly before her 10th birthday. Sabrina had never felt so out of control, and she hated that feeling. There should have been some way to save her mother. The doctors just hadn't thought of it. If Sabrina had been in charge, things would have been different, she was sure.

Her father was a good parent, but he was overwhelmed with his grief, busy at his corporate job, and had no idea how to connect with his daughter the way her mother had. Sabrina's feeling of helplessness and guilt over not being able to save her mother, along with her further isolation, fed her strong-willed determination to excel in school and in pursuing her career. A relationship and children were never in her plan for the future.

Now, she feared all these plans were in jeopardy. She was on track to graduate summa cum laude in the spring with a degree in biology and a pre-med emphasis. She'd been accepted to the best medical school in the country, where she was set to start in eight months. In just a week, during winter break, she was about to start a highly sought-after two-week externship with Dr. Stephens, the head of the Emergency Department at the hospital that worked in tandem with the medical school. This would be an excellent opportunity to make connections and get a leg up on her studies. With any luck, she'd resume working with Dr. Stephens in the summer before she started medical school.

The last thing in the world she had time for was a relationship. But yet, she was contemplating just that. And not just a relationship, but a serious long-distance one. How could this have happened? What was she thinking? Just as important, did he feel the same way? They—or at least she thought both of them—had just experienced the best week of their lives.

"Soulmates" had always seemed like such a stupid concept. It was simply people deluding themselves into thinking they had found their perfect match.

Yet here she was thinking about soulmates.

It had all started last week when she boarded the train to Clarksville. She had always loved trains, so she'd planned a two-day trip by rail to her childhood friend's B&B for some much-needed relaxation. She had paid for a private sleeper car, but there had been a glitch in the reservation system. So instead, she had been booked to share a car with another passenger.

She had protested at first, but the man seemed so nice and desperate to make this trip now.

He boarded the train with his belongings in hand and sheepishly poked his head into the car.

"Miss, where would you like me to stow these? I promise not to be a bother. I really appreciate you letting me share this car with you. I have a lot on my mind right now, and this is my last chance to get away before everything changes."

Sabrina looked up at him. "I was thinking we could each take a side so we can stretch out tonight, and we each get a window that way to see the scenery. So put your belongings anywhere you want across from me. Does that work for you?"

"Yes, Miss. Thank you again. By the way, my name is Jeremiah."

"Nice to meet you, Jeremiah. I am Sabrina."

Both of them settled in quietly and began to read, Jeremiah perusing the *New York Times* and *Wall Street Journal* while Sabrina reviewed her emergency procedures book. Sabrina soon realized they were both spending more time enjoying the scenery than reading.

After a while, Jeremiah excused himself, and before long, Sabrina's curiosity about the train grew—as did her appetite—so she decided to explore a bit before heading to the dining car. She walked the length of the train and spoke briefly with the conductor before stopping in the lounge car. Its large, beautiful windows were perfect for sightseeing, so she decided to stop and have a drink while enjoying the view.

Sabrina ordered a Cosmopolitan from the bar and got a candy bar from the snack bar before she sat down to enjoy the scenery as the train wound its way through the rolling fields. She could just see the mountains in the distance and hoped they would reach them before nightfall. She was trying to identify the many birds she saw flying through the field when she was startled by a voice behind her.

"Would you like some company?"

She looked up to see Jeremiah standing beside her with a beer in hand. She smiled brightly and said, "Sure. That would be lovely."

He sat down across from her. "What are you looking at?"

"I was just doing some bird watching. My mother and I used to do that on weekends—before she got too ill, that is. Uhh... those mountains in the distance are absolutely gorgeous. I hope we reach them while the sun is still out."

"I do hope your mother is better," Jeremiah said. "I wish my parents had spent time with me like that."

Sabrina looked down quickly as a tear slid down her cheek. She turned her head back to the window and carefully wiped it away. Then she met his eyes slowly and said, "My mother passed away from cancer when I was a child."

"I am so very sorry. That was stupid of me to say. Please excuse me," Jeremiah said hurriedly as he moved to get up.

"No, no, no. Don't be ridiculous. You couldn't have known. You were just being polite. Let's talk about you a little. You said when you arrived that you had a lot on your mind and things were about to change. What did you mean—that is, if you don't mind me asking?"

"Well, I just graduated with my master's degree in architecture. I am all set to start at my father's firm next month. But first, I'm taking this trip to clear my head. I have some big decisions to make that will affect my entire future."

"Wow. What kind of big decisions?"

"My family is old money. They have certain expectations about where I work, who my friends are, who I will marry and when... even where I'll live. I have been dating the daughter of my father's best friend since sophomore year of undergrad. Don't get me wrong. Amber is a very sweet girl, beautiful and giving. She will make a wonderful wife... but not for me. We just have different plans in life. She is ready to settle down, have children, and join the boards of local charities. I am serious about my career, but I want to live too. I want to explore the world, ride trains, spend time with friends, and eventually have the 'white picket fence.' My family has already picked out the house they want to gift us as a wedding present. As I said, my start date at my father's firm has already been chosen, but it took a lot of cajoling to negotiate that precious month of freedom. My parents think I just have cold feet, so I'm taking this time to prepare for my engagement. I don't want to disappoint my family, but I'm not sure that I am ready to accept that life. God, look at me going on and on. I'm sure I am boring you. I apologize."

Sabrina felt for him. She could see the stress on his face. Oddly enough, she found she could understand his feelings even though she was on a direct, career-driven path. She wasn't interested in traveling and spending time with friends, but at the same time, she didn't want to be saddled with a spouse and children. She couldn't bear the thought of someone interfering with her path in life.

"I am very sorry, Miss... uh, I mean Sabrina. I don't know what is going on with me today. I'm not usually so talkative, or open, but I just feel so comfortable with you: this instant connection that I can't explain. Shit! Now I just sound stupid, or better yet, creepy. I will just shut up now. I appreciate your kindness in listening to me. I should go."

"Wait! It is OK, really... Now, I should try some of that open honesty. It is more than just OK. I feel the same way. Do I seem like the kind of person who just lets strangers, let alone men, stay in my private sleeper car? I just had this sense about you. Please, sit down and relax."

Jeremiah settled back in his seat with a small smile on his face. Sabrina was looking down, trying to hide the bright red blush on her face.

"Thank you. I appreciate your kind words. Now why don't you tell me more about yourself."

"Well, I just want to say that I don't blame you for your reluctance to follow your family's plan. I'm very independent myself, and I want to make my own decisions about life. While I am very different than you when it comes to my life plan, I would not accept anybody making plans for me."

"How is your plan different?"

"Well, for starters, I will be graduating with my bachelor's degree in biology this spring. I've already been accepted into my dream medical school, and I will be starting in the fall. Next week, I begin a short externship over the winter break that will resume over the summer. My goal is to graduate top of my class, pass my boards in the 90th percentile, become Chief Resident and, ultimately, the youngest Chief of Emergency Medicine in the history of the hospital. I'd love to do research and publish in medical journals. With all that, I just don't have time for a relationship or a family. I am a very career-oriented person."

"I can see that. I don't think I have heard of anyone planning so far ahead in such detail. I respect that though. You know what you want, and you don't intend to let anyone, or anything, get in your way. Does your family support you? "

"My father and grandparents tell me that "every person needs someone to love and support them." They think I will live to regret my decision, and by then, it will be too late to start a family. My father finds it hard to discuss serious topics; he always left that to my mother when I was young. My grandparents just want me to be happy, so they will support me no matter what. That doesn't mean that they don't periodically express their opinion, hoping I will change my mind. I just feel strongly that you should be able to choose how you want to live your life. If traveling and spending time with friends enjoying life is what gives you pleasure, then you should pursue that. You didn't say you're opposed to marriage or a family, just not now and not with her. That is your right."

Jeremiah smiled brightly, showing a genuine sense of relief. He took a deep breath before quietly asking if Sabrina wanted to join him for dinner in the dining car. Sabrina readily agreed: She was utterly famished after such a deep but satisfying conversation. Besides, she wanted to spend more time with Jeremiah.

They each ordered a rib-eye steak, medium-well; loaded baked potatoes (minus the butter); and broccolini. They enjoyed a bottle of Cabernet Sauvignon while they waited for dinner to arrive.

"This will sound silly, but I was shocked when our orders matched," Sabrina said.

Jeremiah laughed heartily and exclaimed, "You mean the butter."

Sabrina nodded her head eagerly.

"Whenever I order my potato that way, people always comment, 'Who doesn't like butter? Who doesn't want butter on their baked potato?' Me, that's who! The butter takes away from the flavor of the sour cream, cheese, and bacon. If I am having a regular baked potato, then butter, and lots of it, is great."

"But loaded is different. I totally agree."

Before they knew it, the hour was late, and the dining car serving staff was cleaning up for the night, so Sabrina and Jeremiah retired to their sleeper car to continue their conversation. Neither one of them was tired yet.

The topic of conversation ranged from politics to TV shows (their shared guilty pleasure lay in watching reality romance shows like 90 Day Fiancé and Married at First Sight) and even their favorite music (they both adored Fleetwood Mac and The Beatles).

They were fascinated by their many similarities, which they continued to explore as the conversation continued deep into the night. As they began to get tired, they set up bedding on their respective seats and continued enjoying each other's company: It was like an adult slumber party.

Sometime past 3, the conversation slowed naturally as they fought to keep their eyes open. Neither one knew who fell asleep first, but they both awoke shortly after 9 a.m. when they heard the other passengers moving noisily through the narrow passageway.

"Well good morning, Sunshine."

Sabrina giggled happily. "I have never had that much fun before. I didn't have many close friends as a child. I spent a lot of quality time with my mother, helping care for her until she passed when I was 10. Then I kind of retreated into myself and my schoolwork, so I just didn't create those bonds. I never had the slumber party experience with girlfriends like that, talking and laughing all night. Thank you very much!"

"Shall we get dressed and go get some grub?"

"Yes, please! I am so hungry I could eat a whole pig... all the bacon. In fact, I just might. In case you haven't noticed, I am a bit of a carnivore. I know, I know. Here I am studying to be a doctor, and I should know better about eating red meat. But come on! You only live once, and I will not settle for anything less. Down with the turkey bacon! That shit is not bacon. Please pardon my French."

Jeremiah burst out laughing. He seemed delighted with her sense of humor. She'd had fun last night, but she hadn't let herself go to this extent. He banged his fist on the armrest as he chanted, "Down with turkey bacon! Down with the faux piggyarchy!"

Sabrina danced around the small sleeper car, pumping her fist in the air, in rhythm to his chant. She giggled again, and then grabbed her toiletries and some clothes before heading to the bathroom to change quickly. When she returned, dressed in a teal pantsuit, her hair was perfectly coiffed, and her makeup subtle but flattering. She knew she looked as stunning as she felt, when she sensed, before she even saw, his gaze upon her. While she had been in the bathroom, he had quickly changed into Dockers, a white and teal-striped button-down shirt, and Skechers sneakers. They looked like a couple, and Sabrina found herself secretly happy about this observation.

They proceeded to the dining car happily, once again engrossed in learning about each other. They enjoyed mimosas at a table by the window as they devoured way too much bacon (extra crispy), scrambled eggs, and biscuits. Once again, their orders matched exactly. Morning passed into afternoon seamlessly, with only a change of location to the lounge car to mark the passage of time. They were so wrapped up in each other that they almost missed the announcement that they would be arriving in Clarksville at 7 p.m. A look of disappointment crossed both their faces as they contemplated their separation.

"Wow. That trip went by so fast. I appreciate you filling the time for me. So... what are your plans this week? Are you staying with a friend or one of the hotels in town?" Sabrina asked, trying to sound nonchalant.

"Oh, let me see. I don't have any specific plans. I was thinking about maybe ice fishing, exploring the town, maybe going on a hike, ice skating... everything, really. I'm staying at this little bed and breakfast... ummm, Fireside Lodge... no, Fireside Cottage."

Sabrina broke into a wide grin.

"That's my friend's place. I'm staying there, too. I don't have any specific plans myself, other than relaxing and having some fun for once. I just thought maybe you might want to hang out a little more—that is if you are interested. I was planning to go to dinner at a cozy, little restaurant my friend recommended, The Lakeside Café. Would you care to join me?"

Jeremiah nodded eagerly.

Both of them hurriedly repacked their suitcases, eager to resume their visit in town. They were the first ones in line to exit the train as it pulled into the station, where Jeremiah had scheduled an Uber to pick them up at 7:15. He loaded their bags into the trunk and jumped in after Sabrina. He reached down to lay his hand on the seat but accidentally placed it on hers instead. He was pleasantly surprised to find that neither of them pulled back.

Dinner seemed to pass in the blink of an eye, even though they were at the restaurant for more than two hours drinking wine and talking. They shared another Uber to the B&B, and he carried their bags up to the check-in desk.

Sabrina's friend Melanie looked up from behind the counter, shocked to see her standing there with a man. Sabrina ignored her friend's questioning looks and stepped back to let Jeremiah check in first. He signed the paperwork, grabbed his key, and then said an awkward goodnight before heading up the stairs.

Sabrina quickly told her friend she would explain everything in the morning and feigned sleepiness to speed up the process, then grabbed her bags and headed up the stairs to her room—which, she realized, was right across the hall from Jeremiah's. As she was unlocking the door, she heard his door open behind her. She hid her smile behind her hair as she realized he had been watching or listening for her.

Jeremiah held out a slip of paper as he said, "Here. I wanted to give you my number. Give me a call if you want to hang out."

Sabrina grabbed the paper in one hand and held out the other, as she asked for his phone. When he handed it to her, she quickly programmed her number into his contacts list.

"There. You can call me anytime. Have a good night."

She whisked herself away into the room, floating on air. She pressed her back to the door as she closed it and breathed deeply. Her head was spinning with all her thoughts about him... about them.

What the hell! Us. There can be no us. I have too much school to finish. A career to develop. Besides, he essentially has a fiancée. He can protest all he wants from the safety of his vacation. But could he... would he really turn his back on everything that was waiting for him back home?

Sabrina unloaded the contents of her suitcase into the bureau and laid out her toiletries on the bathroom sink. She was exhausted by the activity of the day and all the confusing feelings running through her body. She climbed into bed wearily and burrowed into a blanket cocoon. Her eyes had barely closed before she entered a restless sleep, interrupted by dreams of a life with Jeremiah.

Sabrina awoke early the next morning, knowing Melanie would pounce on her as soon as she had a free moment. She headed down to breakfast with a feeling of trepidation, and as she rounded the corner, she heard Melanie talking excitedly about her to someone.

She never expected that someone to be Jeremiah.

She walked up casually as if she hadn't overheard them. They both looked up sheepishly and said good morning.

Melanie quickly rose from the table and rushed into the kitchen, mumbling about getting her breakfast ready. Jeremiah stood up and gave Sabrina a hug, then held her chair as she sat down.

"I trust you slept well. Your friend has the most luxurious beds here. How are you this morning?"

"Oh yes, I slept fine," Sabrina mumbled, stifling a yawn. "How about you?"

Jeremiah nodded. Then he reached out and casually gripped her hand, smiling as her fingers curled around his.

"I was wondering if you would like to go for a hike around the lake in a bit. Then I thought maybe we could go ice skating afterward. I will ply you with hot chocolate and Bailey's," he offered with a wink.

"Well, you certainly know the way to my heart, or at least my stomach—the one who's really in charge. I would love to go. When and where shall we meet?"

"Why don't you eat your breakfast and catch up with your friend? Then go bundle up because it is quite chilly out there today. I will meet you in the lobby at noon. Sound good?"

"Yes, of course."

Jeremiah rose and bustled out of the room, a man on a mission it seemed. Just then, Melanie returned from the kitchen with a steaming plate of food. They quickly jumped into a rapid-fire discussion about their lives the past few months. They had met in their junior year of high school and quickly became friends. They were the kind of friends who might not interact for months but would pick up their conversation again as if they'd never skipped a beat.

Finally, the moment Sabrina had been dreading arrived.

"So....?"

"So what?"

"You know what. How did you meet Jeremiah? And when? What's the story? I want some tea... spill it."

"Oh, stop! There is no tea. We met on the train to Clarksville. There was a mix-up, and we were booked into the same sleeper car. We just enjoyed each other's company on the train, and then we went to dinner afterward. We're just friends."

Melanie nodded with a knowing smile as she said, "Sure."

Sabrina looked at her watch and was relieved to see it was time to get ready. She excused herself and jogged happily up to her room. She put on her thermals under her sweats, donned her coat, then grabbed a scarf, knit hat, and gloves, which she tucked into her coat pockets. She stuffed her wallet into the other coat pocket and zipped it closed. She headed down the stairs, gaining more pep in her step as Jeremiah came into view.

He held his arm out, and she accepted it readily. Arms linked, they headed out the door, and she was surprised to see a horse-drawn carriage sitting out front.

Jeremiah led her up to the steps to mount the carriage and stiffened his arm to support her as she climbed in. He climbed in beside her and reached across to the other seat, grabbing a blanket to spread across their laps—and revealing a beautiful bouquet of roses underneath, which he presented to her with a smile. Then he grabbed a metal thermos and two mugs that were tucked into a basket on the floor.

"I promised hot chocolate with Bailey's, did I not?"

He poured two steaming, full cups and handed one to her.

She closed her eyes and moaned, "Mmmmmm!"

The carriage lurched forward as the horses began pulling on the reins, and they arrived at the park entrance about twenty minutes later.

The day was a whirlwind of activity. Occasional snow showers fell, but a full canopy of large coniferous trees protected them on the path, which wove its way through the forest and around a lake.

As the afternoon skies cleared, they arrived at the pier on the far side. A small cabin near the shore advertised "Snacks, hot and cold drinks, kayaks, and winter sports equipment rentals." So they walked up to the pull-down window on the side, where Jeremiah rented two pairs of skates.

For the next two hours, they skated around the lake, at times racing each other, and at other times pretending they were Olympic pairs skaters. The laughs and merriment flowed freely. When they were done, they began the slow, romantic stroll back around the lake to catch their ride back to the B&B. For the return trip, the carriage driver chose a slower route over winding roads with trees looming overhead.

Sabrina leaned against Jeremiah's chest, her head on his shoulder, as she looked into his eyes, lost in deep conversations that drifted from one topic to the next. Jeremiah leaned down and kissed her softly, their lips grabbing each other and then slowly pulling apart. His hand caressed her cheek softly and then slipped into her hair behind her ear, softly pulling her face closer to his. He covered her face in soft kisses from the tip of her nose to the middle of her forehead. She wrapped her arms around him and pulled him close, turning her body to put her legs across his lap.

When the carriage came to an abrupt stop, they realized that they had arrived at the B&B. They climbed out, and Jeremiah tipped the driver before they walked inside, hand in hand, unable to break eye contact. Melanie saw them enter, but she left the room surreptitiously to avoid intruding. Jeremiah walked Sabrina to her room, then swept her into his arms, kissing her passionately, before bidding her goodnight. The perfect gentleman to the very last moment.

Sabrina drifted into her room in a fog and flopped on the bed with a sigh. She had never experienced a moment like this. She had only been on a few dates in her life—only at the insistence of a friend or family member, and never seriously. Was this love or simple infatuation? Whatever it was, she wasn't sure she wanted it to end. Exhausted by the day, she fell asleep where she had dropped, her mind filled with possibilities.

The next morning, she woke early, eager to get down to breakfast and see if Jeremiah was up as well. She dressed quickly and bounced down the stairs like a teenager. A huge smile spread across her face as she saw him sitting at the table, seemingly waiting for her arrival. He motioned her over immediately and rose to help her into her seat.

"How are you this morning, Beautiful?"

"Perfect. I am feeling absolutely perfect. How are you, fine sir?" she asked with a giggle.

"Great. What would you like to do today? Or, I'm sorry... do you have plans today already?"

"Just whatever you have planned for us. Umm... I mean... umm, that is, if you wanted to spend the day together," she stammered with a blush.

"Of course. I thought we would eat breakfast here. Then we can stroll through the downtown shopping district and catch some lunch at one of the restaurants there. They're having a Christmas festival today, with a tree lighting in the town square this evening at 7. We can go eat roasted chestnuts, drink hot chocolate until we're sick, make our own Christmas ornament or wreath... There will be carolers, games, ice skating in a rink they set up near the tree, and just about any other Christmas activity you could imagine in a quaint small town. I thought it might be fun." He said it all in a breathless rush.

Sabrina giggled, delighted by his enthusiasm.

"That sounds enchanting."

Melanie had been listening through the kitchen door and rushed to bring out their breakfast. They ate ravenously, in a rush to begin the day's activities. Sabrina ran upstairs to grab her coat and purse as Jeremiah ordered an Uber to take them into town. They waited in the lobby in the oversized armchairs by the fireplace as they watched for the car to arrive. Both of them were trying to play it cool, but anyone could see they were falling in love. The adoring looks on their faces as they stared at each other spoke volumes.

They rushed out to the car when it arrived, and Jeremiah opened the car door for her. She had never experienced such a polite man before. When they arrived downtown a short time later, they eagerly began Christmas shopping for their friends and family. Sabrina explained that she bought a special ornament for Melanie each year because Christmas and decorations meant so much to her. They went through every shop in town, each one cuter than the last, until they found just the right one: a small snow globe containing a house, that looked just like her B&B, complete with a welcome mat out front.

Their feet were tired, and they both needed a rest after their epic shopping spree, so they headed off to lunch at Rachel's Place. The menu was full of delicious-sounding home-cooked meals. After much discussion, they both ordered open-face hot turkey sandwiches with gravy and homemade cranberry sauce. Jeremiah excused himself, explaining that he wanted to run back to a store for a moment to pick up a present he had seen for his mother.

Sabrina was watching the snow fall out the window when she saw him coming back. But instead of returning to join her, he suddenly ducked into the jewelry store. She tried to suppress a pang of jealousy, worried that he might be buying a gift for his girlfriend back home. But when he came back a short while later, he wasn't carrying a bag from the jeweler, so she pushed it out of her mind.

He excitedly showed her his purchase, inspired by the ornament they'd chosen for Melanie. His mother had a collection of large snow globes on a shelf in the living room, so he'd bought her a light-up globe in the shape of a lantern with a scene from a town (which looked remarkably like Clarksville) decorated for Christmas. It swirled with snowflakes and iridescent glitter.

After lunch, Jeremiah found a bench near one of the fire pits set up throughout downtown for people to enjoy. They talked about how much they both loved the quiet, simple life they had found in Clarksville. Yet, it was only an hour's drive from a large city if they wanted more excitement or anything they couldn't find in town. The time passed quickly, and the cold set in, so

Jeremiah joined a large line waiting for hot chocolate at a food truck.

Sabrina quickly snuck away and ran into the store behind her. She had seen a fancy artist's valise with a set of professional-grade colored pencils, pastels, and a pen set in a carved wooden box displaying the train entering Clarksville. During one of their many conversations, he'd told her how much he enjoyed art—but that his father had discouraged him from pursuing it when he became a teenager. This gift would allow him to relax and explore his passion, and she just knew he would love it. She managed to get back to the bench before he noticed she had left.

The rest of the day they enjoyed all the activities throughout the square. They decided to make an ornament, rather than a wreath. Without even discussing it first, each of them made an ornament for the other. They skated on the ice rink hand in hand to the music of a live band. They played all the games, and Sabrina even beat him at cornhole. She had an uncanny aim with the beanbag. After the tree lighting, the main street closed and was transformed into a giant dance floor. They danced until they realized the music had ended some time ago and nearly everyone had departed.

Even then, they still weren't ready for the night to be over, so they walked hand-in-hand the mile back to the B&B.

They quietly entered the darkened building and made their way across the lobby and up the stairs. Jeremiah wrapped his arms around Sabrina as she hurriedly unlocked her door. They entered the room and immediately embraced, kissing each other hungrily. Tired as they were after the day's fun, they did not sleep that night, which they spent making love and lying in each other's arms. They whispered deep into the night, proclaiming their love for each other and making plans for the future.

Jeremiah would go home and explain that he was willing to work at his father's company for the next four or five years, but with stipulations: He would need time off to visit Sabrina at college and then medical school, and to travel the world as he dreamed. He would make him understand that Amber was a great girl, but not the one for him. He appreciated his parents' offer to buy them a home, but he wanted to marry Sabrina and buy their own home that they chose together. Most difficult of all, he would need to have that same discussion with Amber.

Sabrina made sure he understood the depth of her need for a serious career, which meant she might not ever want a family, or at least might need to delay it for quite some time. Jeremiah did want a family, if possible, but most important to him was a life with Sabrina. He was not in a hurry for a family anyhow. They finally fell asleep as dawn arrived, satisfied that they had charted out their future.

Around 9 a.m., Sabrina awoke to Jeremiah getting dressed. He told her to go back to sleep; that he would return in a short while. He needed to call his parents because he had looked at his phone and seen multiple missed calls from the night before. He was going to take a quick shower, get dressed, and make his call; then he would return with breakfast for both of them.

At noon, Sabrina woke again to the sound of the 12 resounding bongs from the grandfather clock down the hall. She was surprised to see Jeremiah had not returned. She dressed quickly and headed down to the lobby. Melanie had saved some breakfast for her, so she sat in the dining room, facing out toward the lobby, so she could see if Jeremiah came down. Melanie hadn't seen him all day, so Sabrina became a bit concerned. She spent the next several minutes regaling Melanie with stories of the magical few days she had just spent with him. She looked up, laughing, when Jeremiah entered the room, but her smile faded at the grim look on his face.

Melanie excused herself quickly as Jeremiah approached.

"What's wrong? Are you OK?" Sabrina asked as she jumped up to embrace him.

"Please sit down. We need to talk."

Sabrina slumped in her chair, tears already forming in her eyes.

"My father had a heart attack."

"Oh my God! I am so sorry. Is he OK?"

"Yes, he is stable for now. He is going into surgery shortly for a triple bypass. I need to go home to be with my family and help my mother. But we need to talk first."

Wh... what about?" Sabrina asked as her lower lip trembled

"My mother told me my father has been very stressed out about my life choices. Apparently, I made it clearer than I thought that I am not necessarily interested in taking over his company. He is concerned about 'my questionable dedication to work.' He is also disappointed that I am here on vacation at Christmas, rather than home proposing to my girlfriend, so we can start a family. My mom blames me for his health issues. She's afraid that if I don't come home now and stop being so 'selfish' about my own needs... he will die."

"OK. I understand you need to be with your family now. We can see each other again soon. Maybe you can visit me at Stanford in a few weeks. I will make time..." Sabrina trailed off as she saw a tear fall onto his chest.

"Sabrina, dear Sabrina. If only... if only I could. My father is demanding and controlling, but he really is a good man. I cannot disappoint him. He has been planning for me to take over for my entire life. At one time, when I was young, I thought I wanted that too, so it's probably my fault for encouraging him. As much as what I want matters, I cannot be responsible for my father dying. I cannot destroy my family. I couldn't handle that."

"OK, I understand. You need to go home and take over for your dad right now while he recovers. I will be busy with my externships, finishing college, and then especially with medical school over the next four years. But we can keep in contact. I will wait for you. We can figure all this out with time. There are some amazing hospitals in Los Angeles. Maybe I can apply for a residency at USC Medical Center. They have a top-rated program."

The tears fell faster, as he silently began to shake his head no.

"I will not let you wait for me. You are far too special to waste your life on me. Go back to school, thrive, and most importantly, let yourself live. You deserve it. You are more than honoring your mother's memory. She would never want you to devote yourself solely to work. She would want you happy, just as I do. Promise me!"

"I could never do that. I never wanted to love someone... to get married. It was you, only you that could have ever changed my mind. I can't do this."

Sabrina jumped up from the table, sobbing, as she ran up the stairs. She threw herself on the bed and let the tears flow. She cried her heart out as she mourned the life she could have had, almost as strongly as she still mourned the loss of her mother.

Later that afternoon, as she was staring at the wall in a daze, she heard a light knock on the door and Melanie's voice calling out to her.

She opened the door and fell into her friend's arms, crying uncontrollably once again. Melanie told her that Jeremiah had gone for a walk hours ago, looking broken, and had not returned yet. She tried to console Sabrina, but she didn't know what to say. She promised to bring up some dinner later and finally persuaded her to lie back down and rest in the meantime.

Sabrina remembered the Christmas present she had gotten him. As heartbroken as she was, she still loved him and wished him the best. She grabbed it off the dresser and quickly ran out, setting it against his door where he wouldn't miss it. Then she returned to her room to nap after putting up the Do Not Disturb sign. The sun was dipping in the sky when she awoke to insistent knocking at her door. A quick look out the peephole revealed it was Jeremiah, bags in hand. She couldn't face him again, so she quietly crept back away from the door. He begged her to answer, but she pretended to be gone.

Finally, the knocking stopped.

About half an hour later, she once again heard knocking, followed this time by Melanie's voice. She opened the door to find her standing there with an enormous BLT.

Melanie smiled sheepishly and said, "I didn't know what else I could do to make you happy."

Sabrina cried through her tears and thanked her friend. She found she was hungry after all. Apparently, that much sorrow and tears built up an appetite. Melanie quietly sat with her while she ate, letting her decide if and when she was ready to talk. Sabrina forced herself to engage in small talk and then told Melanie she was ready for bed. She promised to be up early the next morning for Christmas. Melanie turned at the door, seeming unsure about whether to speak or not. Finally, she reached down and grabbed an object off the side table in the hall.

She held out her hand gingerly as she whispered, "He left a few minutes after you didn't answer the door to him. He gave this to me and begged me to make sure you got it. He said it was important that you accept it."

Sabrina frowned but reached out to grab it from her.

"Thank you."

The next day was as dark and gloomy as she felt, with snow falling heavily outside. Her friend was ecstatic for a white Christmas, but all she noticed was the stormy weather that matched the way she felt inside. They had a wonderful breakfast with cinnamon rolls, bacon, eggs, and eggnog... heavily spiked eggnog. Afterward, they opened the presents, and Melanie was brought to tears when she received her ornament. Sabrina excused herself for a moment and went upstairs to get the present Jeremiah had left. She couldn't bear to open it alone. She tore off the paper to reveal a small purple box emblazoned with the jewelry store logo.

He went to the jewelry store for me?

She slowly opened the box to reveal a white gold necklace with two intertwined hearts. The intersecting sides of the two hearts were connected with a double helix, like DNA. The tears poured from her eyes, as she read the small handwritten note tucked inside the box:

We are two complementary strands of the same structure, inseparable soulmates. Truly, you will hold my heart forever, my angel.

Melanie helped her put on the necklace after reading the note.

He will hold my heart forever, too.

The two friends enjoyed each other's company for the rest of the day as they ate way too much of the delicious food that Melanie made for dinner and dessert. Eventually, they fell asleep on the couch watching Christmas movies.

The next day, Sabrina got up and slowly packed for her trip home to Stanford. Melanie drove her to the train station and stayed with her until it was time to board. She had bought some snacks and drinks at the convenience store on the way to the station. She wanted to be able to hole up in her sleeper car alone and not leave until she arrived.

The train ride passed quickly, in a blur of sleeping and staring aimlessly out the window. Sabrina frequently found her fingers running along the hearts, tracing the design, as she silently cried.

Once home, Sabrina jumped into her externship with utter devotion. Every free moment was spent at the hospital, even long after her shift had ended. Those two weeks passed quickly, and she was given a glowing review, just as she had hoped. She then returned to school and immersed herself in her studies with the same single-minded determination to excel.

About a month after the semester started, she received a call one evening. Her mouth dropped open when she heard Jeremiah's voice on the other end of the line.

"Sabrina, please don't hang up. How are you doing?"

"I am doing fine," she stated emphatically, although she truly did not feel that way.

"I miss you. I know you probably don't believe that, but I do. More than you could possibly know."

Against her will, she found herself saying, "I do, too."

"How is school going?"

"It is going well. My externship went perfectly. How is your life going? How is your father? Did you marry her? I am sorry. None of that is my business."

"No, it is fine. We always told each other everything... even from the first moment we met. My father is getting better. He has returned to work full time. I am still running the company for him. No, I am not married. But... I am engaged. I am supposed to get married on June 1st."

Sabrina gulped audibly.

"I am happy for you... if that is what you want."

"Do you really feel that way? Do you not care at all anymore? Would I be calling you if I were happy? I don't know what to do. I don't know how to extract myself from this situation. I don't want this. You know that!"

"Yes, I do. But what do you want me to do? How can I help you? I said I would wait for you. You couldn't make that decision. You didn't choose me."

"I know, I know. I was stupid and wrong. Can we keep in touch and see where this goes? Can you ever forgive me? Do you even still love me? Do you want to be with me?"

"I love you more than YOU could possibly know. It is all I have wanted since that night we spent together. I forgave you that same day you left, even though my heart was broken. I could never be with anyone else but you."

Sabrina and Jeremiah spent hours on the phone that night going over all the details of their lives during the previous two months. The call ended slowly, with great reluctance to let each other go, after many proclamations of love.

The next months were filled with calls and emails. Every spare moment they had was spent with each other. Neither of them had ever been so happy . In those emails, they resumed planning their life together. Their correspondence was filled with details of their hopes for the future. But they were also filled with Jeremiah's concerns about how his father and fiancée would handle the news. Before they knew it, Sabrina's graduation had arrived.

She was surprised to see Jeremiah sitting there, front and center, cheering her on the whole time she crossed the stage. He whistled and clapped louder than anyone else at the conclusion of her speech; she had graduated top of her class, just as she had hoped, so she'd been chosen to give the commencement address.

He joined her briefly at the party afterward, then they quickly went back to her apartment to spend a blissful night together, making love passionately, as if it were both their first and last time together.

Afterward, they lay in each other's arms discussing the plans for the coming week. Sabrina would be busy packing up her belongings and moving into the new apartment they planned to share close to the medical school. Then she had a lot of loose ends to tie up before her summer externship and medical school orientation. After she finished all that, she had one glorious week of free time to return to Clarksville for a romantic vacation with Jeremiah.

He was going to spend this week explaining his change of heart to his parents and Amber. Then he needed to pack up his belongings so he could move them into their apartment after they returned from vacation. He had interviews scheduled at some architectural firms in the area for the week after their return. They were both going to be so busy in the week ahead that they knew they probably wouldn't have time to contact each other, so they soaked up every moment together that night.

As expected, the week passed in a flurry of activity, and Sabrina dropped into bed exhausted each night. Monday, her day of departure, arrived before she knew it. She excitedly boarded the train and passed the time reading from some of her new textbooks, which she had picked up the day before. She would arrive in Clarksville on the morning train Wednesday, and then wait there for Jeremiah to arrive on the 4:30 train.

Melanie surprised her by meeting her at the station upon her arrival. They walked the short distance into downtown and had breakfast together as she waited. Melanie was dying to hear all the news about their reconciliation. She was thrilled to see Sabrina so happy and fulfilled. Afterward, they had coffee together as they sat on a bench and watched the children playing in the park. Melanie had to return to the B&B because she was expecting guests, so Sabrina walked back to the station.

She anxiously waited for the next few hours until the train's arrival, literally popping out of her seat when she heard the whistle blow as it pulled into the station. The passengers disembarked quickly, and her anxiety grew as Jeremiah failed to appear. Ten minutes later, all the passengers seemed to have disembarked. Sabrina ran up to the conductor to ask if anyone was still on the train, and he replied no. Then she ran over to the ticket counter to see if they could find out if he had boarded the train. A short search on the computer showed his ticket had not been used, nor had it been rescheduled, at least not yet.

Sabrina tried to calm herself as she sat on the bench outside the station and called Jeremiah. The phone rang six times before it went through to voicemail. When it did, she tried to sound calm: She didn't want to reveal her actual level of fear and anger.

"Hey, Jeremiah! How are you doing, sweetie? I am here at the station, and they say you didn't get on the train. Is everything OK? I will wait to hear from you and meet you at the station tomorrow, I guess. Call me. I love you."

She needed to work through her feelings, so she walked back to Melanie's B&B. When she walked in the door and saw

Melanie's face, all her feelings burst through the dam she had so carefully constructed.

"Calm down, Sabrina. You don't know what happened. He may just be running late. Maybe he took a plane instead and will arrive here later tonight or in the morning. You need to wait to hear from him."

"He backed out. I just know it. He was so afraid of how they would all handle it. He just doesn't have the guts to break my heart again in person."

"Now, you don't know that. I don't believe that's true. He may be a people pleaser when it comes to his family, but he truly does love you, too. There is no way he would not let you know if he changed his mind. He would call or email you or something. I honestly believe that."

As the hours passed with no word, her depression grew. The hours turned into days, and still she heard nothing. On the first day, she came downstairs to eat and watch television or play card games with Melanie. She left dozens of messages, but not one was returned. On the second day, she just stayed in bed with the blinds closed. She slept most of the day, barely ate, and rarely spoke to Melanie when she came to check on her. The day before she was due to leave, Melanie literally dragged Sabrina out of bed and into a warm shower. She helped her dress and led her downstairs to lunch, where she spoon-fed her soup until she finally started eating on her own.

Soon, the tears began to flow again. Then, after a few minutes, the sorrow turned into anger. While Melanie felt bad for her, she was at least glad to see her reacting again.

"That is it. I am done. We are done. I am not going to let him fuck with my head again. He can't change his mind in a few months, and come back to me again," she yelled as she pulled her phone out of her pocket.

She promptly blocked his phone number and deleted him from her contacts and on social media.

"Thank you for taking care of me, Melanie. You are a true friend. I'm sorry I was so much trouble. Now I need to go pack and see if I can cancel my train ticket, so I can just fly home instead and have a couple of days before my externship starts. Apparently, I need to move again, because I am not going to run into him at that apartment we rented."

Sabrina was all packed up and back downstairs an hour later. She had gotten a refund for the train ticket and found a flight scheduled to leave in three hours, leaving her just enough time to get to the airport.

She hugged Melanie tight to her and promised she would call when she got home. A short time later, her Uber arrived, and Sabrina was on her way.

Sabrina stayed at the Hilton by the airport that night and began to search online in earnest to find a new apartment. When she called a few places in the morning, she was happy to find one she could afford that would let her move in that weekend.

Then she lost no time in taking a bus over to the apartment she had planned to share with Jeremiah, where she went immediately to see the property manager. He grudgingly removed her name from the lease, but only after she agreed to pay a two-month penalty and forfeit her deposit. She was grateful, looking back, that she had been in such a rush before leaving on her trip, so she hadn't unpacked much. Moving would mostly be a matter of just transferring her boxes from one apartment to the next.

Once again, Sabrina dove into her externship. This time, it was much more involved because she had proved her merit during Christmas break. The months passed quickly, and soon it was time to start medical school. Sabrina had always been an exceptional student, but medical school was challenging, as she had expected. She welcomed that challenge, though, because it gave her very little time to feel sorry for herself.

As she started her third year in school, she began her clinical rotations in the school clinic and at the hospital. She had very little free time anyhow, but she found she was thinking of Jeremiah less and less.

All that truly mattered was that Sabrina had learned her lesson. She had been right to never want marriage or a family. Her career was all that mattered to her. There was no longer anything holding her there, so she applied for a residency in emergency medicine at Johns Hopkins Hospital. As the fourth year came closer to the end, she began to get anxious as she waited to hear if she had been accepted.

Finally, word came in and, based on glowing recommendations from the doctor in charge of her externships, her professors, and the doctors overseeing her clinicals, she was accepted.

She graduated from medical school, once again at the top of her class. The next few weeks were insanely busy as she packed all her belongings and had them shipped across the country. She had to make a trip early to find an apartment near the hospital because she knew she'd be working long hours and didn't want a long commute on top of that. She didn't need anything special because she was expecting to sleep in the on-call room frequently.

Melanie came to visit before her move and helped her pack. It was going to be difficult to be so far from her, but they intended to use Zoom to keep in touch as often as possible.

Sabrina drove across the country as quickly as she could. She wanted a few days to get settled before beginning her rigorous residency. Sabrina worked long shifts at the hospital and volunteered for overtime or took on other people's shifts as often as possible. Her dedication to her training impressed her supervisors, who could tell she was studying emergency medicine procedures in her free time. Not surprisingly, in her second year, she was chosen as Chief Resident to serve in that position in years three and four. Those years passed quickly, and she applied to be an attending physician after graduation.

Sabrina was readily accepted for the position. She was an excellent doctor and well-liked by her colleagues, nurses, and support staff. The years passed quickly, and after five years, she was a shoo-in for the Chief of Emergency Medicine position when her boss retired. Sabrina was over the moon when she found out she had finally landed her dream job, especially at such a prestigious hospital as Johns Hopkins. Her days were long and hard, especially when she began a research project. She was hoping to get published in the near future.

Sabrina wasn't shocked when she began having gastrointestinal issues. Between her rapidly approaching research deadline and her long hours in the Emergency Department, she was under enormous pressure . Her terrible diet didn't help either. She was prone to eating whatever was quick and convenient as she rushed from one emergency to the next. When she actually had the time to leave the hospital, she frequently bought fast food on the way home.

Sabrina started to become concerned when the frequent heartburn continued to worsen, even after she started taking medication. Her symptoms soon progressed to frequent nausea and occasional vomiting. When the stomach pain started, she thought she had developed an ulcer. It wasn't until her symptoms became debilitating that she finally scheduled an appointment with a colleague in the gastroenterology department. The doctor scheduled an ultrasound first.

Sabrina became very concerned as she lay on the table and looked over at the screen. There was plainly a mass effect in her stomach. The ultrasound technician feigned ignorance, but it was clear that she was concerned as well. Dr. Burrows called her office that evening and explained he had scheduled her for an endoscopy the following week. He told her not to worry, but she knew better.

Besides, she could hear the worried tone in his voice.

"I don't have time next week. My research project wraps up late this week, and I need to write up my findings. Then, next week, I have a new crop of residents entering the program, and you know I like to be hands-on with them the first few weeks."

"Dr. Sanders... Sabrina, this is serious. We cannot afford to wait. I need you to do this for me. You know as well as I do that a CT is a quick procedure. Make time."

"OK. Thank you, Bob. I appreciate your candor and concern. I will do my best to make the appointment Thursday."

The following week passed even faster than she had expected. Her new residents were greener than she had hoped, so they needed even more supervision. It wasn't until late Thursday night, when she received a call from Bob, that she remembered she had missed her appointment.

"I'm very sorry, Bob. I do take this seriously. I will call the scheduling department and get in as soon as possible."

"Please do, Sabrina. I am serious here."

A week later, Sabrina finally called the scheduling department. She booked her CT for the end of the month when her schedule was a little lighter. Truth be told, Sabrina was scared. Given her family history and what she'd seen on the ultrasound screen, she wasn't sure she wanted to know what they would find. But she realized she couldn't put it off any longer. The symptoms, especially the pain, were becoming intolerable. It was very difficult to eat, and she was losing enough weight that people were beginning to ask questions with concern in their eyes.

Finally, the day of the CT arrived. She barely made it to the appointment, but she did get it done. She ran off to the Emergency Department as soon as she was finished and avoided the computer as much as possible, actively trying to keep from seeing the results when they arrived. Bob—or, as she would refer to him here on out, Dr. Burrows—called around lunchtime and asked her to stop by as soon as possible.

Sabrina finally convinced herself to go down to his office in the late afternoon. When she entered his office, she knew the news was going to be just as she expected.

"I am very sorry to tell you this, Sabrina, but a large area of your stomach lining appears abnormal. With suspicious tissue of this type and size, there is an 80 percent chance of malignancy. Given your family history, I am highly suspicious that you have diffuse gastric adenocarcinoma. Frequently, at this size, it will have already metastasized to either your liver or lungs. There are suspicious-looking spots in your liver and what appears to be metastasis to your lungs. I have scheduled surgery for you at 8 a.m. tomorrow. I have already talked to your boss and explained the situation. I need you to go downstairs and check into the hospital now. Do you understand?"

Sabrina opened her mouth to argue, but then just nodded her head.

"I will see you in the morning, Dr. Burrows."

Sabrina walked down the hall, head spinning with the news she had just received. She went to Admitting, where they helped her quickly and compassionately.

Clearly, they had been expecting her.

One of the nurses on duty, Nurse Andrews, met her and escorted her up to her room. They chatted casually as she changed into her hospital gown, had her IV put in, and settled into bed. Nurse Andrews asked if she needed anything before she left, and then reminded her that she may want to call someone and let them know about the situation.

Melanie was the only person Sabrina could think of to contact. When she heard, she was devastated by the news and offered to help in any way she could.

"I'm fine. I will be fine," Sabrina told her. "This is just a scare. I am sure everything will be okay. I just didn't want you to worry if I missed our weekly Zoom session. I will call you tomorrow when I'm out of recovery."

Sabrina settled in and finally dropped off to real sleep shortly before 5 a.m. She was awakened two hours later when the nurse came in to prepare her for surgery.

She was shocked when she opened her eyes and found Melanie sitting by her side.

"Melanie! I told you not to come. What about your B&B?"

"I didn't have any reservations for this week anyhow. I closed it. I have a friend who will check messages and go by to make sure everything is fine. There is no place else I could or would be right now. Now quit worrying about me and get ready to fight. That is your only concern."

Sabrina awoke from surgery, once again in her room, and found Melanie by her side talking to Dr. Burrows.

"Well, hello there, Sabrina. Are you OK? Do you feel up to talking?"

Sabrina nodded solemnly.

"I removed a sample of your stomach lining and had stat pathology performed while you were under. It came back as I suspected, so I had to remove 60 percent of your stomach. I removed over a dozen lymph nodes, and they all came back positive for adenocarcinoma. I then performed a biopsy of one of the suspicious patches on your liver. It also tested positive. I am afraid you have advanced Stage 4 gastric adenocarcinoma with metastasis to your liver and lungs. I need to see you back in my office in two weeks to assess the status of your healing. In the meantime, I will get you scheduled as soon as possible to have a port inserted for chemotherapy. Fingers crossed, in two weeks, we will begin an aggressive course of chemotherapy for the next three months and then reassess your staging with another CT. Do you have any questions?"

"Let's cut the crap, Dr. Burrows. We both know what we are talking about here. What is my long-term prognosis?"

"Sabrina, I will not tell you that it is hopeless, but I will not tell you that everything is going to be fine either. I will give it to you straight. The five-year survival rate is less than 20 percent with genetic diffuse gastric adenocarcinoma. It all depends on your response to chemotherapy."

"Thank you, Dr. Burrows."

Melanie crawled into bed with Sabrina and just held her. There was nothing to say. They each knew that all they could do was support each other. Melanie stayed for the next week through the hardest part of Sabrina's recovery from surgery. She left reluctantly—and only at Sabrina's insistence when she threatened to end their friendship if she stayed. Sabrina spent the next week at home watching television and reading. At her appointment, she was told her healing was adequate and she could begin chemo later that week.

"Aggressive chemotherapy" didn't begin to describe Sabrina's experience. Her nausea and vomiting increased to the point that she developed an ulcer in her esophagus from exposure to all the stomach acid. Eating became a chore, and her weight loss increased. She was so tired that work was impossible, so she had to take a leave of absence for three months as she proceeded through the course of treatment.

Finally, it was time for her second CT scan, to see how effective the treatment had been. Dr. Burrows scheduled it for early in the morning, and arranged for her to come in late that afternoon to go over the results.

They were not good.

In fact, they reflected the worst-case scenario: The metastasis in her lungs and liver had worsened significantly. Moreover, the cancer had continued to grow and spread through what stomach tissue remained after her surgery. Dr. Burrows explained that they could try increasing her chemo dose, but he was worried that her high level of sensitivity meant it would quickly become intolerable—and potentially life-threatening.

"Sabrina, it is time that we talk about palliative care. We need to make you more comfortable and able to enjoy the time you have left."

"I understand, Dr. Burrows. What is the next step? How long are we talking about? I want to spend what time I have left traveling, and then go visit Melanie."

"It is really hard to say, Sabrina. However, I would estimate you have between one and three months. I can get you set up with a national hospice provider that can get the medications prescribed to keep you comfortable. They have locations across the country, so if you plan your trip carefully, you should be able to find care easily as you need it."

"Thank you, Dr. Burrows."

Sabrina left the hospital and began organizing her affairs immediately. She had always been one to pursue whatever task ahead of her with stubborn independence and deep resolve. This situation was no different.

She packed a few suitcases with whatever clothes and important personal belongings she wanted to take with her. Everything else she either sold or donated to charity. She put in emergency notice with her landlord and paid him the last month's rent. She then proceeded to Johns Hopkins and submitted her resignation and said goodbye to all the colleagues who had been important to her.

She called Melanie and let her know she would be leaving in two days to drive across the country, stopping to see every historical or fascinating point of interest along the way. She then asked her the one question she had been dreading.

"I don't have long. By the time I get to you I will probably only have a matter of weeks. I have taken care of all my belongings and bills. I have made my funeral arrangements. All my assets will be passed to you, and my lawyer will take care of the probate process for you. You are the only person in my life that I want to spend my last days with. Can I stay with you?"

Melanie sniffled as she replied, "Of course. I would never forgive you if you didn't let me take care of you. I love you. You are my best friend. Please keep me apprised of your location and how you are doing as you travel. I will see you soon."

Sabrina drove slowly across the country, making stops in Washington, D.C., the Great Lakes, Mount Rushmore,

Yellowstone, the Grand Canyon, Salt Lake City, and Yosemite. Sabrina was singing along to the Monkees song, "Last Train to Clarksville," as she drove down from Yosemite into the small town of Lee Vining. She was actually feeling hungry for once, so she stopped at a restaurant in a gas station that was well known there.

While she was waiting for her order, she noticed a newspaper open on a table next to hers. She saw a picture of a train, and the name "Clarksville" in the headline beside it. She grabbed it and, when she read the story quickly, she was devastated at what she learned: The train to Clarksville was being discontinued at the end of the week. While that train still held painful memories, it also was the key to the best memories of her lifetime, besides her younger years with her mother.

She called Melanie while she was eating and explained that she would be changing her plans. The trip had been getting more difficult with each passing day as she became more tired, and her pain increased. She explained to her that she was going to hire an automobile transport service to deliver her car to Melanie's B&B. She was going to catch the train and arrive in Clarksville on its last day in service. Melanie was concerned that this trip would be too painful for her, but she insisted that she needed to hold on to all her good memories, regardless of the eventual outcome.

Sabrina boarded the train, having once again paid for a private sleeper car. She enjoyed the scenery on the long ride but found herself sleeping most of the time. She ventured out to the dining car once to get a small bite to eat. Another passenger expressed concern about her when she felt woozy and grabbed onto a table to right herself as she walked back to her car. She thanked him for his concern and told him she was fine. She realized she was still feeling a tad weak, so she settled back into her seat to take a short nap before her arrival in Clarksville in approximately an hour.

Sabrina awoke with a start as the train rumbled to a halt. She saw people bustling off the train, so she slowly gathered her belongings together and began to make her way out. She thanked the conductor for his help during the trip, but he didn't hear her as he hurried by in response to a loud call from another employee. She carefully made her way down the stairs and stepped onto the platform. She looked up as a hand reached out and grabbed her bag from her.

She found herself looking into the irresistible gaze of Jeremiah.

What the hell is he doing here? And damn him! Why is it that men grow more handsome with age? He barely looks like he has aged a day.

Before she knew it, she found herself rushing into his arms, hugging him tight, as he dropped her bags at their feet. Then she sighed audibly before saying, "Hello, Jeremiah. How are you? What are you doing here?"

"I heard about the train. You know how we both love trains, and this particular one holds such fond memories for me. I had to be here for its last trip."

"Me too. I came to visit Melanie. I really need to get going. She is probably waiting for me in the station."

"Wait! I need to be honest with you. I did want to be here for the train's last arrival. But to be honest, I was hoping I would find you here. I needed to see you again. I needed to apologize and tell you how I feel. I need to beg you for one last chance."

"NO! I will not do this again. It is too late... for so many reasons. I really have to go. I cannot keep her waiting."

"She isn't here right now. I am here to pick you up. Please just hear me out on the way to the B&B. If you can't forgive me after that, I will leave you alone... forever."

"Fine. I am not up to arguing with you. Let's go."

There was some kind of issue at the station. Sabrina could hear a woman yelling, and a crowd of people was staring at her. An ambulance pulled up, so it must have been some kind of medical emergency. Jeremiah led Sabrina around the far side of the station to the parking lot, where he had a car waiting. He loaded her bags into the car and then held her door as she got in.

Well, at least he still has some of his gentlemanly manners left.

Jeremiah got in the car and backed out. He was taking the slower back roads to the B&B. She let it go because she wasn't up to arguing.

"I guess I should explain what happened that week."

"You think? Proceed. Not that I care. It is too late."

"I packed up all my belongings and stored them in a pod that was scheduled to be delivered the day after we arrived home from our trip. Then I went to my parents' house and had it out with them. My father was livid. My mother cried. They begged me to change my mind. They threatened to cut me off, and even cut me out of the will entirely. I told them that I did not need, nor want, their money. I told my father that I did not want to run his company, and that he should pass it along to his longtime, loyal employee Mark. I explained that I would be moving up to Stanford with you and finding a job there. They threatened to cut off contact with me, but I did not back down. Finally, they said that they accepted my decision, but I knew they were counting on me to come crawling back eventually when our relationship failed.

"Next, I went to Amber and explained the situation to her. She was not surprised. She knew I was unhappy and did not want to marry her. She had been waiting for just this moment to arrive. She tried to beg me to marry her, promising me to be a good wife. She swore that she would travel more and wait until I was ready for a family. I told her that this would not be a fair solution for either one of us. I explained I had no doubts she would be an excellent wife... just not for me."

"Then what happened? Why didn't you come to me? Why didn't you return my calls?"

Jeremiah pulled up in front of the B&B and turned off the car. He got out and came around to open Sabrina's door. He led her over to the garden in the backyard, and they sat down on the swing.

"That day, I was running late. I loaded my bags into the car and left in a rush to make my train. I was waiting at a long red light, and when it finally changed, I hit the gas. Unfortunately, a semi coming down the hill on the cross street lost its brakes, so the driver was unable to stop at the light. I saw him coming at me as I started across the intersection, but it was too late to stop. He slammed into the driver's side door going about 40 miles per hour. I was killed instantly. That is why I didn't come here to meet you. I couldn't. Wild horses couldn't have kept me away, but death did what I thought was impossible."

Sabrina looked at him in disbelief.

"What the hell are you talking about? Do you take me for an idiot? That is impossible. You are sitting right here, clearly not dead."

Sabrina stood up quickly and turned to leave. Jeremiah jumped up quickly and took her in his arms gently.

"Please wait. There is one more thing I need to explain to you. Please give me one more moment."

Sabrina nodded, and Jeremiah sat down again, pulling her into his lap with his arms wrapped comfortingly around her.

"I can explain why I am here telling you this. I came to meet you at the train to welcome you into the afterlife. Remember the commotion we saw at the station and the woman we heard yelling? That woman yelling was Melanie. The commotion occurred because one of the train employees found you in your sleeper car. When the conductor noticed you hadn't gotten off the train, he sent someone to find you because you'd been sick earlier. They found that you had passed away."

"That's not possible. I feel fine... perfect in fact. I can't be dead."

"Exactly, sweetie. You have not felt 'fine' in a very long time. That is your first clue that things are not as they seem to you. Follow me. I will show you."

Jeremiah stood her on her feet again. Then he got up, taking her hand, and led her into Melanie's B&B. She was not there at the front desk as she should have been. He led her up the stairs to Melanie's room, where they found her crying on the phone. Sabrina stood there quietly in front of Melanie and listened to her talk.

"Yes, sir. I am so sorry. I didn't know she hadn't told you she was sick. She was coming here to spend her final days with me. I went to the station to pick her up. She wasn't there, and when I asked about her, they told me they had called an ambulance because they couldn't find a pulse. The ambulance pronounced her dead upon arrival. I know. I can't believe it. How can she be gone?"

"Melanie! Melanie! I am right here. Please stop crying."

Sabrina reached out to hug her, but her arms passed right through her. Jeremiah grabbed her hand and led her out of the room.

"I am so sorry, sweetheart. I would never have left you alone. In fact, I didn't leave you alone. I have been with you all this time. Through your externship, the long hard years of medical school, and then all the lonely, crazy years since then. Whenever the stress started to become too much, I would find small ways to leave you messages and bring back good memories. Every time you heard 'Last Train to Clarksville,' that was me. Every time, you felt like someone was with you, that was me. Remember when you found those mysterious flowers on your front porch ?"

She nodded.

"That was me. I was always there to support you. I left that newspaper open for you on the table to find the story about the train. I needed to lead you here to me, so we could be together again... here. I needed to be the one to explain to you what had happened. Do you understand?"

"Yes... yes, I do. But what happens next?"

Jeremiah kissed her gently on the forehead, and then grabbed her hand, leading her out of the garden.

"Whatever you want, my dear. Where shall we go? What shall we do? We have eternity to love each other and do whatever our hearts desire."

Sabrina smiled and followed him down the path into town.

Christmas Nightmare's Eve

Bonus story…

Stephen H. Provost

Reindeer Ride

Elizabeth did not know whether to be grateful that the rain that soaked her had ceased, or to be disconsolate about the snow that now replaced it. It hurried and scurried in flurries on the north wind, chasing her along as though it were a border collie nipping at the heels of a wayward lamb.

Snowflakes began to stack up, one atop the other. They fell on the path before her, too, some of them melting partway to create a slushy, muddy mess that looked a bit—but she was quite sure didn't taste—like chocolate ice cream.

The snow shouldn't have surprised her. It was, after all, just before Christmas. Elizabeth had all but forgotten that, however, since—for reasons of her own—she tended to put that particular holiday out of her mind.

"Oh, bother," she said, barely catching herself as she nearly slipped and fell on the icy path.

The snow seemed to fall more heavily, the farther the girl progressed, and through the snowy screen, she saw a large shadowy figure appear up ahead. Somehow, it stood out against the darkness: A silver glow seemed to emanate from it.

Elizabeth stopped where she stood and raised a hand to shield her eyes, not wanting to get any closer without knowing what stood in front of her. It was certainly large, and not in the shape of a person. It was, clearly, an animal of some sort, a fact that made her all the more reticent to approach it. Animals were unpredictable, even the tame ones. She'd been thrown from a horse when she was learning to ride: It had reared at the sound of a hunter's gunshot. Another time, she had gone to visit a family friend near Pocklington, and a friendly German shepherd had bounded out from behind a hedge and leapt at her. The animal had only wanted to greet her, but she'd been very small at the time and, in its excitement, it had knocked her to the ground. She still had nightmares about it, in which the dog was reimagined as a giant snarling wolf.

Whatever stood ahead of her in the labyrinth didn't *look* like a wolf, or even a dog. It was, in fact, much larger and appeared, through the snowfall, as though it wore a crown upon its head. She felt like its eyes were upon her, studying her. Did it think of the girl as prey? Was it getting ready to charge? What *was* it? With the snow falling heavily from the gray-black sky, she still could not be sure. Her curiosity was beginning to make war against her fear, demanding that she know. Besides, she reasoned, there was no way to go but forward, and the animal was blocking her path. She had no other choice, not really.

Elizabeth took a tentative step toward it and heard her foot squish-scrunch on the half-muddy, half-frozen path.

The animal did not move.

She took another step.

The animal seemed frozen in place, more frozen even than the snow and ice.

A third step. She might have been able to see more clearly, but the snow seemed to fall more thickly each time she moved forward. It was so dark, in any event, that she could only see that silver glow surrounding it, and much of that reflected off the soft white, whispered snow.

Still the animal didn't move.

She crept slowly nearer, squinting her eyes as the snow fell still more heavily, until she was nearly upon it. She could hear it breathing; see the chest expanding and contracting. It stood as tall as she was, and the "crown," she now realized, was a magnificent set of antlers. They were almost as long as the animal was tall, and she had never seen anything like it. It was like a deer, only larger, more majestic. She was certain it was not native to Yorkshire, and that it must have been brought here by someone from very far away. Who would do such a thing, and why? She had no way of knowing.

Puffs of steam escaped the animal's nostrils, wafting out into the chill night air. At last, the snow seemed to abate just a little, and she could see more clearly as the animal dipped its head toward her, dark eyes blinking lazily as it stared at her.

It? It must be a "him," with antlers as large as these.

She stretched one hand forward, tentatively, and touched

the great beast's forehead, whereupon he nodded slightly in assent. But then he pulled back from her, tossed back his head, and emitted a sound that was a little like a grunt and a little like a bark.

The girl jumped back in surprise at the sudden movement, but it was clear the animal had no wish to alarm her. Elizabeth steadied herself and waited, and the animal repeated the motion, grunting, it seemed, somewhat more urgently this time.

Elizabeth waited, and so did the animal, but when she did nothing, the creature made the same motion a third time, the grunt more like a honking now. Each time, he tossed his head in the same direction: behind and beyond him, where the path led onward. She realized he wanted her to follow.

"All right, then," she said, and nodded her own head in the same direction.

The animal must have understood her, because he grunted softly and turned around; then, to her amazement, he knelt down right there in the pathway, and a voice inside her head said, "*Climb aboard!*" It was not her own voice, nor was it anything her ears could detect. She realized it must have come from the animal, whatever *kind* of animal it was.

"*Caribou,*" came the response. It could read her thoughts, as well!

"I've never heard of that," she said aloud as she climbed on.

"*Ouch! Don't pull the fur, please! And no need to speak aloud. I know your thoughts the moment you think them.*"

"Sorry," Elizabeth said.

"*Sorry,*" she repeated in her thoughts. She found it mildly disconcerting that the ... Care-i-boo ... which she had never heard of, knew what she was thinking. She was used to letting her thoughts out at her own discretion, not having them taken from her before she was ready to share them. "*What is a Care-i-*

boo?" she asked, enunciating each of the syllables in exaggerated fashion as she settled onto the creature's back. A moment later, he rose to his feet as he stood, jostling her so much that she nearly fell off. She started to panic, recalling the time she had been thrown from the horse, and grabbed on to the caribou's fur again.

"*Ouch!*" he said again, accompanied by an audible grunt of surprise and dismay. "*Please! If you need to steady yourself, use the antlers.*"

"*Right.*" Elizabeth hastily let go of the caribou's fur and placed both hands on his antlers.

"*Much better, thank you.*" The caribou said as he began to amble forward. Elizabeth got the feeling that he was moving quickly, for him, even though his pace was rather plodding. She sensed, too, in his thoughts, a certain urgency. Something was amiss that had him concerned. And, for some reason, her presence was required.

"*A caribou,*" he said, addressing her earlier query, "*is what you might know as a reindeer.*"

Elizabeth vaguely remembered hearing of reindeer, but she could not place where she had heard of them. Had she cared more about Christmas, she might have known, for then she would have read the poem entitled *A Visit from St. Nicholas*, wherein they were first mentioned. In fact, her mother had once read this very poem to her, but she had dismissed it from her mind, as she had all else to do with the holiday. As has been mentioned, she did this for reasons of her own.

"*If you are a reindeer,*" she asked, "*does that mean you like the rain?*"

The caribou chuckled. "*Reins, as in reins on a horse,*" he answered. "*They aren't very comfortable, but they are necessary to perform the task I'm charged with.*" Elizabeth sensed a hint of pride in the caribou's thought-voice at this last statement. He seemed to consider this task, whatever it was, quite important.

"*Oh,*" she thought. "*Do you have a name?*"

"*Most people call me Comet, because I'm so fast,*" he declared. "*But you may call me Cary.*"

As Cary loped along, it seemed to Elizabeth he didn't seem fast at all. Cary seemed a much better name, especially since he was *carrying* her.

"*Don't get used to that,*" he quipped. "*I am NOT a beast of burden!*"

His ability to read her thoughts would take some getting used to.

"*You should be grateful you can do it,*" he said. "*Only those capable of believing the greatest things can hear thought voices. It's a pity you don't believe in Christmas, but I have a feeling that will change. Ha!*"

After a while, Elizabeth's bottom began getting sore. Riding on a reindeer without a saddle was not the most comfortable mode of transportation.

It didn't make her feel any better that it was getting colder, too. She couldn't remember it ever being this cold in Yorkshire, and she shivered and shook in her light dress, teeth chattering as she pulled her arms in close to her—as close as she could while keeping hold of the caribou's antlers.

"*I know you're cold.*" Cary's thoughts invaded her mind. "*It can't be helped this far north. Think of it this way: At least you're not carrying someone on your back.*"

He could certainly seem out-of-sorts at times... but what did he mean by "this far north"? The caribou was not the speediest creature, by any means, and they couldn't have come very far in the time they'd been trudging along. Elizabeth was as certain as she could be that Yorkshire never got this cold.

"We're not in Yorkshire," Cary said.

Not in Yorkshire? This was not possible. There was no way, in the wildest of wild imaginations, that they could have gone as far as Durham.

"We're not in Durham," Cary declared.

Northumberland?

"Keep going. You're getting warmer, but only a little bit."

We're actually getting colder, Elizabeth thought, and if he says we're as far north as Scotland, I'll say he's daft.

The caribou grunted, and the girl took it for a laugh.

"What's so funny?"

"You are. Have you ever heard of the Arctic Circle?"

"Of course I have, you dullard." It wasn't a very nice name to call him, but she didn't appreciate being laughed at.

"We're inside it," he said.

Now it was Elizabeth's turn to laugh. "We couldn't be."

"Oh, but we are. I'd like you to meet someone."

Elizabeth squinted to see through the white mist, which swirled around above the even whiter snow. She could also see three small figures up ahead of them—although, in fact, they weren't small at all. The closer they got, the larger they seemed: larger even than the reindeer who was carrying her.

"Polar bears!" she cried in excitement. She had heard that such creatures existed, living in the great far north, but of course, she had never seen them. They did not live in Yorkshire, or Durham, or Northumberland, or Scotland. They lived in places where the ice didn't melt and snow fell during summer.

They kept moving toward the bears across snow-covered tundra, until they were not a hundred yards away from them. Elizabeth wondered whether they would retreat at Cary's arrival, but on the contrary, they began moving toward the reindeer and the young girl on his back.

"These are my friends Sasha and Olga, and their cub Katriana," Cary said. *"I know they are very large and fierce looking; but do not be afraid. They are some of the kindest bear-folk I have ever known. And they can speak your tongue. If you are considerate and cordial, they will more than reciprocate your courtesy."*

Elizabeth clapped her hands. She was very cold, and her teeth were chattering, but she was also very excited. She was going to talk to polar bears!

The three of them approached Cary and bowed, each in turn: the largest among them first, then the other grown bear, and finally the cub. "Welcome to the North Pole. Well, the *magnetic* North Pole," said one of the adults. From the voice, Elizabeth guessed that it was Olga.

"Is there more than one North Pole?" said Elizabeth. She paused, then remembered her manners and hastily added. "Thank you for your welcome! It's so good to meet you!"

"We are glad to meet you, as well," said Sasha. "It isn't often your kind are seen this far north. By your kind, I mean the young of your species. We have, on occasion, seen humans who have come of age. But they only seem interested in hunting our kind, and in slaughtering our brethren, the harp and hooded seals."

Elizabeth lowered her head. "I am sorry."

"We do not blame you," said Olga. "In fact, we are happy to see someone who is *not* interested in hunting and targeting our kind."

Elizabeth smiled shyly, and Olga saw she was shivering. She ambled forward and held out her arms, and the girl stepped forward, hesitant. The large bear put her arms around Elizabeth, and the girl was amazed at how warm she felt inside her arms. It was a real and true bear hug!

Her teeth stopped chattering.

"Is there *really* more than one North Pole?" she said.

The cub laughed merrily, and her father joined in.

"Of course!" Sasha said. "There is one North Pole at the top of the Earth that stays where it is no matter how many years go by. And there is the magnetic North Pole that moves around from year to year. This year, it is here on King Edward Island—at least that's what your kind call this place. In my youth, it was on a *different* island, a bit to the south of here."

Elizabeth felt confused. "If there are two North Poles, and one is always moving around, how do you know where the *real* North Pole is?"

"It's wherever his Majesty says it is," Sasha answered.

"In fact," said Cary, "at the moment, it's right here."

He nodded his head slightly forward, jostling Elizabeth—who was still on his back—as she tried to keep hold of his antlers.

Once she had steadied herself again, she looked in the direction Cary had indicated and saw a small gatehouse with a gabled roof, alongside which stood a rotating red-and-white column inside a clear vertical cylinder.

"A barber pole?" she said aloud, incredulous.

"Yes, a barber pole. Congratulations for such an astute observation."

Elizabeth scowled behind his back.

"Not just any barber pole, though. This was the first one in the world. His Majesty needed someone to keep that beard of his from becoming a bird's nest and all that hair from getting in his eyes."

His Majesty? Sasha had said that, too. But Queen Victoria was a lady.

"I told you, we're not in England anymore. Weren't you listening?"

"Well, yes, but that doesn't mean I believe you," she said in her thoughts.

"Even after you saw the North Pole?"

"That's not the North Pole. That's a barber pole at a little building for some imaginary king you made up out of your head."

"You're not the first person to say that about him," Cary scoffed. *"He doesn't care, as long as you're nice."*

Elizabeth didn't think she'd ever been mean to anyone, at least, not so far as she could remember. Even if she had, it wasn't possible to be mean to an imaginary person. Or was it? No, of course, it wasn't! And even if there was a Santa Claus, she wouldn't be mean to him.

"Is there really a barber here?" she said aloud.

"Of course there is!" Olga said, sounding offended. "*I* am the barber! And the hairstylist. I also do manicures, but I'm a little rusty. King Nicholas doesn't really go in for fancy nails."

Sasha laughed.

But his laughter was cut short by the arrival of a penguin, who came waddling up, then dove onto the ice head-first and slid the rest of the way. He was clearly in a hurry.

"I thought penguins were at the *South* Pole," Elizabeth said.

"Most of them are," said Cary. *"But humans seem not to realize that some of* us *like to travel, too. And some of us prefer to relocate if we don't like where we happen to have been born."*

Elizabeth had never thought of it that way, and she didn't have time to think on it any longer, because the penguin was speaking very quickly and energetically, flapping his little wings in animated fashion to punctuate what he was saying. And what he was saying seemed very disturbing—even if Elizabeth didn't know exactly what he was talking about.

"The Village is being attacked!" he said. "A sky demon has descended upon us! Come quickly! The Village is under siege!"

"Village?" said Elizabeth. "What village?"

But Cary wasn't waiting to hear any more. Before Elizabeth could even say goodbye to the polar bears, he was taking to the sky again, and she found herself holding on to his antlers for dear life.

"What happened?" she said. "Where are we going?"

He didn't answer, perhaps because he was distracted by the sight of dark smoke rising from somewhere just beyond a high snowdrift a fair distance ahead. The clouds had parted and were rapidly fleeing the north wind, revealing the bright moon almost directly overhead. Elizabeth noticed that they were on a cobblestone road now, and realized there was no sign of the high hedgerows that had formed the labyrinth. They were out in the open. On either side of the cobblestone path stood a row of lanterns, oil-flames dancing, spaced at regular intervals until they disappeared behind the snowdrift that lay in front of them.

The smoke was too heavy to be from a chimney. Something was burning.

"*This does not look good.*" Cary's thought wasn't directed at Elizabeth in particular. It was an observation, behind which lay more than a hint of worry.

The girl wondered what was up there.

"*The Village,*" Cary thought, but he was less focused than usual, seeming distracted.

A village at the North Pole. Wait a minute... It couldn't be...

"*Of course it is,*" the caribou said, irritated. "*I thought the name Comet would have given it away. But I know, you don't believe in Christmas. Just because you don't believe in something, that doesn't mean it isn't so.*"

"And just because you believe in something doesn't make it so, either."

Before the reindeer could respond, their attention was drawn to the sky, where a giant winged creature rose from beyond the snowbank. Ascending in front of the moon, it let loose a scream that, even at this distance, was piercing, breathing fire—yes, fire!—in the next moment from its nostrils.

"*A dragon!*" the caribou exclaimed in his thoughts. "*I did not believe they existed!*"

He believed in Father Christmas but not in dragons?

"*I've met Father Christmas, as you call him, but he prefers Nicholas. That would be King Nicholas to you, young woman.*"

Elizabeth snorted. It was bad enough when grown-ups called her "young woman." To hear it from a four-legged furry animal felt downright insulting.

Cary responded by jouncing her a little more than usual, but the thoughts she sensed from him had little to do with her. As they both watched, the dragon soared high, then swooped low again beyond the snowbank. An orange glow flared, followed by a new, dense plume of smoke.

"*It's burning the Village!*" Cary said. "*That beast is burning the Village!*"

And in that moment, something remarkable happened: The girl felt herself being lifted into the air and noticed that Cary's feet were no longer touching the ground! They were moving faster, too. A lot faster. As they rose, the chill air bit savagely at her face. She held on tight to the reindeer's antlers as he banked sharply right, around the snowbank, and the village he had spoken of came into view. It wasn't a large settlement: A few dozen cottages and farms scattered across the snow-covered landscape. But at the center of it was a large clocktower and a village square lined with shops. None of these, she saw, was on fire. The flames were rising from a bit farther on, from a huge complex at the outskirts of the village that looked like a factory of some sort.

The dragon wheeled high in the air, then dove directly

toward the complex, fire shooting in straight, yellow-hot streams from his nostrils.

To her horror, Elizabeth realized that the flying caribou (flying caribou!) was headed directly *toward* the dragon, as though intending to intercept it. She closed her eyes tightly and clung to Cary's antler's for dear life. "*This is madness! We'll be killed!*"

"*Not if I can help it!*"

Cary flew toward the dragon with such speed the still air whistled like a hurricane in the girl's ears. She opened her eyes just enough to see them rising at the last moment before they reached the dragon, which she saw in that same instant was surmounted by a single black-clad rider. In his right hand, he held a whip adorned with barbed steel spikes—a whip he was using to flay the dragon's scaled skin mercilessly. Each time he brought the scourge down on the creature's flesh, it screamed in pain and released another stream of molten fire. Elizabeth realized that the great dragon was not acting of its own accord, but was in the thrall of this black rider who, somehow, had subdued it.

When he was almost on top of the beast, Cary rose suddenly just above it and kicked violently with his back legs, striking the black-clad rider in the back. Elizabeth heard him shout above the howling wind and saw him topple in from his perch and plummet toward the earth. But in almost the same moment, she lost her grip on Cary's antlers and felt his body falling away beneath her. Then she herself was falling, tumbling through the air and downward, ever downward, toward the earth. The last thing she saw was Cary flying nearby. Or was it Cary? She would have sworn she saw *two* flying caribou. Or three. Or four. But maybe her panicked imagination had just multiplied them amid her tumbling-turning fall.

She heard a voice in her head: *"Open your arms!"* and somehow, she complied. She felt a *thud!* against her chest and felt her arms close in front of her, almost by instinct, around a soft and furry something.

Then, she blacked out.

What she awoke to seemed almost as much like a dream as what she'd left behind.

"Where am I?" Elizabeth said, her eyes fluttering open.

She lay on a goose-down bed, wrapped in a warm quilt, in front of a raging fire. It reminded her of the flames she had seen unleashed by the dragon. The poor dragon! It wasn't his fault. The black rider who had tortured him with that awful whip was to blame. "What happened... to the dragon?" She shivered at midsentence, and realized she had caught a chill traveling, as she had, through rain and snow and the freezing night.

"Rest, child." A woman with spectacles balanced near the end of her nose and gray-white hair tied back in a tight bun leaned over her, smiling a reassuring smile. The girl did not recognize her, but she felt immediately at ease, as though she had known this woman for as long as she could remember. "You are in our guest chambers. You've been through quite an ordeal, I must say, but there were no broken bones, and once you're warmed up, you should be right as rain.

"As to the dragon, he is recovering, as well. He is being attended. It has been ages since we have seen his kind here, and I fear Lord Nigel is behind his enslavement." A cloud of concern drifted across her eyes.

"Lord Nigel?"

"Yes, my husband's older brother. He has been embittered these many centuries since the crown was bestowed upon my husband, Nicholas. Now, my dear husband is missing, and I fear

Nigel used the dragon as a diversion to keep us occupied while he... abducted him."

Elizabeth thought she saw a tear form in the woman's eye, but she couldn't be sure. She was just waking up... or was she still asleep and dreaming?

"Nicholas? As in Saint Nicholas?"

This seemed to brighten the woman's spirits a little, and she chuckled. "No, dear child," she said. "Saints are dead, and my husband is very much alive... or at least he was the last time I saw him." The cloud of worry returned.

"He is not too fond of titles, but he does rather like the name Father Christmas. His brother prefers a different epithet: Father Time. He seems to think all living things must bend to his will, and now he has set out to prove it."

Elizabeth tried to prop herself up on her elbows, but lay back again when her head began to spin.

"I can't believe any of this," she said, hastily remembering her manners and adding, "no offense intended."

"None taken, child. But if I may ask, how is it that you believe in dragons, but don't believe in my husband?"

"I've met the dragon personally," the girl said.

"And you shall meet my husband, as well, if all goes well."

"I pray it will," said Elizabeth, more out of sympathy for the kind old woman than out of any confidence in what she was saying.

"As do I, child."

The woman turned to go, placing a steaming cup of cocoa on a small, circular table beside her.

"Ma'am, one more question, if you please," the girl ventured.

The woman stopped and turned back, waiting.

"How did I survive that fall?"

"Oh, that was Dan. He flew up to catch you when Cary swooped down to save the black rider he had knocked from his perch. Cary won't say it—he's quite ashamed—but he feels terrible that he let you fall off. It is just good fortune that Dan and the others had taken flight at the same time to meet the dragon, and Dan happened to be closest to you when you fell.

"Dan?"

"Some people call him Dancer, because he's so light on his feet, but he prefers Dan. He's very outgoing and doesn't stand on formality, much like my husband." She frowned again, and swallowed hard. "I really must go now, child. It has been a long night, and I fear it will get longer still before it ends."

Elizabeth watched her as she went, then closed her eyes to rest and soon was asleep again.

"Reindeer Ride" is an excerpt *The Talismans of Time*, the first book in *The Labyrinth of the Lost Academy*. Originally published in 2019, it is available for sale on Amazon, along with its sequel, *Pathfinder of Destiny*.

Did you enjoy this book?

Recommend it to a friend. And please consider **rating it and/or leaving a brief review** at Amazon, Barnes & Noble, and Goodreads.

About the authors

Dragon Crown Books publisher Stephen H. Provost has written several books about life in 20th century America, including a dozen books on America's highways. During more than three decades in journalism, he has worked as a managing editor, copy desk chief, columnist, and reporter at five newspapers. Now a full-time author, he has written on such diverse topics as dragons, mutant superheroes, mythic archetypes, language, department stores, and his hometown. Visit him online and read his blogs at stephenhprovost.com.

Sharon Marie Provost, chief operating officer of Dragon Crown Books, is a longtime resident of Carson City and author of the foreword to Stephen H. Provost's *Sierra Highway: U.S. 395 and El Camino Sierra in California and Nevada*. Sharon is the owner of champion of dog-trial poodles, and the creator of handmade dreamcatchers and chainmaille jewelry. You can find her at "Sharon's Dreams" on Facebook.

Also by
Stephen H. Provost

Works of Fiction

Crimson Scourge
The Memortality Saga
  Memortality
  Paralucidity
Academy of the Lost Labyrinth
  The Talismans of Time
  Pathfinder of Destiny
The Only Dragon
Identity Break
Nightmare's Eve
Feathercap

Works of Nonfiction

A Whole Different League
The Great American Shopping Experience
California's Historic Highways series
  Highway 99
  Highway 101
America's Historic Highways series
  America's First Highways
  Yesterday's Highways
  Highways of the South

Highways of the West series

America's Loneliest Road

Victory Road

The Lincoln Highway in California (with Gary Kinst)

Sierra Highway

Roadside Illustrated series

Happy Motoring!

Signpost Up Ahead: The East

Signpost Up Ahead: The West

Mark Twain's Nevada

The Century Cities series

Cambria Century, Carson City Century

Charleston Century, Danville Century

Fresno Century, Goldfield Century

Greensboro Century, Huntington Century

Roanoke Century, San Luis Obispo Century

Fresno Growing Up

Martinsville Memories

The Legend of Molly Bolin

50 Undefeated

The Phoenix Chronicles

The Osiris Testament

The Way of the Phoenix

The Gospel of the Phoenix

The Phoenix Principle

Forged in Ancient Fires

Messiah in the Making

Edited by Stephen H. Provost

The ACES Anthology 2023

Praise for other works

"The complex idea of mixing morality and mortality is a fresh twist on the human condition. ... **Memortality** is one of those books that will incite more questions than it answers. And for fandom, that's a good thing."

— Ricky L. Brown, Amazing Stories

"Punchy and fast paced, **Memortality** reads like a graphic novel. ... (Provost's) style makes the trippy landscapes and mind-bending plot points more believable and adds a thrilling edge to this vivid crossover fantasy."

— Foreword Reviews

"The genres in this volume span horror, fantasy, and science-fiction, and each is handled deftly. ... **Nightmare's Eve** should be on your reading list. The stories are at the intersection of nightmare and lucid dreaming, up ahead a signpost ... next stop, your reading pile. Keep the nightlight on."

— R.B. Payne, Cemetery Dance

"Provost sticks mostly to the classics: vampires, ghosts, aliens, and even dragons. But trekking familiar terrain allows the author to subvert readers' expectations. ... Provost's poetry skillfully displays the same somber themes as the stories. ... Worthy tales that prove external forces are no more terrifying than what's inside people's heads."

— Kirkus Reviews on **Nightmare's Eve**

"**Memortality** by Stephen Provost is a highly original, thrilling novel unlike anything else out there."

— David McAfee, bestselling author of *33 A.D.*, *61 A.D.*, and *79 A.D.*

"The story feels so close, so intimate, we as readers experience the emotions, the events, and the conflicts, in what feels like real time. Gut-wrenchingly so."

— Stephen Mark Rainey, author of *Blue Devil Island*, on **Death's Doorstep**

"If you have any interest in highways, old diners and motels and such, or 20th century US history, this book is for you. It is without a doubt one of the best highway books ever published."

— Dan R. Young, Highway 101 historian, on **Yesterday's Highways**

"Both books are well-researched, nicely written, and illustrated with good black and white photographs, and both contribute importantly to highway literature."

— Wayne Shannon, *Jefferson Highway Declaration*, on **Yesterday's Highways** and **America's First Highways**

"... an engaging narrative that pulls the reader into the story and onto the road. ... I highly recommend **Highway 99: The History of California's Main Street**, whether you're a roadside archaeology nut or just someone who enjoys a ripping story peppered with vintage photographs."

— Barbara Gossett,
Society for Commercial Archaeology Journal

"Profusely illustrated throughout, **Highway 99** is unreservedly recommended as an essential... addition to every community and academic library's California History collections."

— California Bookwatch

"... it contains a lot of information I hadn't heard before. Both books prove well-written with few weaknesses..."

— Ron Warnick, route66news.com,
on **Yesterday's Highways** and
America's First Highways

"An essential primer for anyone seeking an entrée into the genre. Provost serves up a smorgasbord of highlights gleaned from his personal memories of and research into the various nooks and crannies of what 'used-to-be' in professional team sports."

— Tim Hanlon, Good Seats Still Available,
on **A Whole Different League**

"As informed and informative as it is entertaining and absorbing, **Fresno Growing Up** is very highly recommended for personal, community, and academic library 20th Century American History collections."

— John Burroughs, Reviewer's Bookwatch

www.ingramcontent.com/pod-product-compliance
Lightning Source LLC
LaVergne TN
LVHW010052110826
845155LV00028B/303